Goodnight Vienna

Goodnight Vienna

J. H. SCHRYER

Cover Illustrations: (upper) a photograph of a man and a woman kissing, by
Victor Keppler © Hulton Archive / Getty Images, image reference
JJ 6287–001; (lower) *Anchluss with Austria, March 1938, Adolf Hitler enters Vienna*
by permission of the Imperial War Museum, image reference MH 13129

First published 2009

Reprinted 2010

The History Press
The Mill, Brimscombe Port
Stroud, Gloucestershire, GL5 2QG
www.thehistorypress.co.uk

© J.H. Schryer, 2009

The right of J.H. Schryer to be identified as the Author
of this work has been asserted in accordance with the
Copyrights, Designs and Patents Act 1988.

British Library Cataloguing in Publication Data.
A catalogue record for this book is available from the British Library.

ISBN 978 0 7524 4920 3

Typesetting and origination by The History Press
Printed in Great Britain
Manufacturing managed by Jellyfish Print Solutions Ltd

Dedication

For Sheila Hamilton

No greater love can a man know
than the love of a mother

With all my love, J.H. Schryer

Acknowledgements

Special thanks to the following people: Lynsey and Katey Hamilton who stumbled across documents that led to a series of coincidences and the beginning of a career in fiction. Huge thanks to science fiction writer Davide de Angelis and novelist friend Richard Bernstein who spent time with the author developing the creative spark and art of fiction writing; Mary Curry who read drafts of every chapter and whose sharp mind has left no stone unturned; and SOE veteran Eric Sanders who wrote the poem *Core of my Existence* for this book. Thanks to those who cannot be named for their insights into the heroics of the few who saved the many. And finally, to the exceptional Sophie Bradshaw whose breadth of vision saw the possibilities of the novel and agreed to publish it.

To Helen, for making a lifelong dream to write come true.

Finally Howard Hamilton; without his unstinting substantive support this book could never have been.

This is a novel of historical fiction. The backdrop of Nazi-occupied Vienna is as accurate as possible, however, the central characters are entirely fictional and any resemblance to real-life people is entirely coincidental. Scenes which include people like Freud, Churchill and Hitler's niece Geli (Angela Raubal) are the product of creative licence and therefore should not to be taken as factually accurate or true.

Chapter 1

12 March 1938. Katharine scanned the front page of the *News Chronicle*. The newspaper was full of it. Austrian Chancellor Schuschnigg had bowed to pressure and resigned:

> Austria is finally in the glorious hands of our German brethren. Vienna Town Hall taken by SS men. The German SA now in control of all newspapers including the *Wiener Neueste Nachrichten*.

It all seemed surreal. She threw the paper onto the sideboard, obscuring the programmes from her latest concerts with the Vienna Philharmonic. She was gathering quite a reputation in the concert halls of Europe, but would that count for anything now? Outside, spring was waiting to erupt in the window boxes and soften the sharp winter air. Now it seemed postponed indefinitely, as if a law had been passed against it. Summer will not come as usual this year, Katharine thought. If she closed her eyes she could imagine the subtitles under the silent movie:

> The liberation of Austria. A united Germanic brotherhood.

It was Jonathan she wanted now, his strong arms around her, comforting her. He hadn't returned. For a moment, the tolling of the city bells might have been for his funeral. Each tuned to a different pitch, their clamour was incessant. Were they sounding the alarm for the millions of men being condemned to death by this news? Or was it the death knell for those already murdered? She bulldozed these thoughts from her mind. Ypres and the Somme belonged to twenty years ago. It was now 1938. She refused to accept the implications of the gothic headlines, black letters on white, churned out of some newspaper press in a dark Viennese basement. The telephone sounded, soft against the clamouring bells. It was Jonathan. Her heart leapt.

'Have you heard the news?' His voice was distant, distracted.

She couldn't hear the rest. The chanting outside the window became louder: *Ein Reich! Ein Volk! Ein Führer! One Reich, one people, one leader!*

'I can't hear you.' She covered the other ear.

'Have you heard what's happened? Go to Henderson now.'

'Jonny, you're too faint. What did you say? When will I see you?' A click of the receiver and his urgent call was over. He was gone. She knew exactly what had happened; no crystal ball needed to confirm what had been coming for months; no, years. Austria had been threatened by her German neighbour ever since Adolf Hitler came to power five years earlier. The German war machine had crossed the border during the night. Only the previous day Schuschnigg had warned the people not to shed blood, to offer no resistance if it happened. He had sealed Austria's fate as surely as if he had signed a pact with Hitler.

Her thoughts turned to Captain Henderson. She expected that he would have an update. Sir Charles would have sent him at least one if not two telegrams stating the official British position. She must go to him. Her violin remained in its leather case, wrapped in the green velvet cover; there would be no practising that day. She pulled on a pair of white gloves, threw her winter coat over her shoulders and swept her fair hair under a dark brown felt hat. Then it was out into the chill morning.

In the street she couldn't expel the chant from her head, waiting for the start of each line, '*Ein Reich...*' She shuddered, pulling up the thin fur collar of her coat. Heavy grey clouds were thick with unfallen snow. At the end of the street a substantial crowd was gathering. She stood on tiptoe. As far as the eye could see a swarm of bodies moved in the direction of the city centre. Surreptitiously she slipped in among them, hustled along as they pushed down the main street. Their rhythmic chant now replaced with another:

Heil Hitler! Down with the filthy Jews.

A once cultured populace like a herd of rancorous animals was baying for the blood of the city's Jews. Towards the end of Kärntnerstrasse she steered her way into a side street, past the boot-maker's shop now seemingly abandoned; '*The Jews are our misfortune*' scribbled in black letters across the door. Mr Guttmann's once-bustling bakery was closed for business, a swastika daubed on the boarded window.

The word *Juden* had been hastily scrawled across the door, its thick black paint barely dry. There was no sign of the Guttmann family. Katharine shuddered again. This densely populated Jewish street was all but deserted; latent fear tingled down her spine. She glanced up. An eerie silence pervaded the very walls of the buildings. Curtains twitched nervously in the flats above her. She felt the gimlet eyes of the inhabitants gazing down. Moving from door to door, she noticed how each one was smeared with Nazi slogans and swastikas. One last glance back at Kärntnerstrasse, she took a moment to observe lorry after lorry of German storm troopers crawling at a snail's pace behind the crowd, their convoy emblazoned with the new insignia. As if escorting them, the church bells jangled on, announcing the new world order. The Roman Catholic Church in Austria was aligned in unholy union with the Third Reich, trying to avoid the shedding of its own blood. Some priests had already mysteriously disappeared, thought to be in Dachau concentration camp.

Without warning the sky darkened as an eagle spreading its wings across the city, shutting out the weak daylight. Looking up, Katharine saw the aircraft flying low in formation, the droning hum of the engines temporarily drowning out the bells. Wave after wave filled the sky, malevolently disgorging white leaflets from nauseous bellies to a waiting population. Evil rained from the sky, as if heaven itself had vomited. Katharine re-focused on the task in hand. She had to get to the British Embassy on Braunerstrasse.

Half an hour later, the building came into view. The west front housed the Passport Control Office, the back the British Embassy. The queue along the western entrance had doubled overnight. Anti-Jewish decrees which had restricted the public life of Germany's Jews, increasing in intensity over the last five years, had come into force overnight in Austria. Dejected émigrés clutched their papers, waiting for the queue to move a few inches closer to freedom. As her daily work in the office attested, not all qualified for emigration. Quotas were strictly limited. Almost all the available permits to Palestine had been allocated. She had completed the penultimate batch only the previous week. That left Britain as the only next option.

She glanced across the narrow street. The offices of accountancy firm Weiner & Co. had draped a Nazi flag from the lintel. On the glass pane of the door hung new words '*No Jews or dogs allowed here*' replacing the Open/Closed sign. Turncoats, she thought. Every non-Jewish business had rolled over to accommodate the new regime like a dog waiting for its master to tickle its stomach. This was no game. She turned. Hurrying into the main entrance of the building a rush of warm air embraced her. She removed her felt hat, neatly flattening it. Captain Henderson's secretary emerged from the shadows.

'Hugo, how lovely to see you,' Katharine extended her hand. He looked much thinner than she remembered.

'Mrs Walters, it's good to see you too. Captain Henderson and Dr Walters are waiting for you upstairs.' She didn't miss it was one of the rare occasions when he had not stammered.

She raised her eyebrows, surprised but relieved, 'Jonathan? Upstairs?' She pushed past him, faintly hearing Captain Henderson's angry voice floating down the stairs, the words too muffled to make out. Something was amiss. In the few seconds it took to reach the top, the conversation had ceased. Both men were quietly poised over papers strewn across the desk. Neither noticed her. She could observe them and catch her breath. In a matter of a few days Jonathan's face had become sallow and lined.

It was the first time Katharine had ever seen the two men together in the same room. Captain Henderson was the elder by eighteen months but it might just as well have been ten years. His toned body and rugged salt-stained features bore witness to a lifetime at sea. He and Jonathan had trained together at Britannia Royal Naval College, Dartmouth, but afterwards had gone their separate ways. Jonathan as a doctor was posted to the Admiralty as Surgeon Lieutenant, for some strange reason never serving at sea, and then seconded to St Bartholomew's Hospital in 1934 for medical research. He dressed too casually for a doctor, shattering any preconceived ideas of the profession. In contrast, Captain Henderson always wore a jacket and naval tie, impeccably dressed. He had spent time on HMS *Barum* in the South Pacific and once a year he and Jonathan had met in the Royal Automobile Club on Pall Mall, battling out a game of chess in the smoking room. They were very different characters, but neither was ever prepared to give an inch. It couldn't really be termed a friendship, more like hanging on to a nostalgic thread of their past. Katharine couldn't possibly know then that they were bound by a rivalry far deeper than male pride.

Suddenly aware of her presence Jonathan rushed towards her, the tension in his face relaxing. He embraced her, hugging her tightly. 'What did I tell you? I said I would be safe, darling.' She looked at him with relief. She loved his brown curls and boyish good looks.

Captain Henderson coughed. 'Apologies, but I need the attention of both of you now. This is urgent.' His lips were set; his back erect. He had to concentrate, but she should have been in *his* arms. He buried the emotion deeper, trying to focus on the job in hand. Silently they all moved up to the radio shack on the Embassy roof. Inside the makeshift hovel, he spoke first.

'I'm terribly sorry but there are new orders from Sir Charles. I'm going to have to move you to a new place on Berggasse overlooking the Freud apartment. I know you've only just settled into the other flat, but this is necessary I'm afraid. Under the circumstances, his word has to be final on the matter.'

Katharine raised her eyebrows, peering over her spectacles. She was not beautiful in the classic sense but undeniably sensual. Her rich blue eyes danced with life. She dressed elegantly for one so young. He re-focused,

'Yes Katharine, as head of certain operations which overlap with Home Office and Foreign Office policy, Sir Charles does have jurisdiction.'

'Wouldn't it be better to use someone from the other end of the Embassy?' She hoped to appeal to his better judgement, knowing that in the short space of time she had worked with him, he always afforded her a voice, listened to her opinion and respected her in spite of her being his junior, and a woman at that. In this respect he was different from most other men. But then he was bound by Sir Charles as much as she was.

'I really am sorry to inconvenience you at a time like this, after all that's going on, but you are needed to keep an eye on Freud's place until we can get him and his family out. He is at immediate risk. Securing his release is going to be more difficult than we first anticipated. The British scientific community is already engaged in trying to get the necessary guarantors for him, but it's taking precious time. The Americans are also working on the case from their end. There's a flurry of activity at their embassy here. We are trying to make it easier for you and Jonathan. The apartment is already fully furnished. It's a matter of moving your personal possessions which I hope won't be too onerous. But as I said, it is necessary.'

For the first time she noticed how strained he looked too. He straightened his body, smiling to reassure her, 'It will be OK.' His gaze now took in Jonathan, 'Come, it's imperative I bring you both up to date with the latest developments.' They followed him over to a long wooden table. He unfolded a large map of Europe, leaned across it and pointed with the end of his pencil to a single spot on the German border at Kufstein-Kieferfelden. His voice remained calm and authoritative.

'At 5.30 yesterday morning the massed German invasion army crossed into Austria. At 8, the 8th German Army followed. By 7.30 that evening the 7th Reconnaissance Battalion reached the outskirts of Vienna. And at midnight the 8th Army occupied this city. As you well know, the place is now completely overrun by Germans.' He pursed his lips in a rare display of emotion.

Jonathan interrupted, 'This is nothing short of the rape of Austria. Chamberlain should have seen this coming. Now it's too late.'

Captain Henderson straightened his back again, temporarily ignoring his comment. 'After Schuschnigg resigned yesterday the Austrian army fell in behind the incoming Nazi forces. Both are on the streets of the capital whipping up hysteria and popular support. It's a *fait accompli*. The Austrian government has welcomed the Nazis with open arms. As such Europe … no, to be precise Britain, is now powerless to act.' He stared Jonathan directly in the face: 'Yes, now it really is too late.' He pulled another map from the drawer. The Austrian borders were over-marked in red pen. He continued, 'And, at precisely 11.30 this morning, Dr Joseph Goebbels broadcast Hitler's proclamation throughout the whole of Germany and Austria. We have a tape recording. I'd like you to listen to part of it. No doubt you've heard it anyway – who hasn't.'

His statement required no answer. He disappeared for a few minutes. Katharine suddenly felt drained, and sunk into the nearest chair. It had been a long day and yet it was barely two o'clock in the afternoon. She picked up the vacant earpiece of the radio equipment beside her. German High Command barked its orders on and on, no longer in coded messages. She stared across the desk.

'Churchill was right all along. Europe is succumbing to the evil of Nazism and no one is going to be able to stop it.'

Jonathan nodded.

Captain Henderson reappeared, dragging over the trolley of heavy recording equipment. In a twist of irony it bore the name of a German manufacturer. He fiddled a little before loading the reel, then signalled he was ready. Katharine took off the headphones. The wheel of the machine slowly turned the tape. Goebbels' scratchy voice announced:

> Speaking for myself and the Führer as Chancellor of the German people, I shall be happy to be able to set foot once again in this land which is also my homeland, as a free German citizen. I shall convince the world that in these days the German nation in Austria, is living through an hour of blessed joy and emotion.

'I think that's enough,' stated Captain Henderson. 'You get the gist of it. Consequently, we now have a major problem here at the Embassy. The queues outside are becoming desperate. There's so much paper-work to get through that I'm going to need more help. Katharine, I am pulling you off day-time radio duty for a while. I need you here with me on emigrations.'

His clenched fist thrust deep into his pocket barely contained his outrage at the turn of events. His staff couldn't possibly get through more than a fraction of the applications in a day. Lives were at risk. They could only do so many applications in the time – but he reminded himself even that would make a difference. He led Katharine to one side. Jonathan continued to study the map.

Henderson moved closer to Katharine, whispering in her right ear.

'I want you to stamp all those forms regardless of circumstance.' Her enquiring eyes stopped him temporarily.

'Stamp the final box that secures their exit from Austria. Their lives are in our hands. We can't have their blood on our conscience. I for one couldn't live with that.' He paused. 'You may think differently. I'm not compelling or ordering you to do this, but I am asking you.' He didn't miss the flicker of compassionate response. At that moment she understood him. She knew how deeply he cared. He was no bystander. He was prepared to risk his position and his own life to save these people. She waited for him to speak or make a movement. He continued, calmly in control, 'We'll deal with the consequences later and then … then, it will be too late. They at least will be safe.'

Then it happened.

Their glances locked. By God, there was something deeper to this woman than mere physical attraction. His soul cried out to her as it had for the last seven years. What hope was there for him? At twenty-five she was ten years younger than him and a married woman. She stood within touching distance and yet he couldn't have her. How could she ever know what he felt for her? He would never be able to tell her.

She broke his silence in a whisper, 'Don't worry. I'm with you on this one. I'll do it.'

The momentary intimate connection was gone. He withdrew into himself, the cloak of duty around him again like an impenetrable shield. *Be damned to those feelings*, he thought.

'Thank you,' he muttered.

Silently she followed him downstairs. Back in the office he lifted the first pile of papers on the desk. 'Here, you can begin with these. They are the most urgent, if there is such a thing under the circumstances.'

Outside the window the shrill cry of a baby in its mother's arms in the queue was sudden as it was piercing. This was reality, as if either of them needed reminding. She began flicking through the emigration requests. She glanced up, not understanding why he was still waiting. She broke the awkward silence, 'Captain Henderson, I will need full lists to check names against. Oh, and more envelopes please.'

'Yes, of course. I'll make sure of that.' He turned and left.

Several solitary hours later, exhausted, she made her way back to the flat for her last night before the move to Berggasse.

❧

The following day Captain Henderson perused the daily newspapers on his desk, waiting for Jonathan's arrival. His business could not wait until Monday morning. Events were unfolding too swiftly. The chimes struck eleven on the mantelpiece clock. Jonathan would be late as usual. He always was. The weather in Vienna, like the mood of the country, was changeable. A low damp mist hung over the city, shrouding the Danube in an eerie séance. Austrians seemed much more sombre. Was the reality of the *Anschluss* beginning to sink in? An anti-climax to the euphoric celebrations? He detected an apprehension lurking beneath the surface of assured confidence. That morning would be difficult. He hated the grim realities of undercover work; having to inform his network that their brief was being extended into more risky areas.

Dr Walters walked in ten minutes late, a coffee thrust into his hand by a passing secretary. He looked unusually smart.

'Good morning, Dr Walters. Have a seat.' Captain Henderson pointed to a brown leatherback chair. 'How's the research going at the hospital?'

'Very well, George. Thank you.'

Captain Henderson glared back at him. He disapproved of his subordinates using his first name. Jonathan showed no reaction to the momentary displeasure on his face, cheerfully continuing, 'We could always do with more staff for the trickier experiments. Anyway, we aren't here to discuss my new surgical theories are we?'

'I'm afraid not. Tactics are changing. We need you further east to check out a Russian diplomat. He appears to be building a substantial power base. You'll be there for just two days, three at most. I can't stress enough how much alarm he's causing in Whitehall.'

Jonathan straightened his back, 'Gosh George – not much time to penetrate! Hmm, honey trap won't do it then. We need more time to set that up. Do you have an introduction arranged for me?'

'Yes of course, it's all been sorted.' In an unusual gesture during a work situation Captain Henderson also omitted to use his subordinate's surname. 'Jonathan, you're needed in Hungary; Budapest to be precise.'

'When do I leave?' Jonathan stood up, thrusting his hands deep into his pockets. He diffused the tense atmosphere between them with a boyish grin, knowing full well the answer.

'Tomorrow.' Captain Henderson leant across the desk. He opened a silver cigarette box and offered its contents. Jonathan declined. Henderson drew a deep breath, calmly stilling his internal irritation. 'I know it doesn't give you much time to cover your medical work, but you're needed for this. I really don't like this any more than you do.'

'And the risk?' Jonathan stared blankly at the maps on the wall.

'Minimal.' Captain Henderson turned, walked over to the largest map behind him and pointed. 'Here – this is where we need you. Whatever you can gather intelligence-wise. You know – all the usual stuff. But I have to tell you, although the risks are negligible, there's no protection on this one. The government will disavow any knowledge of you.'

Jonathan laughed, determined not to display any negative reaction. 'So what's new? Some things never change. I'd better be careful then!'

'Er, Jonathan …' His face was serious again, his eyes tinged with dark rings, voice a little strained, 'This diplomat, we have reason to believe he may be working for the Nazis, odd as it may seem. Sources suggest that he has been looking out the lie of the land, so to speak. He's visiting Budapest under the guise of a diplomatic junket, but we believe he will be meeting his Nazi co-conspirators there. We believe Hitler has designs to unite all German-speaking countries under his vision of a glorious Third Reich. He's done Austria and now he might make an incursion into the Sudetenland or Czechoslovakia proper. Hungary, of course, is also a potential target. Our concerns are firstly, whether this fellow is a maverick working on his own or secondly, the voice of a larger Russian conspiracy? I know it sounds unlikely given the strong leftist politics there, but we cannot afford to ignore this. Hitler with a power base inside Russia doesn't bear thinking about.' He grunted. 'If this chap is a lone maverick, he needs to be taken out – and fast before he can do any damage. If he's part of something much larger, then the situation is very grave – more than any of us realise. In which case, taking him out will have little effect. We need to know all his collaborators – the whole network. Hitler could march across Europe and we would be totally unprepared. Intelligence is vital.'

'So nothing to panic about then, George! Three days to save the world. Hmm, seems reasonable enough.'

Captain Henderson detested his casual sarcastic humour. This was no game. He drew on his cigarette and reached into the second drawer of the desk. The graphic photographs had arrived that morning from Warsaw. They had been hard to get out of the country, evidence was scarce but now he had the confirmation. His agents were systematically being knocked out. Their mutilated bodies were a horror he would rather not have had to confront. He glanced up. Jonathan was still quietly studying the map of Hungary and Yugoslavia. He closed the drawer again. What was the point of showing him? Sending spies into the east was always fraught with danger. Jonathan didn't need to see the evidence. He had the training. He knew the consequences of failure.

❧

Later that same afternoon Jonathan struggled with a box up the spiral stairs to the new apartment. He reckoned on two further trips and all the books would finally be up; three more and the china would be done. He paused. The celebrations outside on Berggasse showed no sign of abating. Pockets of Hitler Youth strutted around, proud of their new brown shirts and armbands. In a matter of hours Hitler had restored a national pride in Austria's Germanic roots, giving them a united identity. Their chant now all too familiar, '*Ein Reich…*' From the top floor, Katharine peered over the wrought iron handrail, amused at him trying to negotiate the acute angle. 'Jonny…' She chuckled.

'It's alright for you to laugh. Why do these places have such steep staircases?'

'I'll make some tea, darling.' She disappeared back into the flat. It was comfortable enough but much smaller than expected. The flocked wallpaper made the rooms seem almost as claustrophobic as the city outside, now being strangled by the new regime. Waiting for the kettle to boil, Katharine went into the sitting room and over to the window. It had snowed overnight; a light dusting covered the pavement and rooftops. Her eyes followed the line of a single bird's delicate foot marks across the snow-covered slated roof. The group of Brown Shirts having moved on, the street was momentarily deserted except for a solitary figure leaving the building opposite. It was Sigmund's eldest son Martin, a stack of papers under his arm. She sighed. Moving back across the room, she flicked on the radio and began pulling books out of the nearest box, arranging them on the shelf by colour. Somehow it was the easiest way to remember where they were. It was something her mother taught her. She missed her mother; the ravages of cancer had claimed her life at forty-nine, leaving her father to cope on his own.

Katharine paused from unpacking the books. On the radio the constant playing of military band music stopped abruptly, a temporary silence, then the news broadcast which cut through her thoughts. Events were changing by the hour:

In new developments Herr Hitler has ordered Franz von Papen the German ambassador to Austria to join his celebrations in Vienna. There is speculation that Hitler himself is due in this city imminently, even within the next twenty-four hours. Consequently there is much excitement on the streets of the capital.

She sighed. It was to be expected.

Jonathan struggled into the room, depositing the last box of china at her feet, 'Here my dear, this is it. All done.' He paused, stretching his arms in relief. He moved towards her, put his arm around her shoulders, sweeping her hair gently from her face. His kiss on the cheek was tender.

'We'll be very comfortable here, darling.' He walked back towards the adjoining door into the study: 'Things have deteriorated outside. It's endless – Jews, young and old, being humiliated, forced to scrub the streets. Yesterday I saw them dragged from their homes onto the street, front doors smashed down; those detestable Hitler Youths towering over them. "Hitler has finally given work for Jews", they're saying.'

Katharine switched radio channel. Wagner. How appropriate to herald the new regime.

'I know Jonny, what's going on out there is terrible but we are doing all we can at the Embassy. We have to stick it out and pass what information we can back.'

'We all have to get on with our work, including me at the hospital.'

His sudden abruptness caught her off guard and her face fell. 'Come here, my love. I'm sorry. I know I've been a bit touchy recently.'

His arms around her dispelled the uncertainties that had crept into her mind of late. She wished they could return to the carefree happiness and laughter of the days immediately after their wedding. He led her over to the floral-patterned sofa in the adjoining sitting room. She had arranged for her mother's favourite oval table to be sent over from England when they had first arrived in Vienna. It took pride of place in the centre of the room which was already adequately furnished. Even so, she had added a few quintessentially English features: a linen embroidered tablecloth, a china tea set on the sideboard and a clock with traditional Westminster chimes.

'Katharine, come and sit down.' His face was serious again. She dreaded moments like these. Her breathing became shallow as she waited for the bombshell. He moved closer, turned up the music so as not to be overheard, and took her hand. He waited to form his next words.

'There's more trouble in the east. We've lost two more – shot yesterday by a firing squad. My cousin and his mate, you understand.' He winked. She knew he was referring to other agents. Jonathan didn't have any cousins, only a nephew, Günter, and he was still in Vienna.

'They were supposedly involved in the underground resistance. It's a rather foolhardy position to take. Europe needs some restructuring and the Nazis are as good as reshaping the future. We reckon they were under surveillance for some time.' Suddenly the boyish look had returned.

She relaxed, quietly taking it all in. 'And...?'

She strained to hear him against the highs of Wagner's *Ride of the Valkyries*. He whispered, 'I've been asked to go on a little trip – just for two or three days.' Her back tensed. It was her worst fear. He patted her knee, 'Shh, my darling. It will be all right. I always come back. I'm very careful. Trust me. And I have you, waiting for me.'

'Jonny…' He silenced her with his finger. He had forgotten how warm and soft her lips felt to touch. He had not had the time, nor the inclination, to pursue the physical side of their relationship in recent weeks, something he knew she was finding hard. He reassured her.

'Yes, these are dangerous times darling, but I have to do what I have to do. Keep yourself busy. Don't think about me and I'll be back before you know it.' He stood up, gently cupped her head in his hands and kissed her tenderly on the head.

Katharine held back her tears, her lips trembling. 'I have to go to the bakers now. I need bread for later. I won't be long, ten minutes or so but you won't leave before I'm back, will you?'

'No, of course not, my love.'

She reached for her coat, ran down the stairs and stepped out into the cold air. The sky was still heavy with snow but nothing further had fallen. She crossed the deserted Kärntnerstrasse and headed for a side street where she considered the best bread in Vienna was baked. She turned the corner, catching a whiff of the warm dough. She could see the light was on inside. As she approached, the shop was deserted. The usual orderly queue of people chatting as they waited for their bread was not there that morning. As she drew nearer, an uneasy feeling overcame her. Loaves of bread and rolls were piled high in baskets on shelves along the back wall. Clearly no customers as such had been in since it had opened hours earlier. Mr Guttmann scurried out, looking to the left then right. His usually relaxed face gave way to a furrowed brow and pinched lips.

'Herr Guttmann, whatever's the matter?'

'Mrs Walters.'

'Please,' she interrupted, 'there's no need for formalities between friends. Call me Katharine.'

'Your usual? Croissants as well?' He seemed preoccupied as he reached for her favourite loaf.

'Yes, thank you. What's happened, Mr Guttmann?'

How could she even think of asking? She had seen what was happening on the streets. He stopped, took a deep breath, looking beyond her: 'You shouldn't be shopping here any more. It's too risky. Haven't you seen the signs on the shops? No Aryan to buy goods from Jewish businesses. You risk your own safety and that of your nice husband.' He paused. 'When I opened up this morning, well … it was early … as usual 5 a.m. to turn on the ovens. There were two swastikas across my window and a slogan "Down with the Jews". It took me two hours to clean off. Devil if I know what they used.'

She walked around the counter, picking up the bread and croissants. 'Look, if there is anything I can do – just contact me. Here's my private number.'

'We have seen the writing on the wall, Katharine. I told Mrs Guttmann only last month that things would catch up with Austria; that we should leave before the Nazis get here. I said we should leave everything and head for the border but Gelda said, "then what? We have three small children. We can't just uproot". And now … well, now it may be too late.'

She touched his left shoulder. 'You have always been so kind to the folk in this neighbourhood. You are well liked around these parts. It may not be as bad as we all fear. There's widespread feeling that the regime won't last. There has been no referendum.'

'Yet!' His abrupt reply didn't surprise her.

She lowered her voice, 'I do a bit of paperwork with visas at the British Embassy. If you need it, I'll help you and the children. Getting five of you out isn't going to be that easy. There are strict quotas and entry requirements. You'll need a guarantor.'

By now his eyes were moist, touched by her willingness still to associate with him – a Jew. Through his sadness, his loyalty to her was evident, 'You English are exceptional people. Thank you from the bottom of my heart.'

'I haven't done anything yet. But, I must go.' She grabbed the bag of bread and croissants, turned and dashed out. Racing back to the apartment, she passed Jonathan on the stairs, carrying a single rucksack.

'Jonny! You said you would wait for me!'

He reached out to her, their hands clasped momentarily. 'Take care, my love. Be strong. Uncle Jack needs me.' He winked.

Her heart sank. She hated this part of their work. She didn't know how long it would be before she would see him again.

Chapter 2

It was no ordinary day for the people of Vienna. Monday 14 March 1938 would be etched forever on their memories. The radio broadcasts that morning had so far given no confirmation of what was expected; that Hitler himself was due in the city later that day. Katharine stared out of the window, clutching a cup of tea now stone cold. The bells had begun their din two hours ago. Now it was ten o'clock. It was as if the last post was being bugled in memory of the innocent who would soon perish at the hands of the regime. The situation for its Jews was precarious. In her head she listed the prohibitions which now applied to them: Jews no longer allowed to hold public office or buy goods from Aryan shops; not to travel on buses or trams; not permitted to use swimming pools and public parks; teaching Hebrew forbidden; and all passports confiscated to be stamped with a red J for *Juden*. All Jews effectively excluded from public life. Katharine glanced across the street at Freud's apartment. Would that apply to *him*?

How could Jonathan be away – now of all times. She tried not to think of him, silently praying that he was safe. In spite of her training, she felt vulnerable. There was always Captain Henderson. He was the official government protection. It was true, she could always turn to him. He would protect her; that much she had gleaned from the rare emotion he displayed. She tried to dismiss him as quickly as he came into her head. She threw on a small jacket, wrapped a silk scarf around her neck, picked up her purse and left the apartment. The continuous pealing of the bells floated above the narrow street. There were at least a dozen churches in the immediate vicinity, all vying for dominance. Nothing could drown out their declaration. Katharine crossed over, walking briskly and keeping to the left. It did not take long to reach the centre of the city. The droning of heavy military vehicles became louder. From the first floor windows of every shop and building Nazi flags hung from poles, draping this erstwhile civilized city in an unsettling mixture of fear and excitement. Maybe it was her imagination or were their swastikas casting haunting shadows across the pavement? She drew up the collar of her jacket as if to keep at bay the ominous oppression which permeated the dank morning air. It pained her to see SS storm troopers and elite Sturm Abteilung Black Shirts prowling the streets of this beautiful city. They suffocated creativity. A third of the Vienna Philharmonic Orchestra had been dismissed; all of them Jews. She hadn't lifted her violin for three days, let alone played in a concert for several weeks. It was disastrous for her as a professional musician. She should have been practising for at least five hours a day. The extra work at the Passport Control Office had eaten into the little spare time she had. Hailed as a protégé at the age of four, her deep intuitive love of music had been noticed by the master composer Edward Elgar himself. Was it really four years since his death? But that was all in the past. A different life, a different time.

She turned into Central Square. Thousands of people were already along the wide promenade leading to the Hofburg Palace, once the seat of Vienna's Imperial power. Here, too, overnight, huge banners had been hung in rows from every building, their black swastikas on red and white larger than life. So it was true, she thought. This was the day that Hitler would come to Vienna. She moved slowly with the crowd in the direction of Heldenplatz, gradually squeezing her way to the front. The procession had already started. Her ribs pressed up against the temporary metal barriers as she strained to glimpse the beginning of the cavalcade making its way up the street. As far as the eye could see, the route was flanked with troops in both directions. Hushed whispers died down.

Silence.

She held her hand to her chest as if to steady her pounding heart. The procession moved nearer. And then she saw him – the crowd did too and started to chant:

Heil Hitler, Heil Hitler.

It was as if she were in the concert hall, the baton poised to begin the overture. Thousands in unison outstretched their arms in Nazi salute; their guard of honour for one man now passing in the open-top, six-wheeled blue Mercedes. Adolf Hitler stood erect in the front occasionally returning the accolade with like salutation. She had to admit it was awesome. The power he exacted over the people was absolute. Their adoration showed no sign of abating. His entry had been well orchestrated. The crowd's frenzied adulation continued.

Heil Hitler, Heil Hitler.

His car passed before her. Behind him, a single car followed. The black double-headed eagle painted on its side encompassed everything in its piercing vision. In the back Cardinal Innitzer, archbishop and supreme head of the church in Vienna, waved to the faithful flock. Four bishops flanked the vehicle, their crimson red on black vestments symbolising the blood of Jesus Christ. Innitzer had decided to toe the line; he could not risk a Catholic blood bath. He was now at the heart of the celebrations.

Katharine looked to the left. Thousands of storm troopers goose-stepped in perfect timing behind the vehicles. The crowd broke into another chant:

Ein Volk! Ein Reich!
Hail the Messiah, the anointed one.
Führer! Führer! Führer!

Ten minutes later the end of the procession was in sight; three rows of tanks, heavy armoured vehicles and trucks draped in Nazi regalia. This was a war machine, the like of which Europe had not seen before. She strained to see in the distance as Hitler's Mercedes drew up outside the imposing Hofburg. Rumours rippled through the crowd that Hitler was about to deliver his first speech on Austrian soil. Shoulder to shoulder on the balcony of the palace stood his distant silhouette with Cardinal Innitzer. Crozier in one hand, Cardinal Innitzer raised the other to give his blessing to Herr Hitler. Katharine's thoughts were now with the city's Jews. Their future hung with ominous trepidation like the flags around the city. For them the situation was bleak. They had most to fear. In one deft gesture, the biblical Jesus of her childhood had become the Aryan Prince of the Third Reich. She turned, pushing her way through the tightly packed people around her.

The back streets were predictably quiet. She ran most of the way, periodically stopping to catch her breath. As she approached the edge of Leopoldstadt, the Jewish quarter, she could already smell the acrid solution with which the Jews were forced to scrub the pavements. It hung in the air, impregnating her clothing, as if threatening to rot them. She remembered Jonathan's words a few days earlier. This was the work that Hitler had promised the Jews. It pained her to see them on their knees scrubbing the walkway, the grey solution burning their hands. Turning the corner, four Hitler Youths with batons encircled two elderly men and a pregnant woman. Blood as red as the bishops' vestments trickled down the face of the woman, barely able to stand. Which of the four bastards had done that? Even if she had arrived a few minutes earlier she couldn't have prevented it. Protestations were useless. In just two days she had seen what happened to those who defied the Nazis – women gang-raped, men beaten and left to die in the street. Ordinary people could offer no resistance, all forced to become bystanders to Nazi brutality. The regime had subtly but dramatically corrupted polite Viennese society overnight, eradicating centuries of tolerance, culture and learning. These were appalling times, making her work at the Embassy more urgent. Even before she reached there she knew the queue would have doubled that morning. Less than ten minutes later, as she turned into Braunerstrasse, her fears were confirmed.

❧

Captain Henderson sat quietly at his desk inside the Embassy contemplating his next move. He pulled a piece of paper from the drawer, scribbling down figures, calculating how many hours it would take to bring the queue down to even a third. Official visas were strictly controlled and had almost reached their limit. He was powerless without further instruction from Whitehall. He stood up and went over to the window. He was tired. Sleep had eluded him the last two nights. Young children and women were now a daily reality in the queue. His throat tightened. He could not live with his conscience if he effectively signed their death warrants by failing to issue their visas. Then there was the question of Katharine. How long could he protect her in this city? Sir Charles still had no idea who was betraying his agents in the east and insisted on keeping her in the field. Captain Henderson feared she could be next. The uncertainty of it all left him exhausted. Then he caught sight of her turning into Braunerstrasse. Only a few minutes later and she was standing breathless before him, hastily describing the morning's events. He listened without interruption, pulling a cigarette out of a silver case, offering one to her. She declined. He drew in the comforting puff of tobacco, calming his mind, waiting for her to finish. Her face was urgent.

'So you see, Captain Henderson. Things are very grim. What news about it from London?'

'There's concern in Whitehall, naturally, but appeasement is still the name of the game. It makes our job doubly difficult, of course.'

He puffed again on the cigarette, the white smoke curling straight above his head. She followed its line with her eyes.

'Katharine, there are new developments here that you need to know about. I had a visit first thing this morning from Vienna's chief rabbi. The community is concerned … no, terrified, by the speed of events. I discussed with him ways in which our office could help the most vulnerable to get out. He's had an offer of help from a Reverend Hugh Grimes, the head of the Anglican Church here. Grimes has offered to baptise Jews … a phoney baptism, you understand … and thus make the most of a loophole in the current emigration procedures. You are to liaise with him and issue as many papers as possible through that route.'

'Yes of course, I understand.'

He instinctively knew he had her total unqualified support. Again he ventured to suppose that she felt like him, that she believed in the cause. She paused. Agitated voices on the street below signalled an unexpected commotion. They looked at each other. He cautiously went over to the window. Below, an open truck carrying six SS guards had pulled up, its swastika flag flapping in the light breeze. Curt orders were being issued. He turned back to Katharine.

'Well, well, if it isn't Mr Eichmann himself. We are honoured.' His lip curled at one corner.

Katharine turned to leave.

'No, my dear, please stay.' She noticed it was the first time he had ever addressed her as 'my dear'. She moved to the corner of the room just as the door abruptly opened. Eichmann stepped in flanked by two officers, a string of medals weighing heavily across his chest. The soldier on the left took a step forward in Nazi salute: 'Heil Hitler! Captain Henderson, good day Sir. Herr Eichmann has urgent business with you.'

Captain Henderson nodded his acceptance. Eichmann moved forward; the clipped accent the same as he'd heard on the street just moments earlier.

'I have urgent instruction from the Führer himself – our leader of the glorious Reich. I will not beat about the bush, as you say in England, Captain. The Jews are our misfortune and causing considerable concern to us. My position is to ensure that they are removed from this country. That is where I need your complete and absolute co-operation. We have to get rid of these parasites.' He paused and grunted. 'As the Führer says, *Nur in einem gesunden körper kann ein gesunder Geist leben.* It's his favourite saying. I'm sure you know what it means but just in case she doesn't…' He nodded in Katharine's direction. '*Only in a healthy body can a healthy spirit live.* And we all know how unhealthy and depraved the filthy Jews are.'

Captain Henderson said nothing. Prudence dictated it, military etiquette demanded it. Eichmann continued, 'I understand your office is responsible for removing this scum from our country. In this respect, you can rely on my total support Herr Captain. We will give you all the authorisations you need, but we want them out of our sacred country.'

'I understand completely, Herr Eichmann. Rest assured, His Majesty's government is doing all it can to expatriate these people. I assure you, you have my full co-operation in the matter.'

Eichmann pinched his lips, spitting out his final defiant words, 'Scum, Captain. They are the scum of the earth, let's be clear about that. There is nothing lower in this world than a dirty Jew. If you wish to survive in this country you need to understand that.'

Captain Henderson kept his cool, 'I hope, sir, that is not a veiled threat. His Majesty's government takes a dim view of such matters.' Their eyes locked, neither willing to concede an inch of authority. In a rare gesture, Eichmann modified his tone, 'I think we understand each other very well Captain Henderson.' He turned to leave, clicked his heels and saluted.

'Heil Hitler.'

Seconds later, he was gone. Captain Henderson turned his attention to Katharine. 'Come, we have work to do. Let's get down to it.'

She paused, suddenly remembering, 'I almost forgot – this arrived for you earlier today.' She passed the telegram. He scanned the single line:

> Will not be coerced. Who do the Boche think they are. On my way.
> Mother.

He looked up and smiled, 'It's from Sir Charles. Carry on with the forms if you will Katharine. I must see to this.'

❧

Tuesday 15 March 1938. Katharine crossed the deserted Berggasse. Only half an hour earlier it was swarming with storm troopers.

Captain Henderson was right. Freud was not safe. From her window she had witnessed a fair amount of the raid that morning. Less than twenty-four hours after Hitler's triumphant reception in the city, the Gestapo had targeted Freud. He was always going to be at risk. She glanced up. The Nazi flag had been stretched across the double arched doorway of no. 19 – the only visible remnant of the raid. It was to Austria's shame that it had come to this.

She rang the bell twice. Paula the maid answered. Inside the communal hallway of the apartment block the interior was simple: whitewashed walls contrasted with the black wrought iron banisters of the winding stone stairs. At the top, Martha Freud stood waiting to greet her. She recognised Katharine and smiled, 'Good day, my dear. Do come in. Sigmund is in the study recovering from the day's dreadful events.' Martha was a kind lady; her soft lined face displayed compassion. It was mooted in polite society that she held the household together; that she was the main backbone of support which enabled her husband to pursue his theories unencumbered by practical day-to-day matters.

Katharine held out her hand. 'This time I've come on an official visit, Frau Freud. The British government, true to its word, is keeping an eye on you and your family until the necessary paperwork is completed.'

'Thank you, that's reassuring to know. Until today, we've had no urgent desire to leave Vienna. I've been discussing things with Sigmund, but even now he is reluctant to consider emigrating. Although these are dangerous times, he thinks it won't last. Only this morning we were raided by the Gestapo.'

'It must have been terrifying for you.' She couldn't admit that *she*, Katharine, was the one who was assigned to keep an eye on them; that she had seen most of it from across the road. If either of the Freuds were interrogated later, they might blow her cover.

'Yes, it was dreadful,' Martha replied, 'but I tried to keep calm. What else could we do? Anyway my dear, you must come and play for us one day, if we are still here, that is … We can't have a virtuoso violinist living right opposite us and not enjoy her music.'

'Well, things are so grim in Vienna at the moment Frau Freud that I haven't felt like playing. In fact, I haven't lifted my violin seriously for three or four days. That's a catastrophe for me as a professional musician. I've also been very busy with paperwork at the British Embassy.'

'But you could return to England.'

'Not at the moment. My husband is still in demand at the hospital, so we can't return for some time yet.' She glanced around the flat. Nothing appeared to have been disturbed by the raid. Martha had clearly made a good job of tidying the evidence. Walking towards the study, Martha gestured for Katharine to follow. In the corner at a desk sat the grey-bearded figure of the man she had grown to admire at the Imperial Hotel the previous year. His diary was open in front of him. His thin hands had just scrawled two words across the entry for 15 March 1938: 'Gestapo raid'. He looked up, 'Oh, Mrs Walters. What a delight to see you.'

'Professor Freud, what an honour again.'

'The honour is all mine, ma'am.' He took her hand, gesturing for her to be seated on the couch opposite. Was she about to be analysed? Rumour had it that he couldn't help it; whenever he was in the company of others it was second nature. The large bookcase behind him was crammed with leather-bound books. Although she was curious, she felt it impolite to stare too closely at the titles. Around the room, ancient Egyptian and Oriental artefacts adorned every piece of furniture.

'You like my little collection?' He seemed amused.

'Yes.' She smiled. 'It's very unusual.' She turned back to face him. 'Herr Professor Freud, have you suffered from this morning's events?'

'Ah the raid, you mean. Well, none of us came to any harm if that's what you mean.' He closed his diary. 'They didn't lay a finger on us. One young lad rifled through Martha's linen cupboard and threw it all over the floor, but that has been tidied up now. I've lost a little money from the safe – that's all.'

'Sigmund! It was hardly little,' called Martha, now walking back in from the other room.

'Please Martha,' he stared ahead, feigning a smile through his deformed jaw. The recent operation performed by Dr Pichler made it difficult for him to form certain words. 'Let's not alarm our guest. We are safe and that's all that matters.'

'All right Sigmund, have it your way. We did agree afterwards that there was much worse that could have happened to us.' She turned to Katharine, 'Many of Sigmund's friends now live in fear for their lives, they don't have his reputation or the backing of the international community for protection.'

'We are doing all we can at the Embassy.' Katharine assured her, but her reply seemed shallow. Getting him out would be tougher than anyone expected.

Freud leant forward, 'I've just had a telegram from my dear friend Ernest Jones. He's flying in from England today; obviously concerned for our safety. He is an advocate for my cause. He still talks about getting me out but I'm not sure it will come to that. This regime may not last, or at least that's what's being suggested in certain circles.'

'There is a lot of concern now over your safety, sir.' Katharine couldn't help thinking how this great man, whose pioneering theories had helped so many people, now stood to lose everything. Was he naive or in denial? She focused her gaze on the heavy white stone bust of Buddha on the table next to her.

'Is that your favourite in my collection?'

She looked at him quizzically. 'Yes, sir, I think it is.'

He smiled. If they could, the Gestapo would interrogate Sigmund ruthlessly. His subversive ideas were counter to pure Aryan ideology. Given half the chance they would have him disappear, but they had the Americans and the British on their backs warning of the consequences of any arrest. He looked directly at her. 'Of course, Austria has come to this because of the Great War. My three sons fought in the war. For nine months we thought we'd lost Martin in the Battle of the Piave until we learned he was in a British POW camp in Italy. And then at the end of it all, Germany was humiliated by huge reparation demands exacted by Britain and her allies. Now our country has been overrun by an insane leader who has grandiose ideas of power. Not that I am totally blaming Britain and her allies, you understand.' He looked beyond her, suddenly far away in another time and place. 'I have the highest regard for England.'

'Yes, sir.' Katharine knew it would be impolite to disagree with him.

'Remember what a member of the British War Cabinet said back in 1918?'

Katharine shook her head.

'No, you're not old enough. He said the Germans are going to be "squeezed as a lemon is squeezed – until the pips squeak. The only doubt is not whether they can be squeezed hard enough, but whether there is enough juice." Britain is a great country. As I said, I have the highest respect for her and have followed British politics all my life, but a country like Germany can't afford to be humiliated. A nation needs its pride. Deep within everyone's psyche is a proud tribal sense of belonging. It goes back to one's childhood. The heavy price of peace exacted by Britain has led to the Germany we have today. Britain enabled this ogre Hitler to gain power, first in Germany and now here in Austria.'

Katharine stood up, 'Indeed, sir. Please don't think me rude, but I have to get back to the office. Professor Freud, if you or your family are ever in danger please ring this number at the Passport Office. It is the diplomatic telephone line, only for special circumstances. There's always someone there, twenty-four hours a day.' He didn't miss the twinkle in her eyes.

He nodded, taking the slip of paper. It was the last time she spoke to him in Vienna. She wouldn't see him again until the following year – in London.

❦

The following morning, back at the British Embassy, Captain Henderson turned to face Katharine across the desk. 'What update on the Freuds?' For all her show of brash independence, he occasionally detected an innocent naivety.

'They've had a bit of a shock from the raid, but everything seems to be in order now. I've reassured them that both the British and American governments are doing everything possible for them.' She looked at him afresh. His aloofness hid a sadness deep within. What secrets he harboured, she couldn't even begin to imagine. What she saw was not what was thought. She was beginning to realise that all Sir Charles's agents were no more than a mask, or at least so it was with the ones she knew about.

'Can I offer you tea?' he asked.

'Yes, thank you.'

'Please, sit down Katharine; we have some extra things to discuss today.' He gathered half a dozen files on his desk, before straightening his back into the chair.

'As you know, we had some new equipment delivered last week, before all this blew up outside with the Nazis. Gibbons, the American, has been trying to get it working. We've had a few problems but now it's up and running, but not very smoothly.'

'And you want me to…?'

'Yes. We're having trouble with some of the decoding. I'd like you to come and take a look.'

She reached for her cup of steaming hot tea just brought in by the secretary and followed Henderson out. At the far end of the corridor they passed through double doors. At the end of the narrow passageway an iron door led to two flights of steps up to the Embassy roof; outside, what seemed like a hastily constructed wooden shack with crooked chimney squat in the far corner. It puffed out a continuous trail of thin grey smoke, blowing gently across the roof terrace. The chill air was biting around her neck and shoulders. She wished she had grabbed her coat. Once inside she saw that he hadn't exaggerated about the amount of apparatus that had been installed. From floor to ceiling radio equipment and gleaming metal lined the shack. An impossibly tall slim man whom she assumed to be Gibbons stepped forward to greet her. He stooped to bring himself to eye level. He seemed out of place in his tweed jacket and baggy flannel trousers, both a size too big. Dark brown bushy eyebrows protruded over the top of his large round black-rimmed glasses. They revealed matching dark brown eyes making him look very much like an oversized owl. She half expected his head to swivel round at any moment.

'How can I help you?' she asked.

He surveyed her, much as an owl might watch his prey before swooping. His voice was deep. 'Well ma'am, it's not so much a problem as a possible misunderstanding. The young guys here keep picking up loads of babble. A few messages are in Morse but most not, usually we pick it up on the shortwave. The consensus here is its gibberish, lasting anything from twenty minutes to an hour. Possibly amateurs messing around, but I'm not so sure.'

'I see. Can you pinpoint any particular time of the day?'

His eyes widened, 'No, ma'am. It can happen any time of day or night. We have no trouble picking it up now that the equipment has been set up. The issue is the fast speed at which it's being transmitted, making it impossible for our boys to decode.'

'Have you any idea where it's coming from?'

'That's just it. We don't because it's in dialect. It could be naval, although we are a good way from the sea. We suspect German army command, but we can't be sure.'

Captain Henderson interjected, 'We've noticed that these coded messages occur about half an hour before a major national German broadcast.' He passed her the earphones. The rapid irregular bleeps had begun again. She concentrated for several minutes before taking off the headphones. 'Could I have pen and paper, please? And has anyone photographed the frequency?'

'Er, what?' said Gibbons as he rummaged through the nearest drawer, pulling out several scraps of paper.

Katharine turned directly to him, 'Look, each time you get a new message do this, and this, and then hold it … done. Now we have a perfect photograph of the frequency.'

She listened again, scribbling notes. After fifteen minutes she placed the earphones on the table. 'That transmission has finished for now.' She paused. 'It's definitely German military high command, probably the Abwehr, which we all know is Hitler's innermost circle. Could you pass me a map? I need to confirm my guess. Now watch here – all aerials are directional. Signals appear stronger or weaker depending on the direction of transmission, so if we listen to known broadcasts we can roughly judge the direction of any other transmissions. Our office is here on the map. Now if I draw a con-tinuous straight line from this address along the frequency, we can be certain that the source is somewhere along this route. On the next transmission, we need to tune in the other listening radio sta-tions to this frequency. Do the same, draw the line between them, and we can confirm the address to within a few yards. What you have been picking up recently, I'm still certain, is within the region of the Bavarian Alps. Now, where are the other radio stations, so we can cross reference?'

Gibbons looked lost: 'Er, there are no other stations.'

'What? Surely you understand the principles of radiographs?'

'Er no, not really.' His eyes widened, reminding her of her first impression of him as an over-sized owl. 'I came over with the kit to set it all up. I then sort of ended up staying. I only know the basics – I don't really need any radio know-how to put the things together, just a screw driver.' He gestured to the other young lads in the shack. 'And this lot know even less than me.'

Katharine stared in disbelief. She shrugged her shoulders and passed the paper to Captain Henderson. She would get more sense out of him with his naval training. 'Here, these are their transmitted codes that I couldn't decipher immediately.'

'Thank you, Katharine. They'll go off to the station in Britain for them to work on further.'

'Judging from the little I was able to decipher from the other codes,' she added, 'I've worked out that the locations are all German cities which appear to have been transliterated into girls' names. They must be of some consequence.'

Gibbons punched the air, 'Well done, ma'am. I just knew it.'

'I'm glad someone's happy.' She smiled. 'Now I need another set-up like this in another location please.'

Captain Henderson turned to Gibbons, 'Please take care of that would you? And soon. You have my verbal authorisation. I'll sort the official paperwork out in the morning.' He turned back to Katharine, 'What do we know about that region of Bavaria?'

'Not much at the moment, but I would suggest that you and your team keep on top of the transmissions. Accuracy is everything. Keep the logs, cross-reference everything and then pass it to me to look over if you get stuck.'

Gibbons nodded in approval, turned, then left with the other lads to retrieve the rest of the equipment from the Embassy base-ment. Alone in the shack, Katharine moved closer to Captain Henderson. He could smell her lilac perfume. How intoxicating it was. He clenched his right fist in his pocket. Her soft voice was already whispering. 'I need to speak to you, Captain Henderson. We are alone, but is it safe?'

'In here, yes.'

'It occurred to me that the link between the cities in coded girls' names could possibly be munitions factories. If so, then the re-armament programme is continuing in spite of the incursion into Austria. Other neighbours could well be at risk. We could be head-ing towards war.'

He nodded, 'I am well aware of the implications, but thank you. We ought to get these coded transmissions off to M immediately. It can't wait Katharine. You know the procedure – use the double-sealed envelopes please. And…' He smiled. 'Thanks for everything. You can leave the rest to me.'

He began to walk towards the battered door. As he opened it he turned, 'I need you to do a bit up here every day for a while, if you can. The guys are going to need your experience. I want you to bring everyone up to scratch, and train the radio operators for the new location. Only *you* have the training. I … *we* need you.'

Could she detect a tenderness in his voice? Katharine dismissed it as quickly as the notion entered her head.

Chapter 3

Katharine swung around; the shuffling behind her took her by surprise. Her hand tightened around the wooden coat hanger of the dress she had just pulled out of the wardrobe for that evening.

'Jonathan! You startled me. I wasn't expecting you back for another three hours. Your telegram said four o'clock. Why do you have to creep around like …' He leant against the bedroom doorframe, the light emphasising his dark sunken eyes. Her heart raced, 'Darling, what's the matter? … Jonny?' He moved unsteadily forward. Her fingers loosened their grip on the chiffon dress and its hanger.

'Come here, my dear.' He held out his arms, held her tightly. She looked up into his face. He barely whispered, 'It's Cecil. He's gone.'

'Gone? Darling, what do you mean he's gone?' He didn't miss the tremor in her voice.

'I saw Sir Charles early this morning in Linz. He brought the news to me personally.' His broken voice stuttered through the silence. 'He's been shot … Cecil's been shot.'

'Your friend Cecil? Hutchinson?' She felt his cold hands wrapped in hers begin to shake. 'What do you mean? He can't be … isn't … Jonny, talk to me.'

He sank back into the small sofa, his hands drained of colour covering his face in guilt and grief. 'Somewhere in the east – thought to be a firing squad. We don't know. Sir Charles thinks it was betrayal, but we're not sure. The mission, the contacts – were all safe. I made sure of that. That's the awful thing.'

'You mean he was one of us?' His silence was confirmation. 'I had no idea.'

'Why should you? We … I … can't reveal the network, not even to you. And now he's gone. We were so close at Eton … and since.' He tried unsuccessfully to hold back the tears. 'Sir Charles is trying to recover his body. The government has disowned him of course, but there are ways of getting him back. Then he'll have a quiet burial on his estate near Bath.'

Katharine glanced down at her crumpled dress trailing over the arm of the sofa, a reminder of that evening's engagement. She touched his arm, cutting through his pain, 'Look darling, I don't think either of us are up to going out tonight. Let's cancel.'

'No, Katharine. We have to continue as if nothing has happened. We can't let the buggers see they hurt us.'

'But we can't just blot out Cecil's life,' she implored, her lip trembling. 'He was so kind to me, especially at our wedding, lending his estate for the occasion. He made me feel like one of the family.'

'Remember him as he was, my dear. It's best that way and always hold in your thoughts that he gave his life for his country. There is no nobler sacrifice. It's what we are here for, including you and me.'

She hadn't seen this side of him before. They had only been married for six weeks after a whirlwind romance. She still had so much to learn about him. Beneath the playful humour was a sensitive and deep-thinking man. He suddenly looked up, managing a weak smile, 'I quite forgot, my dear. Captain Henderson has asked to see you early at the office tomorrow. Now, powder that pretty nose of yours and after I've refreshed and changed, we'll go off to the Herz's for the evening, as arranged.'

Travelling across the city from Berggasse to Leopoldstadt should have taken half an hour on two tram routes. Jonathan, subdued, quietly held Katharine's hand. Images of oppression flashed passed the window. The swastika and double-headed eagle's presence was evident everywhere as the symbol of Austria's supposed liberation. It was all rather depressing. She wondered how a whole nation could be indoctrinated so quickly. She glanced at Jonathan. He hadn't said a word since they boarded the tram, now trundling its way through the streets of the Third District. It was only a matter of minutes later and the wheels jolted, slowing down, the brakes screeching to a halt across the icy track. Katharine strained to see ahead. Three SS officers stood at the helm of the road block. One stepped forward holding his hand up, another came on board, his eyes darted furiously as he scanned the carriage.

'Herraus! Everyone out.'

Hell, they're coming for us. Katharine couldn't erase the news of Cecil from her mind. Jonathan squeezed her hand. She averted her eyes, avoiding any direct contact with the officer.

With half the passengers now off, he finally spotted his suspect. 'You there!' The object of his interest cowered in the back seat.

'Show me your papers.' In seconds the officer reached for his trouser belt, pulling out the baton. The strike was swift. The young teenager clutched his cheek, blood trickling through his parted fingers.

'Get off, you scum. Jews aren't allowed on buses or trams. What insolence!'

The hands of the two other officers now standing behind him grabbed his collar, dragging him off. A few minutes later the passengers filed back on. Katharine stared ahead, clutching Jonathan's hand tighter. 'Is it really a good idea for us to be heading for the Jewish quarter?' she whispered.

'We've nothing to be afraid of, darling. We're British citizens. The laws of segregation don't apply to us. We can travel in and out of the quarter.' It was hollow comfort. Slowly the tram pulled away again.

'I know but ... under the circumstances why don't we wait until things have settled down? Besides, you never told me you had Jewish relatives.'

'Does it matter?' His harsh response pained her. She had every right to be concerned.

'I'm sorry Jonny. I shouldn't have said that. Forgive me. After all that's happened today, I've got rather overwrought.'

Another road block ahead slowed the tram. This time the officer waved them on. Katharine tried to relax. Through her thoughts Jonathan's voice was distant: 'One doesn't talk much about such things these days – the way it's going here. But I've nothing to be ashamed of. It's my sister's husband who's Jewish. She married a Jewish businessman. Remember I told you ages ago – he exports glass, mainly objects d'art.'

She squeezed his hand, 'Yes, I think I do. It's OK, really darling. I'll be fine now.'

His eyes clouded over. 'It's all rather unfortunate. He has relatives in Berlin. It could be risky for them both, if things turn any worse. But tonight, we'll enjoy ourselves in their company. We're going for a traditional Friday night meal to mark the start of their Sabbath. Here, this is our stop.'

A group of children played in the street outside the tenement block. One boy bent down to pick up his *kippah* that had fallen into the gutter. They were all oblivious to the regime now suppressing their community, their innocence somehow able to shut out the oppression in moments of tranquillity. Katharine sighed, following Jonathan up the stairs to the top floor. The children's voices echoed in the stairwell, their Yiddisher songs a throw-back to a lost eighteenth-century world. Beyond the open door of the apartment a table was neatly set; in pride of place at the centre stood a pair of ornate silver candlesticks with matching goblet. The crimson red wine was so full to the brim that Katharine was sure drops would spill over at the slightest movement. She thought back to her religion lessons at school, marvelling at the similarity between the two faiths, knowing that for Christians the wine in some way represented the blood of Christ. How much more blood would be shed in this city before the Israelites would taste true freedom? Next to the wine, two plaited loaves peeked out of an embroidered cloth.

'Welcome, my dears. We're so delighted that our Jonny has married at last.' The voice belonged to a wizened man with greying beard, dressed in black suit and crisp white shirt. Hermann Herz extended both hands, his wife Ilse close behind. She smiled, wiping the last remnants of flour from her hands down her apron. 'He's a very lucky man, I can see,' she said; her slightly wrinkled face hid years of turmoil and struggle. 'We're so sorry that we couldn't be at the wedding but Hermann was sitting *shiva* for his father who passed away suddenly.'

Hermann coughed, taking Katharine's hand, 'Come, my dear, and meet our eldest son. Günter's back home from studies in Germany.' Katharine's eyes rested upon a tall lanky youth of about eighteen warming his hands by the fireplace. He turned and smiled, his cheeky grin making her feel completely relaxed.

'Come and sit down, both of you,' Hermann gestured to the table. 'Ilse is about to serve chicken soup – it's a Jewish custom on a Friday night.'

Günter seated himself next to Katharine. The candles already lit, Hermann raised the silver goblet. '*Baruch ata Eloheinu.*'

'Blessed are you, Lord our God, king of the universe, who creates the fruit of the vine.'

Katharine closed her eyes; the melody not unlike the Greek Orthodox liturgy she had heard as a child on holiday with her father in Athens. The two traditions had so much in common and yet history had driven them poles apart. The blessing over the platted loaves followed. The bread was surprisingly moist and sweet to the lips in contrast to the wafers used in church. She turned to Günter, 'Jonathan tells me that you're studying at university.'

'Was.' He frowned, 'I was in my second year of Law at Heidelberg.'

'And?' She should have guessed what was coming next.

'Last month I was called into my tutor's office. Professor Berg was my mentor for nearly two years. I had huge respect for him, but that day I stood before him a different person. He looked at me across the desk with hate in his eyes. The university had discovered my father was Jewish and that was it. I'm out. No one with a trace of Jewishness is allowed in German universities.'

'That's terrible. I knew things were bad in Germany, but surely not for you?'

Günter leant back, rocking on the back legs of his chair, 'It makes no difference to them. As far as they're concerned if just one grandparent on either side is a Jew, practising or not, then your bloodline is tainted. For the last couple of weeks I've been helping father sort out his affairs. The Germans now refuse to buy goods from any Jewish exporters. Father's had to get rid of all his staff.'

Across the table, Hermann nodded, his face solemn. 'The business is done for.'

Günter's tone suddenly changed. His fist thundered to the table, 'I'm no bloody Jew. I've been baptised in the Protestant Church, mother insisted on that. The bloody Nazis are doing all they can to destroy those who would give their lives for their country. Father fought for Austria in the Great War. And what for? Austria has been laid bare, raped like a whore. I'm for the old Austria. Red-white-red Austria! Until death!'

'Günter, that's enough.' Ilse put down the soup spoon. 'No one should be ashamed of their roots – least of all you. And, I'll have none of that socialist nonsense in my house. You'll bring destruction on us all with your reckless idealism.'

'It can't be any worse for us or Austria,' he snapped. Seeing the discomfort of his parents, he relented. 'I'm sorry mother, but I just get so frustrated by it all. Let's change the subject. Katharine, tell us about your concerts.'

'What's there to say?' She smiled. 'I play my violin. They seem to like me, especially in London's Queen's Hall. I've done a number of concerts there every season for the last three years.'

Jonathan interrupted, 'She's far too modest – and it's not like her at all. She's usually full of confidence, aren't you my dear? All musicians are self-assuring; they need to be to survive in a man's world. We actually have a famous fiddler in the family!'

Under the portico of the British Embassy Katharine shook the rain off her umbrella. It hadn't stopped all morning.

'Lovely day is it not,' the deep voice behind her was unmistakably Captain Henderson's. He held the door open for her.

'Yes, if you're a duck. It's pouring outside.'

He loved her wry humour. It raised his spirits in seconds. 'It's been an all-nighter for me. I haven't been out at all today.'

She wasn't sure if he was serious or not. Turning, his face gave nothing away. 'Here, let me take your wet coat.' His hand briefly touched hers. She looked puzzled. What *was* it about him? He led her into his office, brushing the worst of the rain off her coat. 'Sir Charles has secured a concert for you at Berchtesgaden. It'll mean just a couple of days away from here.'

'Berchtesgaden?'

'Yes.'

'That's where Freud wrote *Interpretation of Dreams*. It's also Hitler's summer retreat.'

'Precisely,' he replied. 'It's also within the possible region where those transmissions are coming from. That's where your concert is going to be. Hitler won't be there of course, but we want you to sniff around if you can.'

'Me?'

'That's why Sir Charles recruited you in the first place. Your reputation as a musician is the perfect cover … and your proficiency with radios. There aren't many women quite like you Katharine.'

Was he serious? She knew better than to question him. He wouldn't open up anyway. Beneath his formal reserve lay an ocean of secrets which she could barely begin to fathom. He was somewhat mysterious. She was beginning to like that in a man. Maybe that was what first attracted her to Jonathan. Although he was very different from Captain Henderson, he also hid so much beneath his playful cavorting. She dismissed sentimentality. She had to, especially where Henderson was concerned.

'When do I go?' She paused. He was miles away. It worried him to send her away. At least in Vienna he could keep watch over her. If only she knew that he was her ultimate protection. At least, I am with her now, he thought. He tried to concentrate on what she was saying; her presence distracted his keen analytical mind, tugging at his emotions.

'Captain Henderson? When do I go?'

'The middle of next month. I'm getting Hugo to sort out your travel arrangements. He's not around at the moment. He's off on some course with Sir Charles. Talking of Freud, there's been another raid on his home. I got a call from the American attaché about five minutes before you arrived.'

'Oh, no, not again!' she retorted. 'It's exactly a week since the last one. I didn't see anything this morning.'

'You must have already left. Martin Freud is under arrest at the office of the International Psychoanalytical Press at 7 Berggasse and his sister Anna has been taken into custody. She's at Gestapo Headquarters in the Hotel Metropol. Ernest Jones and Princess Marie Bonaparte are doing all they can to get her released.'

'Is there anything I can do?'

'Not at the moment but I'll keep you informed.' Katharine turned to leave.

'Wait, please. There is just one more thing.' He stared directly at her. 'Freud's friend Friedl Stadlen has committed suicide. He's been under house arrest since the annexation. Rather than risk being taken to a concentration camp he took his own life early this morning. I hope it isn't setting a trend amongst the intellectuals here. It's the third suicide in as many days.'

꩜

That evening, Günter slipped the leather-bound book into his pocket and stepped out into the dimly-lit street. He glanced at his watch, straining to see the time. He could just make out that it was nearly ten thirty. The moon was as good as ineffectual now hidden behind the clouds, its celestial light useless to him. He yawned. He had been sleeping badly and the recent late nights had made him overtired. He ran through the deserted back streets towards Heldenplatz; the heavy book pulling on the lining of his trouser pocket. The ceremony was due to start in half an hour. As he approached the square, burning torchlights were visible, illuminating the black silhouettes which held them. He slowed down, walking closer. Some two hundred students and their professors encircled an enormous heap of books. Around them storm troopers and Brown Shirt youth had formed a guard of honour. He pushed his way to the front. The familiar chant rang through the still night air:

He scanned the scene before him. On the other side, Professor Ubertal of the Anatomical Institute was deep in conversation with Professor Stuhr of the University of Heidelberg. He grunted. Stuhr must have travelled especially for the ceremony. He was the one who had signed his final dismissal notice from the university on the advice of the tutor. Professor Stuhr had cited academic reasons, 'failure to complete the required standard'. Günter knew otherwise. Now these two academics stood at the helm of impending operations. Professor Ubertal raised his hand to signal the start. The first flaming torch fell onto the mound of books. Within seconds the pages were a blaze of yellow flares. Hitler Youth rhythmically waved their flags above the mob. Hand to hand the students shunted more books down the long line from the back of the crowd. Silence momentarily descended, anticipating the climatic moment. In one unifying strike, the front row flung their loot into the funeral pyre. Pages splayed open in a last defiant attempt to show their contents to a blasphemous and unforgiving audience. Günter turned to the student on his left, saw he was clutching a copy of Freud's *Interpretation of Dreams* ready for the next sacramental move. It was his classmate of three years ago.

'Hi, Thomas. Warming your hands by the fire?' He did not hide the sarcasm.

'Günter, what are you doing here?'

'The same as you. Committing degenerate ideas to the annals of history.'

Thomas raised his hand, the silver lettering of Freud's name on the spine of the book shimmered in the bright light of the bonfire. He began chanting with the crowd, dedicating the book to the flames with a single thrust:

> Against soul-disintegrating exaggeration of the instinctual life,
> for the nobility of the human soul,
> I commit to the flames the writings of Sigmund Freud.

Cheers signalled the deed complete. Günter eyed up the situation, biding his time. The ritualistic slaughter of academic learning, the desecration of intellectual freedom was now complete in his beloved homeland. He took it all in, determined to stand up for Austria, for liberty. All hands raised, books held high, the next in line was Karl Marx, his hero. He stepped forward, reached into his pocket, pulling out the book. In a gesture of final satisfaction, he hurled it towards the burning pile citing the last rites:

> Against soul-disintegrating exaggeration of the instinctual life,
> for the nobility of the human soul,
> I commit to the flames *Mein Kampf.*

Thomas gasped beside him. Four firm hands landed on Günter's shoulders, pulling his collar tightly around his neck. They dragged him to the back of the crowd, pushed him to the ground. A steel-capped boot headed for his face. He blacked out.

❧

Jonathan looked up at the top of the building for the vital clue. The slanting weathervane on the crooked chimney signalled that this was the place. Around him the main square of Linz was lined with cafés; inside, along their window fronts, pockets of SS officers relaxed over coffee. He glanced at the monumental town clock in the centre of the plaza. Sir Charles would probably be late. He always was. He strolled around the back and into the kitchen. The chef and his two assistants ignored his presence. He made his way upstairs to des-ignated room 16. It was less than a week since his last mission in Hungary. Now he was meeting Sir Charles in the birthplace of Adolf Hitler. To his surprise, Sir Charles was already pacing the confines of the tiny bedroom, the buttons of his shirt straining over his paunch. 'Ah, about time. I was wondering where you had got to.'

'By God, Sir Charles, why here? The place is swarming with SS officers. I assumed they'd all be in Vienna.'

'Where better? No one is looking for you here in Linz. In the heart of the lion's den, you're as safe as you can ever be. Now, let's get down to business.' He cleared his throat, keeping clear of the window overlooking the main square. 'Your assignment has changed. Passages to the east are increasingly being compromised. We need an alterna-tive – and pretty damn quick.'

'So, it's not Budapest this time.' Jonathan's eyes scanned the room in search of clues. Sir Charles was meticulous, no papers left any-where on show.

'We need you in Danzig.' He began slowly brushing his moustache in meticulous long strokes. Jonathan was perched on the edge of a dressing table. Sir Charles loathed his childish smile and casual demeanour. He was the most relaxed of all his agents. Sir Charles muttered to himself, 'Where's the coffee I ordered?'

As if anticipating his master, Hugo suddenly appeared, 'Coffee, S…sir Charles. No biscuits I…I'm afraid, only croissants.'

'I'm sure your stammer is getting worse Hugo. Get it sorted lad. No biscuits? Erh. Never mind, you can leave us now please.' Sir Charles pulled a crumpled map from his bulging trouser pocket. 'As I was saying Jonathan, it's Danzig. We need to establish a safe route to the east that is right on the German border. If you open that tall cupboard over there, you'll find your uniform and papers.'

Jonathan fingered the dark grey uniform hanging in the wardrobe. A Gestapo identity was a new one on him. It felt well made, comfortingly heavy. 'Probably made by a Jewish tailor.'

'No doubt. Someone has to make uniforms for the Nazis. I've secured you as acting Burgermeister of Danzig. A temporary measure – the current mayor has had a heart attack. You're the stand-in until they appoint another. You're in for a week at most.'

'A week? That's a pretty tall order.'

'We'll pull you out earlier if needs be.' He noticed Sir Charles's eyes cloud over, the jugular in his neck throbbing. It was never a good idea to challenge him. He watched as he fumbled to unravel another crumpled map. 'That's not all, Jonathan.'

'I gathered as much. It never is. There's always more.'

'We need you to get information from the SS gauleiter of Danzig. He will be your immediate boss while you're there. You will be reporting directly to him. It shouldn't be too hard for someone like you to worm your way to his table. He controls the whole region, right up to the border and that's where we need a new safe house, eventually fully staffed with our people.'

Jonathan shrugged his shoulders, 'The assignment seems straightforward enough.'

Sir Charles prepared him slowly for what was to come. 'We need you to get close to him.'

'How close?'

'Sleep with his wife.' He studied his face waiting for a flicker of reaction. There was none – good – he was well trained. 'There's a society ball in Danzig at the weekend which will be attended by all the dignitaries. Here's your ticket. Find a way to get that woman into bed; use your charm to find the information we need, you're good at that. Locate which areas are uncovered – and that'll be our route in. There has to be one somewhere. We intend to use it.'

Jonathan pulled the uniform off the hanger, 'I'd better put this on now then, hadn't I. It's going to be a busy week.' Sir Charles missed the sarcasm, he always did.

Less than twenty-four hours later at the British Embassy, Sir Charles stared at Captain Henderson across the desk. 'Before I left Linz this morning, I installed two more in the field.' He pulled a bundle of files from his case. Silently he leafed through the top of the pile. 'So far we've lost three operatives on active service in as many months. The king's men are going down like flies and we are still no nearer to ascertaining how or why.'

Captain Henderson moved to the window, gazing down on the street below. The visa queue now snaked around the back of the building. His eye caught the weary figure of a woman and crying child. For the last two days she had faithfully stood in the queue, edging nearer the front. Every few hours a teenage lad brought them food. He turned back to Sir Charles.

'Could it be an inside job?'

'Not sure. So far the evidence is ambiguous. We need to keep an open mind on the matter.'

Captain Henderson walked over to the corner cabinet, pouring them both a brandy. 'What do you suggest next? I've had every one of our personnel double-checked, including their recent movements and contacts. It's thrown up nothing out of the ordinary.'

Sir Charles looked up. 'Long term we may have to test the water with false trails, but doing that would de-stabilise confidence amongst our agents. The trouble is we don't know for sure that it is a mole. In the meantime, watch your back and your staff.'

'Do you want me to recall all operatives?'

'What? And leave the place uncovered? No, they're the eyes and ears of our government abroad. The worse it gets out there, the more we need them. By the way Henderson, your emigration quotas have been increased. That should ease the pressure on that queue outside.'

'Thank you, Sir Charles. That's welcome news.'

❧

The next person quietly slipped into the interview room waiting for Katharine to turn around. She was filing the previous applicant's emigration papers in the cabinet behind her, pencilling the registration number in the top left-hand corner of the first page. It was number seventy-eight for that day alone. She had now reduced each interview to less than five minutes. The work was exhausting, concentrating for long periods, and the emotional side of dealing with so many distraught people drained her. She turned back to her desk, 'Günter, what a surprise!' The 6ft lanky lad looked tired and strained, his left eye blackened, his right cheek red raw and slightly swollen. 'You look in a right state. Here, come and sit down. I don't have long – you've seen the queues outside.'

He thrust the papers across the table.

'Oh Günter! Not you too. I'm so sorry.' Her eyes betrayed an awkward embarrassment at her misjudgement. 'What's happened?'

'I've been in a spot of trouble. I was arrested last week and slung in prison. It was dreadful, absolutely dreadful.' He slumped into the chair opposite her. 'The place was so cold and damp; water running off the walls. I got pushed around a bit … you know. I thought that was it for me. I don't know how, but father secured my release – at huge cost I think. He has agreed with the authorities that I will leave Austria before the month is out.'

'Can I ask what prompted the arrest?'

He studied her carefully. Would she approve of his action? No matter, he would have to tell her. 'I was involved in subversive activities.'

She raised her eyebrows.

'Alright, I consigned *Mein Kampf* to the flames at the book-burning affair in Heldenplatz.'

'I see.' She flicked through the pages of his form. The reason for emigration cited as 'political'. She paused. He was doubly at risk with Jewish ancestry and being an active member of the Resistance. She gathered he couldn't be trusted to keep quiet for long. He was prone to being rather impetuous, idealistic and outspoken. He waited, watching her face carefully for any clues that a resolution was forthcoming. In the silence the clock on the mantelpiece ticked away an eternity. She carefully considered her response.

'The problem is this, Günter. Because of your political activities, you need an extra stamp from Eichmann's new office. And I guess that's impossible with your involvement in the movement.'

He fidgeted in the chair, 'Spell it out, Katharine. I'm not ashamed of my part in the resistance. Someone has to stand up for Austria. Our country is being pillaged and raped without mercy.' His eyes challenged hers.

She held her own, 'I was merely trying to be discreet. Emotions are running high, I know.' She lent forward, her face now within a few inches of his. She remembered Captain Henderson's words. She held this lad's life in her hands. She had not bargained on this kind of work when she had signed up with Sir Charles. She lowered her voice, 'Look, without the right papers, my hand are tied.' He noticed their slight tremble as again she leafed through his papers. She was unable to reveal to him her part in false documentation, stamps and money deposited into bank accounts; even that couldn't help him. He still needed the extra stamp from Eichmann's office. She sat silently contemplating her next move. At last she looked up, 'There is a way out, Günter. One that doesn't need the extra stamp, but it does require you to be baptised with official church documentation as proof.'

He shrugged his shoulders, 'I've been baptised before, a few days after birth. Mother made sure of that, but we've lost the certificate.'

'Yes, I know, but I need the documents to prove it. Are you up for this?'

He laughed, 'Jesus was a Jew, so were his disciples, and his mother and almost certainly his father. Jews all of them, although the Church tries to deny it.' He waited, enjoying a chance to court controversy. There was not a flicker of emotion on her face. He continued unabated, 'Jesus Christ gave his life for a cause – for the freedom of his people from oppression. Why should I be any different? My people are oppressed and living under an evil regime.'

In that moment, Katharine realised that Hitler had turned this lad from a political agnostic into a Jew with a single stroke of the pen. Culturally it was hard for any Jew, even a half-Jew, to deny his roots. There was something deep within the Jewish psyche, however far they had strayed from their heritage. Katharine gathered her thoughts.

'Would your father be upset if the only way out was for you to become a Christian? Would he see that as betrayal?'

He thumped the desk, reminding her of the same action during the Friday night meal. 'My father wants me safe *at any cost*. I'll do it. And when I come out the other side, I'll get my own back on the Nazi bastards.'

'Very well. I'll stamp the necessary forms for you to take to Revd Grimes. He's a vicar in the Anglican Church across the other side of the city. Here, this is his address. If you give him these papers and mention my name, he will know what needs to be done. And don't worry, I've heard that his baptism doesn't involve any water. A kind of phoney baptism, but if it buys your freedom, who am I to criticise?' She stared at him across the desk, breaking into a smile. 'And good luck Günter. Just in case you ever need it, here's my address in England.'

He got up to leave. 'Thank you.'

'Günter.'

He turned. 'Yes?'

'Be careful. And call me when you are safely on British soil.'

Chapter 4

Five hundred miles from Vienna as the crow flies, on the northern coast of Germany near Borkum island, the biting North Sea air whipped around Captain Henderson's face penetrating his thick coat. The vast expanse of grey choppy water rolled away into the distance, the demarcation between sea and sky barely distinguishable on the horizon. The sea was temporarily devoid of any shipping. High above, the seagulls cruised in reverse gear on the wind.

'Over there, Captain Henderson.' Hugo pointed to an area on the peninsula secluded by sand dunes. A lone German policeman watched their approach. Captain Henderson's pace quickened, his shoes sank into the wet sand. 'When exactly was it found, Hugo?'

Hugo tried to keep up. He began wringing his hands, slightly breathless, 'This morning, s…sir, around six o'clock. A sea patrol spotted it floating near the peninsula.'

'What state's it in?'

Hugo would rather not have had to explain. 'A complete mess, only some of the uniform remains s…sir, and … his skin's completely shredded. He's severely bloated, one eye is badly gouged and the other one missing. Er … most of the fingers are gone.' Hugo felt a lump rising in his throat. He swallowed hard and continued, 'His teeth appear to be intact, so we can use dental records to confirm identity.'

'He's in a bit of a state then, Hugo.' They finally came up to the gelatinous mound of the body in tattered shreds of a naval uniform. The policeman gave them a single nod of acknowledgement. Captain Henderson looked down, trying to contain an involuntary gag. The colour drained from his face. He took a deep breath, finally crouching down beside the body. Instinctively he pulled a handkerchief from his pocket to cover his nostrils. It was too late – the putrid smell had penetrated the cloth.

Hugo ventured, 'As you can see, the feet are missing.'

'Yes, I can see that Hugo.' Captain Henderson grunted, his face drawn in a tight grimace. 'If you notice, they're clean cut. That means it was done before he was in the water.'

'Same job as the last lot then, s…sir.'

'That's enough idle speculation, Hugo. Hold your tongue.' Captain Henderson's patience suddenly snapped. 'And stop your infernal shuffling from foot to foot. Between that and your hand wringing it's enough to drive me to distraction.' He turned the body over; suppressing the urge to vomit. He had seen some gruesome things in his time, but this was different. He hesitantly fumbled in the tattered sleeve lining, barely covering the corpse's right arm. Pulling out some sealed documents, a map of the region was attached.

'Do we know who it is, s…sir?'

'Yes, Hugo. I am afraid I do. He's one of ours. As soon as we leave the scene, please would you notify Sir Charles? Tell him the Rear Admiral has had his contract prematurely terminated. He will know what it means.'

'Yes sir.'

Captain Henderson peeled the brown leather gloves off his hands inside out to exclude himself from any possible contamination from the corpse. Together he and Hugo walked back in the direction of the town. Captain Henderson paused for a moment to take in the coastline, not unlike the vast expanse of Saunton and Woolacombe on the North Devon coast back in England. He straightened his back, inhaled the cool sea air. As he stared out to sea again, flanked by dunes on either side, one question remained uppermost – how on earth was he going to tell Katharine about the Rear Admiral?

∾

Two days later Captain Henderson returned to the British Embassy in Vienna. He had been away a total of only four days but in that short space of time the visible presence of SS patrols had increased. Now they passed under his window every twenty minutes singing their euphoric military songs. People were being encouraged to spy on their neighbours and report any suspicious or subversive behaviour. He was expecting Katharine at midday. She was prompt as usual. She stood in the doorway, waiting for him to acknowledge her presence. He turned, as if he had heard her breathing.

'Katharine, come in, please have a seat.'

She didn't like the sombre tone of his voice. She had no idea what was coming but knew it must be serious for him to call her off the midday radio duty. She anxiously surveyed his face for any clue of what he was about to say. Her eyes betrayed a little apprehension, dampening her usual sparkle. God, how beautiful she was – even now.

He cleared his throat. 'I really wish I did not have to be the bearer of bad news.'

'Jonathan? Is it about my Jonny?'

'No.' He stared momentarily beyond her. It was to be expected that she would still be hoping he would return. He had hoped that he, Henderson, was making a difference to her life. She had appeared much more open towards him in recent weeks. 'Katharine, as head of Section in Vienna, and … I hope as a friend, it falls on me to break the sad news. We've lost another agent.' He paused for her to take in the news. 'It's not just that. I need you to formally identify the body.'

'Me?'

'Yes … Katharine, I wish I could spare you this. It's the Rear Admiral. Your brother-in-law's body was washed up on the beach near Borkum in northern Germany a few days ago.' He watched her face for a flicker of reaction, knowing the shock would take a few minutes to sink in.

'Kenneth? Oh my gosh.' Her lip quivered, 'Does my sister know?'

'We've delayed telling her until you have identified the body.' At that moment he wanted to reach out, comfort her, hold her tight against his body, make her feel safe. She had no one else here in Vienna. Etiquette prevented it.

'Are you sure it's him?' Her words broke his thoughts.

'Yes, we've recovered his papers from the remains of his clothing. It wasn't easy to decipher but his identity card had been encrypted with invisible ink. It's standard procedure, as you know. His coded poem was also amongst the papers. But … we need a family member to perform the official identification. I'm so sorry that that duty falls upon you, if you will do it.'

She titled her head, looking directly up into his eyes. Hers then welled up with tears. She stepped closer to him. Without thinking she buried her head in his chest. Instinctively he put his arms around her, holding her as he had wanted to do since an eternity. At last he was as close to her as he could possibly be without contravening her position as a married woman.

Her sobs became uncontrollable, 'Laura … what about Laura? My sister will die without him. How can she ever…'

'Ssh, ssh,' he reassured her. 'I'll authorise for someone to be sent to look after her for a few weeks, give her the necessary support – you have my word on that.' He released her from his grasp, wiping the corner of her tears with his handkerchief. 'I am so very sorry. Believe me if I could have spared you this, I would Katharine.'

She flung back her head, her feisty defiant spark evident. 'I'll get whoever did this if it's the last thing I do.' Then a flicker of realisation passed across her face. He didn't miss it. 'That's it, isn't it? Sir Charles is keeping me here in Vienna because it's the same mole. The one that betrayed Cecil has done the same for Kenneth, hasn't he?'

Captain Henderson nodded, 'Yes, we believe so. Now it's a race against time before the next one is taken out. The situation in Germany and here in Austria is very grave. Hitler is re-arming at an alarming rate. We need our eyes and ears here and we can't afford to lose any more.' He strode across the room to pour a brandy for her. 'Here, this will help to calm you.'

Her hand trembled as she raised the glass to her lips. In one gulp, the warm liquid hit the back of her throat. She coughed and spluttered, 'gosh that was strong.'

He smiled to reassure her, and passed her coat. Gently he took her arm. 'Come, let me accompany you to the mortuary.'

1 April 1938. Jonathan had barely been back a week from the Danzig operation. Whilst he had been away, Katharine had undertaken the painful task of identifying the body of her brother-in-law, Rear Admiral Kenneth MacPherson. She had tried to erase the terrible sight from her mind but it still haunted her in quiet moments. Now she had Jonathan back. He was her comfort. He had accomplished his mission in less than four weeks. She knew better than to ask him about it. He wouldn't reveal anything to her, he never did.

Things were deteriorating dramatically for Vienna's Jews. Men of all ages were disappearing daily without trace, women forced to scrub the pavements for several hours a day, their hands burnt and scarred from the acid solution. That acrid smell was everywhere. How she detested it, clinging to her nostrils. It was all entertainment to the young Brown Shirts who towered over their defenceless victims. As Katharine walked into the sitting room, Jonathan was still sprawled out asleep on the sofa. She moved into the dining room. She *had* to practise. The concert in Berchtesgaden was three weeks away. She picked up the violin propped against the sideboard, then reached for the tuning fork on the mantelpiece with a cursory glance at the black and white photographs of her ancestors. She reached for the rosin to give the bow grip, then a few exercises to get started. She adjusted the instrument under her chin, slowly moving the bow across the strings. Her fingers felt stiff from the cold weather and lack of practice. A few octaves and arpeggios would cure that. If only she admitted it, she was exhausted from trying to juggle long hours at the Embassy with stints on the radio transmitter for Captain Henderson, listening for any orders from German High Command. The haunting melody of her music matched the melancholy of her mood. At regular intervals SS patrols passed under the window, the clip of their boots always in perfect unison. This was military precision to perfection. There was no respite for the city; they were everywhere. By now she barely noticed that Jonathan was awake and reading in the next room. From the open door he interrupted her playing, 'Let's go to bed, darling. You're looking exhausted. If you don't, you'll be no good to anyone.'

'You're right, dear.' She replaced the violin in its case and followed him into the bedroom. Sleep came easily.

❧

It was 2 a.m. The sound of revving engines suddenly filled the narrow Berggasse. The faint smell of exhaust fumes filtered through the hairline cracks in the window frame. Barked orders broke the night. A woman's scream pierced the air. Katharine sat bolt upright. Jonathan rolled over, facing her. 'Oh God, what time is it darling?'

'Two o'clock,' she replied, suppressing a yawn.

'Ignore it.' He pulled the bed sheet over his head to block out the disturbance. She made as if to get out. He threw back the cover. 'No! I said ignore it.'

'Jonny,' she hissed. 'It might be the Freuds. Remember, I'm supposed to keep an eye on them. I'll be discreet, I promise. I'll just peep through the blinds. No one will see me.'

'Well if you insist, but put some clothes on please – that gorgeous body is for my eyes only.'

'Jonny, how can you be so flippant. These are dangerous times.'

He grabbed her wrist. 'Be careful.'

The banging on the doors below became more persistent. '*Achtung,* open up! *Schnell.*' She rushed back to the bed, grabbing a dressing gown. 'It sounds a bit too close, Jonny.'

'I said ignore it.'

The blinds cast vertical pyjama stripes over the walls like prison uniform as the searchlights shone through their slats. Now he sat bolt upright, holding her hand tightly. 'Don't worry. Whatever it is, leave it to me.' He couldn't admit his fear to her.

Metal boot studs echoed in the corridor outside.

'Stay calm,' he reassured her with a squeeze of the hand. 'It's probably nothing. We have diplomatic immunity, remember that.'

One massive crash and the front door was broken down. Jonathan reached under the mattress for their passbook and papers. Two Gestapo officers barged in, a third waited in the open doorway.

'Get up!' The uncompromising face of the other man in a long grey coat glared at him.

Jonathan held his ground, 'How dare you barge into our apartment. We are both British. You have no jurisdiction over us.' He thrust their papers at him as proof. Next to him the officer in a leather coat smirked, ogling Katharine's semi-naked form.

'We are checking you aren't sheltering any bloody Jews. Search the place, Heinz.' The third young officer stepped forward. Jonathan reached under his pillow. The young Gestapo officer drew his revolver, his finger on the trigger. 'Stop or I'll shoot.'

Too late. A single bullet cracked the air from the direction of the doorway, grazing Jonathan's right shoulder. He flinched as blood seeped through his pyjamas. The other two officers lurched forward, dragging him from the bed. His body collapsed to the floor. The full force of a metal toecap hit his ear. The pain seared through his eardrum; their malicious laughter distant and muffled.

Katharine grasped the second officer by the arm. 'What…' With a rough movement he turned, striking her hard across the cheek, knocking her to the floor. 'Frau, I suggest you keep quiet unless you want to come with us.' She was powerless, knowing that her self-defence training at Aldershot barracks would jeopardise both of them.

They spread-eagled Jonathan on the floor, handcuffed him. One heaved him to his feet, wrenching his shoulder blade. He had learnt in training to suppress any reaction to pain. Their manic laughter mercifully stopped. 'We have orders that you are to come with us.'

'No!' Katharine struggled to get up. 'What has he done? No!'

The third officer stepped within an inch of her. His left hand moved around her back and down her thigh. With malicious self-confidence he squeezed her buttock, 'We'll come back for some of that when we're less busy.'

'Get your filthy hands off me or you'll regret this.' In that moment she realised how precarious life was. Through brutality and psychological fear the new power had instilled terror into everyone. It was so easy to achieve. She took deep breaths to regain some calm control.

He laughed. 'This time you're safe.'

She sank back onto the edge of the bed. As Jonathan was dragged from the room, he managed one backward glance, even a half-smile. 'I'll be back, my love.'

The officers' laughter became distant as they reached the bottom of the stairwell. She stared at the broken door, numb with disbelief. Then steadily, slowly, she moved to the window, her legs no longer seemed part of her body. She pulled back the blinds. She had to see for herself. Jonathan was being pushed into the back of an open army truck. He was not the only one. Through blurred tears, she counted a dozen other men. The bent figure of Guttmann the baker from the next street was unmistakable. Her heart sank. His wife and children must be distraught. She would go to them in the morning.

Just why she looked further down the street at that precise moment she couldn't tell. At the far end, a sleek black saloon car waited in the shadows; the silhouette of two heads clearly visible in the back seat with chauffer in the front. She didn't see their faces but could tell that they wore no uniform. Then the truck drove off with its detainees in the direction of Kärntnerstrasse. The saloon pulled out and followed. She turned away. Reaching into the bottom drawer of the dressing table she pulled out Jonathan's personal coded poem for posting. M would get it within hours and know that he had been taken.

The truck pulled up outside Gestapo Headquarters in the Hotel Metropol. An SS guard stepped forward, opened the latch and ordered the bare-footed men to file out. Their movement slowly snaked unsteadily towards the grey building in front of them. Jonathan's shoulder ached. He fought to keep focused. By now the graze had stopped bleeding but he was cold and nausea churned his stomach. He tried to glance sideways at the others. He wasn't moving fast enough for the SS officer. Without warning the officer struck him on the back of the neck in a single blow. Jonathan barely heard the ensuing orders. 'Move it! *Schnell!*'

He tried to regain his balance.

The detainees were marched into a large entrance hall, dingy and bare except for a large portrait of the Führer bearing down on them. Each man was searched, all valuables, watches and rings removed. Pushed along the dark gloomy back corridor they came to half a dozen cells, devoid of any furnishings. The stone floor was their only resting place. Two or three men were shoved into each cell, the heavy metal doors slammed behind their victims. Total isolation from the outside world; fear for the future.

Jonathan's eyes gradually adjusted to the dim light. He knew interrogation was the only certainty. It wasn't a question of if but when. His two companions hadn't spoken a single word; one looked to be a middle-aged businessman, the other a non-Jewish lad who was almost certainly part of the Resistance. Hours seemed to pass. Time indefinitely suspended. It was all part of the psychological disorientation. He took a pencil stub from his jacket pocket, the only item they missed after the initial search. He began to scratch words on the plaster of the cell wall. Slowly, with determination, he formed each letter carefully with the charcoal. Facts would keep him sane. He had to fight what was coming; safeguard his sanity and thereby protect his cover story. He listed everything he could remember: first countries, then their capitals. In an act of defiance, he decided to omit Vienna and Berlin. Silently the young lad joined him, inscribing mathematical symbols on the other windowless wall. Their encyclopaedic compilation was suddenly interrupted by a prison guard as the key grated in the lock. He stood there scanning the cell.

'You,' he beckoned to Jonathan. 'Herraus!'

Jonathan shoved his pencil back in his pyjama pocket; his treasured implement to retain his sanity. Marching down the corridor, the combination of damp and cold air caught his breath, causing a sharp pain in his lungs. Drops of water dripped from the ceiling above, soaking into the blood stains on his pyjamas. He hadn't noticed the two Brown Shirts fall in behind him. Claustrophobic walls closed in on him everywhere – metaphorical and physical. He tried to suppress the sinister dread which threatened to engulf him. He tried to re-focus on his training at Anderson Manor. His Commanding Officer's words rang in his ears: 'Never let the foreign blighters know you're scared. Keep your nerve. You're British. Remember that.'

The austere room beckoned as an octopus about to wrap its tentacles around its prey. As Jonathan looked around he noticed the light bulb had been removed from its socket. Two waiting SS officers stood rock-still examining him from behind a small wooden desk; a single chair the only other furniture. A shiver involuntarily ran down his spine.

The senior SS officer was the first to move. He stared at Jonathan, assessing his figure. He began rhythmically tapping the back of the chair with his stick. 'Sit down!' His agitated movement with the baton moved to the palm of his hand in slow regular intervals. Jonathan walked towards the chair, trying to relax his shoulders to relieve the tension.

The questioning began: 'Name, rank and number?'

Jonathan stared ahead, not making eye contact with his interrogator. 'Dr Jonathan Walters, medic at the general hospital.'

'I said, rank and number?'

Jonathan cleared his throat, 'I am a doctor and a British citizen. You have no right to arrest me. His Majesty will take a dim view of my treatment. I say nothing more until the ambassador arrives.'

'Is that so? What insolence! Well, the British ambassador is asleep and is not going to get out of bed for you.' He bent over him, his mouth close to Jonathan's ear, 'If you do not co-operate, we have something in mind for you which may just alter your perspective.'

Jonathan could smell the faint garlic on his breath. It was hard to imagine that this man was just like him: he ate, drank, slept; probably even had a wife and family. But fundamentally they were worlds apart; at opposite ends of the spectrum of good and evil. The sudden crack of the cane across his thighs was unexpected, cushioned a little by his pyjama trousers. He held back from any reaction, gritting his teeth to absorb the shock. His head felt light, he was slipping away. The last thing he saw was the distorted hand coming towards his face. A few seconds later, dazed, his head spinning, he heard the officer's words distant, 'I will ask you one more time: rank and number.'

Inside he rallied his strength.

The SS officer took a step back as he cracked the cane against the back of the chair. 'We have reason to believe that you know someone by the name of Sir Charles Basil. He and his friends have been causing us some bother.'

Jonathan sat still, his body burning with pain, staring ahead. The agitated officer, his face now red, the vein in his neck bulging, glared out of round metal spectacles. His eyes blazed as he continued, 'You have one last chance – do you know this man, Sir Charles?'

'No.'

'*Lüguer!*' He struck him across the ear. His head rocked with the impact. Instantly blood stained the baton.

The officer turned to the other guard, 'Take him away! Separate him from the others. He leaves on the 4 a.m. schedule. He's going on a little holiday.' He smirked, then saluted: 'Heil Hitler, Dr Jonathan Walters.'

He turned, his boots clipping across the stone floor. Jonathan was marched out to an unknown fate.

❧

Inside the hot sweaty cattle truck, Jonathan opened his eyes. He had fallen asleep where he stood. He breathed in deeply before realising his mistake. Packed so tight that he was not able to sit, like every one else he had defecated where he stood, the stench horrific. The rickety jolting of the train journey accentuated the pain in his shattered body. He was almost pleased they had finally stopped. They must have been travelling for some time; it wasn't possible to tell because the Gestapo had confiscated his watch. Their destination was anyone's guess. The dawn's first light now seeped weakly through the cracks in the wooden doors, enabling him to glimpse the barren dusty ground outside. One by one, the doors were wrenched open, spilling the remnants of humanity within. The silence was broken by shouts further down the outside of the train.

'*Juden Schwein, Herraus!*'

'Jewish pigs get out – stand to the left.'

'*Schnell Juden Schweinehund.*'

'All other degenerates, to the right.'

The voices came closer to his cattle truck.

'Open up!'

The door slid open, the light now blinding his eyes.

'*Juden Raus* – Jews get out!' The SS officer randomly struck at whim the heads of the men clambering down, spitting in their faces. One by one, the last of the Jewish occupants gingerly climbed out, their identity shown on the left breast. The dulled yellow star's black lettering marked *Jude* could never be forgotten.

'*Staats Feinde*, enemies of the State, get out!'

This was his cue. Jonathan shifted unsteadily, cramped up against the wall. He clambered down, trying to straighten his aching body. His movement too slow, the SS officer raised his baton hitting him across the back. '*Schweinehund*; dirty dog. Get in line!'

Jonathan stumbled alongside the other political prisoners. Like him, they too had a blue star on their left breast, no thick black lettering for them. They were marched the short distance towards the gates of the camp. As he passed under the wrought iron arch, his heart sank. Overhead, the words *Arbeit Macht Frei* rang through his head. Looking beyond the words he glimpsed the heavy spotlights set on the square wooden watch towers, vigilant guards peering out, guns to hand. When would he taste freedom again? It was a luxury that now had to be fought for. Ahead of him dozens of rows of huts encircled a large parade ground, surrounded at the perimeter by an electrified barbed wire fence. The camp already held five thousand inmates. In the distance, the sound of a single gunshot cut through the chill air. He glanced at the other political prisoners; for some their only crime had been protecting their Jewish neighbours or friends from attack by the Gestapo. Now they all paid a heavy price. He tried to focus, using the technique he had learnt in training. P.O.T.S. Over and over he repeated the words in his head:

Positive thoughts,
Observe everything,
Think,
Survive.

Every minute alive, every breath he drew, would bring him nearer to freedom. That day *would* come. He promised himself he would survive. Every morning he would thank heaven for new opportunities: he would devise a way of living through it all. Through his thoughts, he was pushed towards one of the huts by the guards flanking him. The new inmates were lined up a few metres from the whitewashed wall. Orders were brief: '*Sich nackt ausziehen! Schnell!* Strip naked! Off with your clothes! Hurry!'

No one moved; too stunned to react. A senior SS officer, short and pompous, brushed the guard aside. 'Off with your clothes! Twenty-five lashes for the man who fails to obey.' The other guards raised their weapons in support.

One by one the prisoners stood naked, shivering in the cold dawn. Jonathan moved closer to the elderly man next to him to provide some bodily warmth. He wouldn't be able to withstand the cold like Jonathan. The final order rang through their ears: 'Out onto the parade ground now! *Schnell*.'

For the first time, as Jonathan waited for the others to get into line on the concrete square, he noticed the desolation. No birds sang to hail the start of spring. Nature had deserted this place, its absence epitomising the reverse of life. Here death reigned. Even before he could see it, he could smell it everywhere.

Two more guards approached: '*Achtung*, stand still!' Their water hoses pointed at the men on each end of the line. Waiting in the middle, Jonathan glanced down at the bloody wheals on his naked flesh. Unflinching, he took the ice cold water against his bare skin.

'You're done, to the left.' The guard gestured to a large table at one end of the parade ground, piles of folded clothes neatly laid out on the top. Silently, each naked man filed passed to collect their new identity; their individuality stripped; their humanity trodden into the ground. The blue-and-white striped flannelette suit looked more like pyjamas. Socks and underwear were luxuries no longer afforded to them. The guard marched them to hut 28.

'This is your abode gentlemen,' his lip curled in mock courtesy. 'Morning roll-call is 5 a.m. sharp; breakfast at 5.30 a.m.; work until one o'clock; lunch followed by more work. Final roll-call is at 8 p.m.; lights out by 8.30 p.m. Failure to obey these simple rules has consequences.'

Jonathan stood at the hut entrance observing the depressing scene. The stench of overcrowded humanity invaded his senses. It was impossible not to breathe in the putrid air. What seemed like hundreds of eyes peered from small wooden bunks lining both sides of the hut, three layers high, too tight to move easily between. So many souls, too many to count, crammed into each section; no mattresses or pillows, only straw. Standing in front of him was Mr Guttmann the baker. Guttmann turned around. Recognising Jonathan, he whispered, 'Dr Walters, not you too.' Jonathan acknowledged his comment with a nod.

'See that man over there,' he hissed.

Jonathan's eyes followed Guttmann's line of sight. Leaning against the end bunk was a thin lanky man, his age indistinguishable because of his shaven head. His over-large sunken eyes in hollow cheeks betrayed years of torment. 'He's called a "Capo". He's been here the longest, probably since the camp opened. Although he's a prisoner, he's in charge of our hut. He has all the power in this hut. Get on the right side of him and you'll be okay.'

The Capo stepped forward, 'There's room for you two over there on the top bunk. You call me Capo Fritz. You…' he pointed at Jonathan.

Jonathan stepped forward, 'Yes, sir.' He eyed Jonathan up and down. 'You look strong enough. You and him', he nodded towards Guttmann. 'You can both collect lunch today for our hut.' He passed Jonathan a single pair of gloves. 'Here. You'll need these. The handles of the cauldron are hot and it is quite a distance from the canteen.'

'May I have gloves, sir?' Guttmann was braver than most to ask the question.

Capo Fritz stared around the room, 'Fat fool, this is no holiday. You're lucky we even have this pair. Share them.'

'Sir, where are the toilets?' Guttmann had been desperate for ages.

'Can't you see with your own eyes? There are no showers, no toilets, nothing. Do you think we look and smell like this through choice? As for defecating, do it where you have to but keep it away from the walkways. Then at roll-call throw it under the hut as you leave. One thing you learn very quickly in this place – keep your head down, obey orders and you may see another day.'

Katharine waited impatiently in Captain Henderson's office. Unable to stay alone in the apartment after Jonathan's arrest, she had gone straight to the Embassy. She felt the walls of this place were her only real protection. Although she had sat for several hours in his office waiting till daybreak, she was not quite alone. A skeleton staff manned the building during night hours. She glanced at her watch. It was now nine o'clock and still no sign of him. Unusual for him to be late for work. The clock on the mantelpiece had stopped. She walked over to wind it up. The rhythmic tick would comfort her and break the world of silence around her. She knew that Captain Henderson was often at the office early, usually before eight in the morning. Now she feared the worst. Had he been taken too? Her thoughts raced. She put her hands to her head as if to stop the pounding. *Please, not him*, she thought. He was the only reassuring presence left in her life, her one constant. She gazed sightlessly at the picture of the Battle of Waterloo hanging over the fireplace, numbed by the early morning's events. She barely heard the footsteps coming along the corridor.

He appeared flustered as he entered, none of his usual upright composure. He was unusually distracted. 'Katharine, ah, I'm so sorry I'm late.' He stopped in his tracks, noticing the graze on her cheek and reddened eyes. She could not hold back the emotion. Her eyes welled up. She opened her mouth, but no sound came. Her bottom lip quivered. He walked over to her, putting his hand on her shoulder. It felt strong and comforting. Tears now streamed down her face. Emotionally she clung to him.

His words were comforting, his deep voice tender, 'Katharine, I know. I know what's happened and I am so very sorry.'

Through the tears, she spluttered, 'What … news of him? Where's my Jonny?'

His shoulders tensed. Jonathan was the one thing which stood between him and happiness. Wasn't this what he had always hoped for? That Jonathan would be off the scene and he himself would have a chance with her? Yes, but he never wished this fate – not even on him. He took a deep breath, 'We are trying to find out. Sir Charles has everyone on alert and is doing his utmost. We have no reason to believe that he's not still alive.' He moved away to pour them both a brandy, passing her a double measure. 'Here, take this. It will steady the nerves.'

Her hand trembled as she took the half-filled glass of amber liquid. With the other, she fumbled for a handkerchief. He was quicker and drew one from his pocket. 'Here.' He continued gently, 'When you have finished your drink, we can go over the latest papers. Foley has sent us some new official stamps from Berlin.'

She drew back, shaking. 'What?' She flung back her head. Her quiet tears turning to uncontrollable anger, 'I … I have just lost my husband to – the Nazis. The bastards have taken my husband, beaten him in front of me – and you, you want me to work as if nothing has happened?' Her impassioned face pulled at his heartstrings.

'Katharine … please, I was only trying to…'

She didn't allow him to finish; still shaking she let out a tirade of rage, 'You heartless man. How could you?'

He had never provoked such anger in a person before. Now the woman he cared for most in the world had been mortally shaken to the core by his attempt to distract her from her pain. She still hadn't finished, glaring straight at him, eyes glistening; she challenged him, 'How can you know what it is to love someone – you with your stiff upper lip and British correctness? You never show any emotion. Never! You don't know what it is to love someone and lose them.' She fixed her blazing gaze defiantly on his face. Her emotion finally spent, their eyes locked in something beyond the present. A flicker of pain flashed across his face. At that moment he would give his life to have her.

'Oh my goodness! Captain Henderson, I'm so sorry.'

He abruptly turned and walked out of the room.

Alone, she was left with a mixture of confused emotion. How could she have been so insensitive? She had gone too far. So he did have feelings. He had loved – that much she now realised. What love that it should provoke such pain in a man? Now she would never know. She would never be able to raise the subject with him. He had always been a mystery, hiding so much within his reserved exterior of polite etiquette. Whoever she was, she probably didn't deserve him. She rushed into the corridor to see him turning at the bottom. She couldn't go after him. It was too late.

It had all started with her first trip to Berlin for a concert in September 1937. Berlin had hosted the Olympic Games the previous year. For Britain, 1937 was the year of the Coronation of George VI in Westminster Abbey after the rocky abdication of Edward VIII who had given up his throne for the American divorcee Mrs Simpson. For Katharine, it was the year she met and married Jonathan, her beloved 'Jonny'. She had also come to the attention of Sir Charles Basil after a chance introduction to Berlin high society and the Führer himself. It had all happened so quickly. The events of the last few months flashed before her.

Chapter 5

Berlin, September 1937. Inside the Philharmonic concert hall Thomas Beecham raised his baton. Wagner. That'll get them, he thought. On stage Katharine wiped her brow and adjusted her violin, any thoughts she might have drowned out by the chanting.

'Ein Reich! Ein Volk! Ein Führer!'

She could hardly believe she was here. Germany, Goethe, the land of Heine's poems and musical dreams, Bach and Beethoven. Schiller and Schubert. Germany – now the land of Adolf Hitler. New anti-Jewish laws had deprived the country of its Jewish musicians. Most had left four years earlier when Hitler came to power. Germany's loss was Britain and America's gain. No one here cared about that. Hitler's psychological indoctrination was almost complete.

'Deutschland, Deutschland über Alles!'

Her acute musician's ear noted a moment's hesitation, a quaver? Then, as if to send the notion crashing to the ground, the audience began its hysterical mantra. Somewhere in the tumult, she felt her fingers twitch gently on the fingerboard, her head throbbed with tonight's musical rhythm, her eyes glued to the conductor. She was almost too afraid to look up, to see. She chided herself that this was ridiculous. She was, after all, a British subject; well-bred and educated in Bath; none of this pompous German bravado for her. She glanced up. Standing erect in the State Box she saw Herr Adolf Hitler dwarfed by his aides. Swastika banners draped from every balcony. But now to music; Beecham raised his baton once again. All eyes watched. Steadying her hand on the bow, she was lost to the music for the entire concert. At the end, amidst rapturous applause and calls of 'encore', Beecham smiled and muttered, 'The old bugger seemed to enjoy that.' He hadn't realised the microphone was still switched on and his comments echoed around the globe on the BBC radio service. He was lucky this time. No diplomatic crisis ensued.

Backstage there were the usual courtesies. Katharine would have preferred to return to the hotel but Beecham beckoned her:

'Katharine, come here my dear, now if you would.' His voice gentle but firm, the exertion just expended on the concert had caused beads of perspiration on his face. He mopped his brow with a pure white handkerchief, telling her, 'The Führer is on his way and wants to meet the orchestra and soloists. Our playing of *Lohengrin* was a masterpiece and you were perfection incarnate; a triumph, my dear.' She couldn't take in fully what he said. Hitler was already moving along the line of the orchestra. In a second he was silently passing her; his face sombre. She tried not to stare, frozen in the moment. He was thinner and considerably shorter than she had expected. He looked very ordinary, but his presence gave an air of authority in spite of his slight stature. She took in the moment. This was her first sight of the man who was instilling fear across Europe.

❧

At the end of that same week, Sir Charles paced the temporary office inside the makeshift headquarters on London's Shaftsbury Avenue. The wiry figure of Hugo, flanked by two men, was standing nervously facing him.

'I want that woman on my team!' bellowed Sir Charles, his baritone voice echoing off the walls. 'She has made substantial inroads into German high society. Why wasn't I told? Last week she came within a hair's breadth of the Führer himself. It has taken me years to get near him and she waltzes in without so much as a smattering of training. She was flagged up a year ago. You were supposed to keep an eye on her. Why didn't you track her? It can't be that difficult. What do they teach you at Blenheim? I should have sent Hugo, the office junior.'

Hugo tried to keep a straight face.

Sir Charles swung round, pointing to a map on the wall, its pins and flags at odd angles. 'Here – this is her next destination. The first flight to Vienna, you're on it. And I want her on my team before the week's out. Do you understand?' He sank back breathlessly into his leather chair, the heat of the room overwhelming him. He needed time to compose his thoughts. The two men scurried out. Hugo turned to follow but Sir Charles leant forward, his voice softer: 'No, Hugo. Stay a moment. How long have you been with us lad?'

'Six weeks, sir.'

Sir Charles smirked, 'Well, Hugo … we will both take the train. I'll deal with that woman myself. She is too valuable to lose and you can keep me company.'

'But sir, I don't have a passport.' Hugo waited anxiously for reassurance.

'These are mere details, Hugo. See Captain Henderson, he'll take care of everything for you.' He stroked his moustache, 'Oh and Hugo, on your way out please show in Dr Walters.'

'Yes sir.' He barely had time to summon him as they passed in the doorway. Dr Walters strolled casually into the office, his slightly dishevelled hair belying his age, his tie not altogether straight. Sir Charles preferred a much smarter dress-sense. He could time Walters to the precise second with his watch; always ten minutes late no matter what. He knew his agents better than they realised. He could predict their every move and reaction.

'Jonathan, have a seat.' He gestured to a chair covered in newspapers. 'Move that lot and tell me, how's the doctoring business?'

'Not bad. Fair enough.'

Sir Charles swivelled round in his chair, 'Let's not beat around the bush Jonathan. I need you full time. How was Prague?'

Jonathan surveyed the chaotic room, his face not betraying the seriousness of the situation in the east. 'There's no progress. None at all. We didn't even get close to the old blighter. He's gone deep.'

'We don't have much time, Jonathan. Russia is unstable, you know that. The PM's getting agitated and I need results.'

'We all want results M, but under the circumstances we might have to move operations. I have a hunch they're closing in on our lot.'

'Hunches aren't good enough man,' he muttered, moving to the cabinet and pouring out two brandies. 'I need concrete evaluation of the situation, and I need it *now*.' He turned to face Jonathan again, 'Take these new reports, they arrived this morning. They make sober reading. Study them carefully. Action them as you think fit. I trust you on this one and we'll debrief after I … no, after *we* return from Vienna. I have a little job for you. You'll like this one.'

Jonathan had learned from past experience never to contradict the boss. Things were rarely as he portrayed them.

❧

Captain Henderson stood by the window of his Whitehall office on one of his rare trips back to England. He pondered his rapid rise within the ranks of the Secret Intelligence Service. In the past year he had been promoted to Head of Operations in Vienna. All the cloak and dagger stuff of childhood fiction suited him well. He felt like a spider in the centre of an intricate web, waiting, feeling the tender vibrations of counter-espionage; at the ready to pounce.

'Captain Henderson?' The voice was female, familiar, alluring. He turned. It was her. Katharine! She didn't seem to recognise him, but she was as beautiful as he remembered. His throat inexplicably tightened. 'Good morning, how may I help you?' He stared far too intently for comfort.

'Yes, I have a problem with my passport. There seems to be an error which caused a terrible row at the airport. They actually refused permission for me to board my flight. I've got an important trip, and now … well, it's all a mess and there's every chance that I'm going to miss my concert.'

He hadn't seen her since 1932. That was five years ago. Her face was softer than he remembered, her wavy fair hair cropped in the modern style. It suited her.

'Concert?'

She looked puzzled. 'Yes, I am a …'

He interrupted without thinking, 'I see. Right, hmm. Let's see your papers.'

She stood awkwardly as he flicked through the pages of her passport. He paused at her photograph, remembering the first time he had set eyes on her. After a few minutes he finally looked up, 'I'm so sorry. How impolite of me – please have a seat.' He continued to scrutinise the documents. 'Well, according to this you're taking up permanent residence in Austria. But from what I see I assume you're not planning emigration, but a short stay. You've inadvertently filled in the wrong forms to renew your passport.'

'Really? How silly of me.' She looked down at the relevant page. She bit her bottom lip in frustration. 'How long will this take to put right? I'm terribly late and still need to make alternative travel arrangements.'

He regained his thoughts. Now was not the time to be lost in the past. 'Quite. Where will you be staying?'

She tried not to show her irritation at his slowness to grasp the urgency of the situation.

'Vienna. Where else do we cultured violinists hope to play but in the heart of the city of dreams?' She smiled to diffuse the tension. He surveyed her facial expressions, angling for any clue as to her perception of him. This was not a good start. He needed to change his tone, be less formal. 'Yes, of course.' He returned her smile, softening his approach. 'I meant – where in Vienna? Which hotel?'

She blushed. 'Oh, I'm sorry – I'm staying at the Hotel Imperial.' Now she had taken the formal tone.

'Where better. Well, I have some discretion in these matters and I can actually stamp your passport. You shouldn't have any more trouble.'

He leant towards her as he reached for the official stamp. Looking down he inadvertently noticed her breasts.

'You must know that you're gathering quite a reputation in the music world after your triumph in Berlin.'

She raised her eyebrows, her mouth slightly pouting, 'So you do know who I am! Why did you pretend otherwise?' She seemed even more sensuous.

'I didn't link the name with the face.' He lied. He hadn't stopped thinking about her for a moment, but masculine pride and naval training prevailed. To her, he was probably just another functionary. How could she possibly know his real status? No one could really discern what lay behind the stone façades of Whitehall. She gave a wry smile.

'Oh, Berlin! That was a whirlwind tour. I intend to stay in Vienna a little longer. I couldn't refuse an invitation to be guest violinist with the Vienna Philharmonic. Herr Furtwängler is such an eminent conductor and it's a privilege to play with him.'

At last he had caught her attention positively, 'Ah, please give him my regards. We're old friends. Maybe I'll come to hear you one evening. I do enjoy a good concert.'

'You visit Vienna, Captain Henderson?' Her eyes suddenly sparkled. She had a life and vitality, which it was rumoured in social circles, had already attracted several hopeful suitors. How could he make a difference? How could he capture her attention such that she would never forget him?

'I have an office in Vienna, doing pretty much the same work as I do here. I'm pretty nifty with these stamps.' She didn't miss his sardonic humour. She laughed. He had finally broken through her reserve. Encouraged by her response, he continued, 'I love Vienna, it's my second home. Beautiful Vienna – a cultural heaven.' He shuffled the papers on his desk, noting how she silently observed him. He would love to know her thoughts at that moment. 'I'm actually based there most of the time now. I only come back to England occasionally. How did you meet him?'

'Who?' For the first time, she looked around the room, taking in the scene; maps of Europe covered the walls, each section a different colour. Drawing pins and flags protruded from lines and borders. In the corner she noticed a large drinks cabinet and a gentleman's umbrella propped against the side. The heavy velvet curtains were partially drawn against the bright early September sunlight.

'Furtwängler. How did you meet him? You must have been to Vienna before?' He had lost the connection again. She shifted slightly. Outwardly, she remained cool – the future of her trip to Vienna depended on him. 'No, I've never been there. He came to Bath last summer and heard me playing first violin virtuoso with the local orchestra. He's such a charming man. I obviously impressed him because he came to find me afterwards and invited me to play in "his little orchestra" as he likes to call it.' She momentarily found herself back on the stage, Furtwängler striding towards her. She had been struck by the slender formally-attired gentleman of an undisclosed age. She loved the way he clicked his heels as he bowed from the hip and offered his hand.

Henderson coughed. 'Well, your papers are now complete. Here.' He had that look in his eyes again. She frowned and glanced away. 'Might I suggest the Orient Express? It's an excellent way to travel for someone in your position. You can use my telephone to make the booking.' He passed it to her.

She accepted. He discreetly studied her as she made her call. When she had finished, he smiled, 'And now, I wish you every success with your concerts in Vienna.' As he passed the documents across the desk, their hands touched briefly. She stepped back.

'Thank you, Captain Henderson. I'm very grateful to you.'

He offered his hand. Hers felt so warm. He wanted to hold her forever. She turned and walked confidently out. He returned to the window. On the streets below His Majesty's civil servants rushed between their government offices in Whitehall. The room suddenly felt empty, he was hopelessly in love with her. Her vitality was irresistible. He smiled to himself. Why, on occasion, he himself could be less serious and was even known to have a sense of humour. Why hadn't he tried harder? Next time he would be less reserved, less formal.

There *would* be a next time. He would make sure of that. In his peripheral vision he caught sight of his secretary passing the door.

'Dorothy! I leave for Vienna on Wednesday. Book a ticket for the orchestral concert at the weekend, would you? Furtwängler is conducting. And…' He lit a cigarette and drew breath, '…please, don't tell me they're all gone.'

'Very good, sir.' She paused, 'By the way, sir, as you requested, I've sent off the visa applications to Berlin this morning. Mr Foley should have them within the week.'

❧

Katharine boarded the train for London clutching her copy of *The Thinking Reed*, Rebecca West's latest novel. She admired this forthright female writer, once a lover of H.G. Wells. There had not been time to travel back to Devon before her trip to Vienna so she had stayed overnight with an aunt in Reading. As she glanced back, all along the platform people were elbowing to get to the carriage doors. She settled into an empty compartment, not sure how long she would be able to enjoy the peace and quiet. A few minutes passed. The carriage door slid open, the morning's chill air rushed around her ankles. A handsome gentleman in his early to mid-thirties stepped inside, Gladstone bag in hand. She smiled, returning to the page in her novel. Avoiding eye-contact she ventured, 'The Railway gives such marvellous service these days. I see we're supplied with our very own physician.' She glanced up, her eyes sparkling. He might be a challenge. She extended her hand, 'Katharine Simmons. Pleased to make your acquaintance.'

He returned the gesture and shook her hand, 'Dr Jonathan Walters, at your service. Is it wise to be travelling alone? After all, this could be a very dangerous journey, especially for one as delicate as yourself.'

She smiled. She was anything but delicate. Beneath her slim repose, she was tough. She had had to be at school to protect her younger sister when the other children teased her about the leg-irons. Laura had contracted polio when she was just seven, affecting her left side and necessitating the dreadful restrictions. Katharine had always come to her defence. Now she was somewhat more refined. A year at Finishing School in Bath had taken care of that. She raised her eyes, peering over her glasses. 'How do you know I'm alone? My husband is, this very minute, getting me a cup of tea.'

'Because you don't have a wedding ring.' He surveyed her momentarily before continuing. 'You only have a single case stored above you, your tone is more flirtatious and daring than a married woman … do you want me to carry on?'

'No.' She laughed. 'Good gracious, for someone who has only just clapped eyes on me, you're very observant.' She liked him. His mischievous grin was deceptive. He might be older than he appeared. It was hard to tell. His youthful manner could place him in his late twenties, just a few years older than her. However, as a doctor he would have had a number of years at university and medical school, making him in his early thirties. Two can play at this game, she thought. 'Well, Dr Walters, your clothes although functional lack the care of a woman's touch. You also have no wedding ring and from your unruly lock of hair, I'd guess you were a bit of a rebel.'

'Very good,' he replied, surprised by her forthright honesty. 'Please, do call me Jonathan. I much prefer to do away with formality. You could spend hours in this tiny compartment in the company of some dreadful bore, thus forcing you to listen to heaven knows what idle chatter. And I judge that you are not the kind of person to endure such nonsense.' He had a twinkle in his eyes.

She laughed. 'So Jonathan, where are you travelling?'

'Vienna.' His cool relaxed smile lifted his countenance.

'What a coincidence, so am I.' She had to admit she was rather pleased. It would liven up a rather long journey.

'I know.'

She shot him a look, challenging his apparent clairvoyance. He laughed, 'It's written on your suitcase.'

She had nothing to lose in being a little bolder. He already knew she was no meek girl. 'What takes you there, if you don't mind me asking?' There was something about him and it was not just the lack of a wedding ring. She glanced discreetly over his lean body. Her sister Laura would definitely approve of him.

'You're very forthright, but I like that in a girl.'

She studied him carefully, 'Well Jonathan, I was never one for too much small talk over tea. I prefer to get to the heart of things, none of the old Pump Room stuff for me. We have the vote now and a woman needs to find her way in this modern world.'

He nodded, 'Yes, I suppose you're right. It's just a bit of a shock when one's not expecting such maturity and honesty from someone so young or, dare I say…' he whispered just loud enough for her to hear, '…striking.'

She lowered her eyes. 'Thank you.'

He continued observing her reactions. 'It so happens that I'll be spending a couple of months on a new research programme. I've developed a new surgical technique. Some British practitioners pooh-poohed the whole thing, but quite a few surgeons abroad are eager to learn my methods after my paper was published in *The Lancet*. So until the scepticism has died down in London, I'm off for a while. I've been seconded to the general hospital in Vienna where I'm hoping to consolidate my work.'

'Isn't that where Professor Sigmund Freud works?'

'Well – used to. He's now in private practice. What do you know of his work anyway?'

'Nothing really.' She had over-stretched her knowledge in aiming to impress him. 'But I do read the newspapers.'

His face became unexpectedly sombre. She preferred his lighter mood. His sudden seriousness bothered her. She couldn't quite place why. She broke his sudden pause, reverting to their conversation about women travelling unaccompanied, 'Considering the possible dangers for me on this train journey, maybe you're right Jonathan, I shouldn't travel alone. After all, if I was to swoon suddenly, from the dangers you understand, at least I would have the benefit of you to attend me. That is, if you have no other companion …' How could she be suggesting such a thing? Her sister would be mortified by her forthright suggestion. She discreetly moved her eyes over his body again. What would it be like to seduce him?

The station master's voice interrupted, 'London Victoria. All change please.'

Katharine steadily made her way down the platform, jostled from side to side by chattering middle-aged women. At the far end of the station the Orient Express was already waiting for its twelve noon departure. Its well-polished maroon and green carriages edged with thin gold trim were quite a contrast from the shabby Reading to London train.

Jonathan was suddenly beside her. 'Here, Katharine, let me help you into the train.' A uniformed attendant approached them, taking their suitcases, 'This way please.' He led them slowly along the carriages. 'Here you are then, I've put your cases by the bunks. If there's nothing else I'll take my leave.'

Katharine scanned the compartment. To the left a discreet door off the cabin revealed a tiny compact toilet. On the opposite side a sumptuous sitting room. She adjusted her hat in the mirror before entering the adjoining sitting room. She removed her jacket.

'Jonathan. Thank you for …' her voice trailed away as she looked down. The attendant had brought in two suitcases. 'Oh, I'm terribly sorry, Jonathan. This is so embarrassing.'

'Well, I don't know about embarrassing … er well, yes, yes, maybe it is. I'll call the guard immediately.' A different attendant came in. Jonathan began his complaint, 'Ah yes, look, there seems to be an error. This young lady and I have been inadvertently put in the same carriage.'

The attendant was unperturbed by the potential disaster, 'Let's see ya tickets then. Nope, no mistake sir. That's what it says on ya tickets. Look, 'ere, one berth sharing. Now I sees two people, two berths, both sharing. All sorted, anyways we's too full to bursting. Can't change nothing this late in the day, nothing spare anyway, guvnor.'

'But, dash it man! We are single man and woman. We can't possibly share.'

'Very sharp if you don't minds me saying, sir, but if you reads your ticket it clearly asks gender, and neither of yous has bothered to fill it out. So there *yous* are then. We ain't mind readers you know. Now if there's nothing else sir, I am off. I've lots of others to sort out.'

Katharine turned to Jonathan, 'Well Jonathan, it's you and me. Under the circumstances I suppose we'll have to make the best of this error.' She raised her eyebrows in mock shock. It wouldn't do to show amusement at the situation.

Jonathan nodded, 'Judging from the number of people and luggage on the platform, the attendant was telling the truth. The train is going to be pretty full.'

'Well…' Katharine looked at him intently. 'We both have our reputations to protect, but I suppose we all have to compromise on our standards from time to time, and this is obviously one of those situations when … *I must*. After all, it is possible to be too fussy, don't you think?'

Jonathan returned the gaze, not sure who was teasing whom. She was so easy to converse with, no airs or graces, just plenty of good British humour and highly spirited. 'We could try again, another attendant? Maybe a small bribe might help sort out the issue.'

She shot a glance over her spectacles. 'If we did, we might both get some ghastly character to share with. Lord only knows what horrible habits they might have. I'd rather spend the journey in your company.' She lowered her voice, 'and, I don't doubt for one moment that you're a trustworthy gentleman, Jonathan. Besides, I might get some old woman who will snore the entire night.'

'Now you put it like that, I agree. That's decided then. We'll have to share, but if we are, you'll have to be my younger sister. You can't afford to risk your reputation.'

'That's sorted then. Shall we go straight to the dining car? I'm starving.'

The dining car was nearly full but Jonathan had managed to reserve a table as compensation for the error over the sleeping berths. He was engrossed in explaining as simply as possible his latest medical theories. Katharine listened intently taking it all in. A deep clearing of the throat interrupted their conversation, 'Excuse me. I apologise for the intrusion, sir and madam, but may we join you?'

A tall portly gentleman in a dark blue suit towered beside them with a much younger slim-built male. 'May we share your table? The rest of the dining car is full. You appear to have the only table with spare seats.' Jonathan gestured in agreement. He turned to Katharine. 'You don't mind, do you?'

'Well, er, no. Of course not.'

The gentleman extended his chubby hand, 'I'm Sir Charles Basil and this is my companion, young Hugo Rose.'

Katharine glanced at Hugo Rose. He couldn't have been more than nineteen or twenty. The poor lad looked overwhelmed. Sir Charles promptly sat down.

Jonathan tried to find some common point of conversation. 'It's rather busy for this time of the year, don't you think?'

Sir Charles nodded, 'Everyone seems to be travelling at the same time. I take it you've been on the Orient Express before?' He fixed his stare on Katharine. 'What about you?'

'I'm a musician.'

'Are you indeed! What's your name?' He feigned ignorance.

'Katharine Simmons.' She sipped her wine, returning his stare.

'Oh! You're the violinist. Well, what a pleasure for us.' He turned to Hugo and nodded. The evening's conversation over the meal flowed as freely as the wine.

Two hours later, Katharine stood up. 'Gosh, is it 10.30 already. Please excuse me gentlemen, I think I need to retire to bed while I can still stand up.'

Jonathan stood up, winked at Sir Charles and followed.

Finally alone back in their compartment, Katharine beckoned Jonathan into the sitting room. She felt light-headed from the wine. She opened the window, momentarily forgetting the train was anchored within the hold of a substantial ferry crossing the English Channel. The chill air still percolating around the ship's hull washed over her, doing nothing to clear the worst of the alcohol from her head. The meal had been good.

'I'll change first.' She watched for his reaction. 'And by the way, I prefer the top bunk.' She disappeared into the bedroom compartment. He waited, not sure what his next move should be. This wasn't the way he had planned it. She wasn't quite what he was expecting. The tick of a gilded clock on the wall penetrated the silence. Slowly the door opened. He contemplated how he could turn around the situation but it was already too late.

He gasped. 'You … are … You are … so *beautiful*.'

The afterglow of the alcohol had induced her seductive mood. She moved slightly, rustling the clinging silk folds of her sheer nightdress against her thighs. Standing in the doorway seeing his reaction she smiled to herself, bathing in his lustful confusion.

'Katharine … I…'

'Shush,' she beckoned him closer. She came within touching distance and looked into his face. He breathed in the heady scent that was her. Intoxicated he stood still, not daring to move. She wrapped her arms around his neck, pulling him tight to her body. She kissed him softly on the mouth. Her lips were moist and sweet from the alcohol. How young and naive her kiss. Or did she know what she was doing? Was it all a façade? He wasn't sure and didn't care. His plan had gone to the wind. She moved tightly against his thighs, his manhood giving up the ghost of respectability. He let out a whimper. She held his head firmly, now kissing him hard. He dared to move his hands slowly over her back, then to her breasts, the slippery silk of the negligee enhanced the heat of his excitement. Gradually she pulled away, shaking her head, holding her bare ring finger to her lips. She deftly slipped past him. She entered the adjoining sitting room, silently closing the door behind her.

He was alone again. He would have to salvage the situation somehow; get back on track. He told himself he could do it. He had the experience. It was just that she had affected him. He hadn't bargained on this reaction to her. With conflicting emotions, he kept staring at the closed door that separated him from her. At least the physical attraction would make it easier for him.

In the next compartment Sir Charles squeezed Hugo's shoulder to stop him falling over. 'You've drunk *far* too much lad. Here, into the carriage. It's lucky you're sharing with me. Stand up! You can't possibly sleep in that suit. Your mother will kill you if you take it home wrecked.' Hugo climbed unsteadily to his feet, struggling with his jacket. He tried to undo his trousers.

'Hic.' He shrugged his shoulders and fumbled, 'Can't sir, can't.' He fell clumsily onto the bed. 'Hic. Sorry, s…sir, if you wouldn't mind, hic.'

Sir Charles moved next to him, 'Hugo these buttons of yours are damned tricky. Sorry can't seem to unbutton them without touching you. There we go, off in one swift movement.' He shoved his hand deep inside Hugo's underpants, pulling them down. 'Got to get them off lad.'

'Sir … hic … wha–at are you, hic …' Hugo clutched his forehead. 'Ooh, my head.'

'You know you want it really.' Sir Charles ran his other hand down Hugo's pale white chest towards his flat stomach until they finally came to a halt. 'You like that don't you. I knew you would.' He began unbuttoning his own trousers.

In the next cabin, Katharine stirred at the muffled cry. Was it the wind or her imagination? She turned over and slept solidly on.

❧

The following morning, after crossing the French border, the train gathered speed through the Swiss countryside. Having finished breakfast Katharine struggled to open the narrow sliding door to the public toilet. She found it difficult to hold her balance. Unheated, the room was uncomfortably cold. She reached into her bag. Make-up wasn't her thing, but she liked to add some rouge to her otherwise pale cheeks. She turned abruptly at the door sliding open behind her. 'You startled me. Can't a woman powder her nose in peace?'

Sir Charles chuckled, 'Call me Mother, everyone else does.'

'With the greatest of respect I have no objection to calling you *Sir Charles* but Mother is definitely out.' This was the first test of will power. He decided to give her an inch, make her feel she had the upper hand. 'Then call me M. Does that suit you better?'

'Er, well…' She couldn't quite decide yet whether or not she liked him. He could be rather pompous, self-assuring, but he was probably well-meaning.

'Stems from my school days. Everyone said that I clucked like a mother hen. I didn't mind. It was nonsense of course but the *nom de guerre* has stuck ever since.' He moved nearer to her, pulling the door closed. 'Miss Simmons, I need to ask you something that requires your absolute discretion.'

'Of course.'

He cleared his throat. 'I am head of, how shall we call it … one of His Majesty's departments. We're interested in news of foreign dignitaries and their governments. As such we're always on the look out for new people to help us. In short, are you willing to do something special, something different for King and country?'

'That depends.'

'On what? You are fiercely patriotic. That much I know. I've heard you on the radio speaking about the role of women in politics and society.'

Her eyes scanned the tiny compartment. There was no escape. She wished she didn't have to give an answer at that moment. She had enough to think about with the forthcoming concerts in Vienna. She knew he was angling towards some kind of undercover work.

He continued studying her, 'I am impressed with your discretion at breakfast this morning over the state of my companion Hugo. He drank too much last night, poor lad. You also have a sharp wit and an even sharper tongue. Not to mention your uncanny ability with foreign languages.'

'Well, yes. I can speak German, French, Italian and a smattering of Russian.'

Now he had her attention positively. She was warming to his suggestion. Experience told him as much. He personally had recruited most of the agents working for him. 'Your aptitude for languages together with your intellect is a credit to you. You are an established violinist which gives you the perfect cover to travel and mix wherever you wish without arousing suspicion. You'd be ideal and you'll be very well remunerated.'

'I'll think about it.'

It was the answer he was expecting. They all said that. He thrust a card into her hand. 'Contact me, my dear. Don't leave it too long. I am waiting.' He slid the door quietly behind him. She reached for her powder box and pulled out the pale pink puff. She had to admit she quite liked the idea.

❧

Vienna was everything it promised to be – cosmopolitan, elegant and home to the best of theatre and music. Jonathan was exceptionally attentive to Katharine in the coming days, meeting her every evening for an early supper, although pressure of work meant he hadn't been able to attend any of her concerts. He appeared to be besotted by her. She in turn found herself swept away by an unexpected whirlwind romance. Stolen kisses as they parted, she couldn't wait to see him again. She found it difficult to focus on her work. Leaving the front porch area of the Hotel Imperial for the evening performance she reflected how these very steps were once swept by Hitler in his younger days, poverty-stricken. And just a month ago she had come within inches of the man himself. Now he was causing consternation across Europe, but appeasement was still the name of the game with the British government trying to avert another war.

An hour later she was seated on stage for the start of the recital. Tonight she would be playing solo just before the interval. The concert hall was hot and stuffy. Scanning the upper circles she caught sight of Dr Freud arriving with his wife. She smiled. He had promised to come in spite of ill-health but she had assumed he was just being polite. The conductor entered after the leader of the violins. As the applause died away the lights dimmed, all eyes on Furtwängler's baton. The immortal sound of *The Blue Danube* filled the Baroque hall. Halfway through, Katharine adjusted the position of her violin. Glancing up towards the inner circle she saw the unmistakably erect figure of Captain Henderson seated three boxes along from the Freuds. He hadn't seen her looking. Her hands relaxed, she flowed through the last bar of the waltz. The audience stood in rapturous applause. Furtwängler brought the orchestra to their feet. They took the encores and bowed. Exhilarated but exhausted they filed slowly backstage where the social elite of Vienna were gathering. Furtwängler was already greeting the mayor and local aristocrats. He came towards Katharine, taking her hand: 'My dear Miss Simmons, let me introduce you to Baron von Lücken. He's very appreciative of this evening's concert.'

'How do you do, sir?' She had put her hair up for the evening's performance, enhancing her air of elegance and sophistication. Visual presentation was everything. She would play her way into the hearts of Europe and carry the music of modern composers with her. There was no better place to start than Vienna. 'Are all concerts so rewarding?' she asked.

'I like your sense of humour, ma'am.' His voice was clipped, almost Prussian. 'Indeed, it is we who have been rewarded. You honour us with your brilliance in our beautiful city.' He bowed and took her hand. 'Maybe you'll enchant us further. My wife likes to hold a little soirée now and then. You must be my guest and play for us. You were delightful tonight; your solo piece quite wonderful.'

'That would be my pleasure sir.'

He took her arm leading her towards an elderly gentleman of slight build with curling moustache. He was not unlike the late King George V. 'Herr Dr Brücker, meet Miss Katharine Simmons. She's going to play at one of our soirées in the summer. Soon the whole of Austria will know her name. I'll invite Lady von Stellen and Baron Inglestein as well as the usual crowd. Naturally, you will join us, I hope.'

Brücker's voice matched his frail physique. He was barely audible, 'We don't know how much longer we can sustain our social life. Let's enjoy it while we can.'

Katharine watched them closely. 'Gentlemen, what do you make of the ban on musicians in Germany? Isn't it a worrying affair?' she was rash enough to ask.

'Well, the Baron and I disagree on that,' replied Brücker. 'He has Nazi sympathies.'

'Steady on, Brücker. That's putting it rather bluntly. It's not that simple. You know that full well. You see...' He looked directly at Katharine, '...the situation is far more complex. If you take into account the economic position of Germany – the country has never quite recovered from the war. Huge reparations imposed by the Allies means that the Fatherland is paying a heavy price for defeat. It affects us all. Even today, we in Austria are feeling the impact of the Great Depression of ten years ago. Inflation is as high as it's ever been. As to the musicians, it's only the Jews. Some people believe they brought it all on themselves. They control everything, Miss Simmons. Thank goodness we can say that our Emperor had no Jewish blood in him.'

Brücker responded, 'There's a widespread feeling even in Austria that the Jews have too much influence on society. I wouldn't go so far as to say they're the cause of all our ills, but they do seem ubiquitous. Germany can't breathe without the Jews interfering. One might, I suppose, say the same of Austria.'

She prudently listened, deciding it best not to offer an opinion. How long would it be before their freedom would be restricted? It was December 1937 and Hitler had been in power in Germany for five years. He had designs on Austria but whether it would come to anything was an open question. None of them could have predicted that annexation was just three months away. Things were so much different in England.

Von Lücken looked directly at Katharine again, 'I'm not saying, Miss Simmons, that the ban on intellectuals in public office should be enforced so stringently, but Hitler may well be onto something.' He paused to sip his champagne, 'At long last someone is injecting some much needed pride back into the German nation. The country has been submissive for far too long. It's time to move on. We may well need some of Hitler's magic touch. Don't you agree?'

'Gentlemen, I am no politician. Music is my metier.' She offered the answer as a way out of the awkward debate, hoping they hadn't heard one of her radio interviews. Why should they?

Katharine began to wonder how she could extract herself. She could make an excuse to use the ladies room. It was unnecessary. A deep voice behind came to her aid.

'Katharine!'

She turned. Captain Henderson in full naval uniform was walking in her direction. There was no escape. Now she would have to face him. As she watched him approach, she couldn't help admitting his regimental repose was impressive, even if his presence was unnerving.

'Captain Henderson – what a surprise to see you.' Her tone was level, despite her emotional confusion inside. She didn't let him see it.

'Is it? I promised to come and hear you in concert. I am a man of my word. Can I offer you a drink?' He stared directly at her, wishing to fathom her secrets.

'Thank you Captain. Something tall and cool would be most refreshing. I rarely drink after a concert, but orange and tonic water with just a hint of vodka will suit me very well.' Did he detect a softening of her voice? He couldn't be sure. He was inexperienced with women. She waited, her eyes following him across the room. He was better looking than she had previously noticed. She could usually sum up a person at a glance, but he was a mystery. What lay beneath?

He returned and raised his glass. 'Here's to more success for you in Vienna. You were marvellous this evening. And I'm not one to pay compliments quite so readily.'

'Thank you Captain. I shall prize it all the more knowing its scarcity.' She was gracious in spite of her youthfulness. She scanned the room, slipping in the next comment, 'I must thank you. This is the second time you have rescued me.'

He knew exactly what she meant. 'Think nothing of it. I noticed your agitation and thought it best to intervene. Nab the prisoner, so to speak, and make good the escape without injuries or loss.'

She laughed. She couldn't help but like him. 'You have quite a wit,' she said. At last he had roused his humour for her. He gently took her arm, led her to the nearest table, pulling out a chair.

'We can observe a great deal from here.' He sat opposite, desperate to reach out to her. To tell her that he had admired her since the first time he glimpsed sight of her at the tea dance in the Pump Room in Bath all those years ago. He wanted to tell her that to him she was the most enigmatic woman he had ever met. He had not looked at another since, nor would he. Instinctively he felt that she was his soul-mate. But duty prevailed first and foremost. He held it all in, his face impassively giving nothing away. Instead he referred to her success again, 'Katharine, you appear to have been very well received in Vienna.'

She silently ran her fingertip around the edge of her glass. In the momentary silence between them, she began discreetly observing him. She imagined that he could so easily drive women to despair with his mysterious façade and rather good looks. Why hadn't she noticed before? His apparent ice-cold distance could be a challenge to any high-spirited young woman, and yet he seemed very alone, if not aloof with life itself.

'I'm so sorry. I was daydreaming. How rude of me. What did you say?'

'I was commenting on your being well received in Vienna.'

'Thank you.' She smiled, knowing that now she could befriend him, maybe even prise open one of the pages. 'That has much to do with Mr Furtwängler, but I'm still somewhat surprised by it all. It's not what I expected at all. And what about you?' She returned his gaze, noticing that his deep brown eyes had a life of their own, an unusual depth, not lost in spite of the late hour. 'What kind of Captain are you?'

'I'm not in the habit of talking so readily about myself.' He straightened his back, slowly sipping the red wine.

'You haven't answered my question.' She persisted. Her eyes challenged him.

'You're very direct. But since you ask, I will give you the official, but brief synopsis of my career to date. I started in the Royal Navy at the age of fourteen. I always wanted a life at sea – read one too many adventure stories of the high seas, I suppose, and formed a rather romantic view. So I lied about my age to join up; but then I hadn't expected to be sent to war. I'm talking about the Great War of course. I'll never know why they call it that. Anyway…'

She nodded, running her finger again around the rim of her glass. Her sister Laura had told her that men found such action seductive. He appeared not to notice, but nothing escaped him. 'The ship was involved in some minor skirmishes. We survived, obviously. Churchill was Lord of the Admiralty at the time. He was an extremely fine leader, in spite of the rumours. He made mistakes, but then who doesn't? He was our rock. After the war, I made my way up through the ranks to Captain. And here I've been ever since.'

'But you don't command a ship now. There's not an inch of sea within a hundred miles of Vienna.' She waited for his response, wondering whether he was ever capable of unbridled passion.

'Your tenacity appears to know no bounds. When you reach a certain age, having developed a level of experience and maturity from travelling the seas, it is not unusual to be offered other work. I was assigned to the British Embassy here in Vienna. Who am I to argue with the powers that be? Here I am expected to mix freely with a certain level of society. It's good for the image of our country. I suppose here they prefer the breeding of the blues and whites rather than the khakis.' He drew breath. It was the most she had ever heard him say in a single conversation. That was to be all. He was already standing up.

'Well Katharine, duty calls. You must excuse me. If I can be of any further help whilst you're in Vienna please do let me know. You can contact my office any time.' He reluctantly stood up, turned and walked towards the Italian ambassador. She watched him circulate with ease amongst Austria's social and diplomatic elite.

❧

Waiting at the foot of the grand staircase in the lobby of the Hotel Imperial, Hugo hoped that Katharine would co-operate. It was his first lone assignment for Sir Charles. The splendour around him was palatial. The black-and-white marble tiled squares gleamed across the floor. A polished elm circular table stood at the centre, its crystal vase charged daily with fresh white lilies, their scent in the air. A huge chandelier hung low, casting shards of light across the foyer. Louis XIV chairs adorned the edge of the grand hallway, standing to attention like an imperial army waiting for its orders.

'Miss Simmons!' Hugo nervously extended his hand. She glided towards him in pale green jacket and floral skirt. She had the same bright freshness that he had warmed to on the Orient Express. Her soft voice gave him confidence. 'Hugo, what brings you here?'

He smiled, palms sweaty in his pockets and stammered, 'Y…you're playing magnificently if the Viennese press are to be believed. S…ir Charles is so proud of you. He often mentions your name.' He began wringing his hands and shuffling. He wouldn't dare shatter her youthful confidence with the truth that he often brought up her name followed by a dozen expletives for not yet taming her spirit.

'Here, let's move into this side room. We are guaranteed absolute privacy.' She followed him across the entrance hall. The last of the evening's light was filtering through the windows. A group of chic women chatted idly in the far lounge, their long cigarette holders held elegantly between their fingers. Their clothes tasteful but different from the Bond Street elegance Katharine was used to. She looked away, the memory too painful; it was reminding her of fun-filled evenings at the Savoy Grill with her beloved friend and writer Arnold Bennett.

Hugo cut through her thoughts, 'H…have you thought about what S…ir Charles said to you on the train? You remember? The increase of Hitler's power base is causing some bother in Whitehall. Prime Minister Chamberlain has ordered Sir Charles to increase staff.'

His face clouded over, anxious for her response. He was terribly pale and thin, his eyes ringed with dark shadows. He was stammering more than she remembered. She contemplated the situation. She felt pity for him. She let out a sigh, 'I'm tired after the concerts, Hugo. I'm attempting to build my reputation further as an international musician. But I have to admit, I am patriotic and want to serve my country.'

'So you'll do it?' He could barely contain his delight.

She paused. 'Yes, I reckon I will.'

'When you return to England, you will need to sign special forms and undergo some training.'

Curiously he had stopped wringing his hands and shuffling his feet. She liked to think it had something to do with her acceptance. He turned and walked out of the hotel; his step much lighter and confident.

❧

Upstairs in the hotel bedroom, Katharine picked up the receiver, 'Operator please. Can you connect me to the Hotel Ambassador?' She hadn't seen Jonathan for a couple of days. The memory of the train kept coming back to her. The last time she had seen him he had been exceptionally tender. She could almost feel his warm breath on hers, the sweet taste of his kiss. The sensual tension, the teasing and the wanton passion captivated her. Was she in love? She certainly missed him. She closed her eyes, hearing his infectious laughter. She wanted to feel his lips on hers again. The telephonist seemed to take forever. Then his voice came clear over the phone. 'Hello?'

'Jonathan, it's Katharine.'

'Who?'

Her heart missed a beat. 'It's Katharine. Jonathan, how could you forget me? It's only been two days.'

'Of course I know it's you! I'm only teasing. How could I possibly forget? I've thought of nothing but you.' He lied. He had been too busy to give her a single thought. 'How are things going? The concerts. Tell me all.'

'I was rather hoping you might have come to one of them. I looked out for you. The whole of Vienna was there, but *not you*. Shame on you! And I've got quite a reputation now.'

He cleared his throat, 'Look, I'm really sorry Katharine. I've been rather busy with medical duties, teaching, and I had to go out of town for a couple of days. But I've … I'm sorry, really I am. When is your final concert?'

'It was last night. I'm returning to England the day after tomorrow … Jonathan?'

'Katharine, what can I say? I'm so sorry. Let me redeem myself. How about dinner tomorrow night? I'll make sure it's a memorable occasion, I promise. After all, you can't spend your last night in Vienna on your own, can you? I know a wonderful restaurant near the river. It's small but delightful. I'll send a cab to fetch you at 7.30.'

Her anger was dispelled. He was so easy to forgive, perhaps because he was making an effort and she found him compelling.

❦

Slightly off the tourist track in a quiet side road, the restaurant was almost invisible except for a nondescript door nestled between two fashionable dress shops. It was but a stone's throw from the river Danube. Jonathan was already seated at a corner table, reading the menu. He looked up as Katharine approached.

'Gosh, Katharine, you're looking lovely this evening.' He pulled out a chair for her. She had made a huge effort to look seductive. The fabric of the pastel yellow dress with high mandarin neck was paper-thin, falling in light folds over her thighs. The slender gossamer sleeves added sensuality yet simple elegance. Her tiny waist was enough to exaggerate the fullness of her breasts held tight within the lace bodice of the dress. It wasn't what you showed, but what was imagined nestled beneath that was so attractive to a man. Or so her sister Laura had always told her. She should know. She had spent years reading every romantic novel ever published. Laura had even managed to obtain a copy of the illicit book *The Perfumed Garden*, a euphemism for the female parts. It was a collection of erotic letters written by an older woman to her much younger lover in a bold attempt to keep his passion and interest in her. Katharine was not usually interested in such books but the letters were captivating, even if a little too explicit.

'Thank you Jonathan.' She glanced around the room taking in the subdued tones of purple and cream wallpaper which gave it an entirely intimate atmosphere. Crisp white linen covered the tables, each with simple candelabra and a single spray of carnations. 'How did you discover this charming place?'

His eyes twinkled. He was in high spirits. 'Quite by chance when a grateful patient brought me here for a meal after my new surgery saved her life. It's not the grandest of rooms. It reminds me of my aunt's sitting room, but the food is excellent. The owner is a Mr Jacob Gruber, an exceptional chef. The literary elite of Vienna meet here on a regular basis.' He passed the menu. 'What will you have? I can recommend the *Gebratene Bachforelle mit Petersilerdapfel* as the main course. You'll be surprised. Fried trout – it sounds so plain, but it is cooked to perfection.' She trusted his judgement. It would be impolite to do otherwise. 'We mustn't forget the hors d'oeuvre. What will you have?'

'For me, *Eierschwammerin*. I had it in the hotel the other day. I just adore wild mushrooms.'

He noticed her emphasis on the word *wild* with a hint of teasing in her voice. When it came to dessert, he tried to guess what she would have. He believed it possible to tell a woman's character from the pudding she chose. She was not the kind of woman to order something mellow or light.

'I'll have *Mohr im Hemd*. I simply can't resist rich dark chocolate.' He smiled. His judgement confirmed. He liked educated women with a free and decisive spirit. He had gathered from their conversation on the Orient Express that she was widely read in the latest literary works, as well as possessing a broad knowledge of politics and world affairs. It was still not so common for the modern woman finding her voice in the public arena, even though they had won the vote twenty years earlier. He had done his homework and ascertained that she had had close, somewhat flirtatious, friendships with the late D.H. Lawrence, H.G. Wells and novelist William Gerhardie. Age seemed to be no barrier; only the latter was closest to her in years. Before his death it had been writer Arnold Bennett, who had been instrumental in introducing her to the literary world.

Jonathan stood up and moved to her side. The quickness of his movement betrayed an unusual nervousness. He stumbled, banging his knee on the table leg.

'Jonathan…' She held out her hand to steady him but he was already on one knee. She would be naive if she didn't know what was coming. She had thought to seduce him further. A proposal of marriage was not what she was expecting.

'Katharine, would you … that is, will you marry me?' He looked into her bewildered face. 'I know this is all a bit sudden, but I … well … I love you, Katharine. Ever since the train … I can't get you out of my mind. Will you?'

She peered over the rim of her glasses. He was still on one knee, rubbing the other one.

'Yes.'

'Yes?' He leapt up, headbutting the passing waiter. The silver tray of drinks spun around. The waiter reached for the corner of the table, glasses sliding around the tray just as he regained his balance. The tranquillity momentarily disturbed, the entire restaurant burst into applause at his apt rescue of the drinks and the proposal of marriage.

❧

The New Year of 1938 hailed a Vienna knee-deep in snow. The atmosphere was tense with pro-government supporters clashing periodically on the streets with Nazi sympathisers. Using Nazi slogans was still illegal, but times were changing. All eyes were directed at Germany and what Adolf Hitler would do next. It was well-known that he would move into Austria if he could. At the British Embassy, Captain Henderson looked up from his desk. 'Sir Charles, I wasn't expecting you in Vienna until next week. Brandy?'

'Yes, thank you George.'

Sir Charles had replaced his usual tie for a cravat, precariously balanced between dark green braces attempting the impossible over his substantial girth. His jacket strained under protest at the single button holding the ensemble together. Taking his drink, he gulped the measure in a single mouthful and passed it back. 'Another one please George. The atmosphere seems tense here in Vienna. It's quite different from my last visit and that was not so long ago.'

'Yes I agree. There's serious concern about what Hitler might do next.' He glanced down at the pile of immigration requests still waiting for the official British stamp of freedom. 'We've seen a fair number of professionals here in the office in recent weeks; all have crossed the border from Germany, requesting visas – doctors, lawyers, architects, surgeons and so forth. They're mainly Jews, of course, but not all. Some are political opponents of the state. They've all lost their jobs in Germany and have flocked into the city hoping for a new start, albeit temporarily. The ones we see know that there's no future for them here and want to move on to Britain. Palestine is still an option but only just. Quotas for there are more limited.'

Sir Charles began meticulously stroking his moustache. Captain Henderson recognised the sign. Something significant was about to be revealed. 'I have some important information for you, George. I'm about to bring a new recruit into the family. They're on nodding terms with Hitler, well not exactly … but you know what I mean, and half the Austrian elite. I had to bring them on board. It took a devil of planning. I need you to smooth the edges. It couldn't wait until our meeting next month. I need you to be prepared for her.'

'Her?' Captain Henderson leant back in his chair.

'Yes. The girl needs training up. I've decided that Aldershot will do for her; somewhere tough to tame her unwieldy spirit. Then she will be joining your team initially on an *ad hoc* basis here at the Embassy. She's rather proficient with radios. For operational reasons she'll work here with you undercover.'

The scenario sounded familiar. There was only one such woman Captain Henderson had met that fitted the description. Surely he didn't mean Katharine. It couldn't be. She was too busy developing her career as a musician. 'Who is she?' he asked.

'Katharine Simmons, a…' Sir Charles paused, choosing his words carefully, '…a free-spirited, fearless woman. But just perfect for our set up.'

Captain Henderson was motionless. His heart pounded. His unruffled exterior hid the turmoil in his chest. He finally muttered, 'More brandy?'

'Yes, thank you George.'

He poured a shot for both of them, feigning calmness. 'She's a musician of some reputation, isn't she? She makes quite an impression wherever she plays,' he remarked casually.

'You *have* heard of her then, good. She'll do us proud, but she needs handling carefully.' He smirked, 'believe me, I should know – I was the one who brought her on board.'

'We could certainly do with a new recruit. It's the devil's own job keeping our heads above the parapet here in Vienna. When do I meet her properly?'

Sir Charles hadn't expected him to be quite so co-operative without personally vetting the woman himself. 'She starts her training next week. We've got to get it in before her wedding in a month's time.'

'Wedding?' Captain Henderson's shoulders tensed. 'She's getting married?'

'That's right, George. She is going to marry our doctor Jonathan Walters. And what a match that will be. She'll get more than she bargained for from him.'

He barely heard the last words. His heart felt wrenched in two. He had hoped … knew that deep down he was meant for her, but he had never really had opportunity to tell her. He barely knew her socially, yet he trusted his judgement. It had saved his life many a time. He loved her. He knew he loved her. Now it was hopeless.

His stomach knotted, almost retching. He could taste his own despair. He would not be seeing her again until it was too late. She would be Mrs Walters and he was powerless to stop it.

◆

The car taking Katharine to the barracks finally skirted the edge of Aldershot. The garrison town had served the needs of the British army for over two hundred and fifty years. Katharine had been back from Vienna for three weeks. In that time, so much had happened. She had signed the Official Secrets Act, started training for Sir Charles and completed her final wedding preparations. Her sister Laura had married Rear Admiral MacPherson in a lavish affair, the likes of which the village of Georgeham had not seen for twenty-five years. Jonathan hadn't been able to attend, having been called away on an urgent medical case. In four weeks time it would be their wedding.

She stared out of the car window. The mist hung in cool droplets. The daffodils drooped their heads in disapproval. For the whole journey the driver refused to be engaged in conversation, not even on the weather. Then the rows upon rows of uninspiring Nissen huts of the army camp came into view. Through the fence, she could see ranks of soldiers drilling on the parade ground. Everything looked dreary and drab. Her heart sank. What sort of God-forsaken place was this? What had she let herself in for? At the gate the young guard thrust his rifle at the half-open window. 'Papers, please. No admittance without documentation.'

She wound down the window further, looking down the end of the barrel. Another soldier stepped forward and lent into the car. The putrid smell of his breath gave away his identity.

'Miss Simmons,' he grinned. She remembered him from the Orient Express. Through blackened teeth and several gaps Spike smiled in greeting. 'So the guv 'as sent you to me. Ain't that sweet.' He turned to the guard, 'Let 'er in man.' He peered closer, his face just inches from hers. 'You're under my protection in 'ere. The guv wants you looked after right and proper. It's infantry training for you.'

She detested that leer. She hadn't liked him on the train, but now she hated him.

Once through the gates, Spike opened the car door and escorted her across the complex to the lines of huts. 'Here, this is yours. You're sharing with one other woman. At 0500 hours I'll see you back on the parade ground for roll-call. We like it punctual.'

The hut was stark, utilitarian. Ten identical bunks lined the walls, each with mattress covered in a beige-coloured blanket, white sheet turned over the top, and a single white pillow. Another woman stood bemused, watching her. She had already laid her own personal things on the bedside table. Her confident posture was immediately evident, an air of toughness betrayed from her brown dungarees and short white shirt. She stood with toned arms crossed. She was curvy, her face softer than her body language, her brown eyes peering at Katharine.

Katharine spoke first. 'Hello, I'm Katharine Simmons. I believe we're sharing.'

'Yeah, we are. I'm Susie, Susie Norton.' She leant back against the bunk, arms still folded. Her head tilted, her mousey brown hair fell in curls around her face. She looked Katharine up and down.

Katharine smiled, 'And which part of Section are you from?'

Susie faked a gasp. 'How did you know? We aren't supposed to tell anyone.'

'Deductive logic and a bit of woman's instinct. And, there appears to be no one else in the hut.'

'Very clever. We've got a right smart one here.' But Susie liked her. She moved towards Katharine, spontaneously hugging her. 'We are in this together. From what I've seen already, we're not in for an easy time.'

'So it would seem.'

Katharine reached down for her tiny suitcase. She figured she wouldn't need too much stuff in the camp. She began placing her folded jumpers and shirts in the middle drawer. She glanced up, 'From your slight accent you're not British, but your name certainly is.'

'You're observant Katharine. No one else ever spots it. I speak perfect English, or so I thought until now. I was born in south London. My father worked in medicine, doing research or something ever so clever. He went to Germany for a number of years and we followed him. I spent my childhood travelling between the two countries. I take it for granted you're English.'

'Yes, through and through. For more generations than I can recount. My ancestors have always lived in Devon. In fact, we all come from one small village.'

'And no one ever escaped?'

Katharine was beginning to like her. Susie was blunt, had a wry humour that was endearing but she was easy-going and relaxed. She pulled Katharine's pyjamas out of the suitcase and threw them onto the bed; then took her arm. 'Let's finish this later. Here, come on, let's go get your kit.'

⁓

At 0500 hours the following morning the door of the Nissen hut burst open. The screaming voice pierced the darkness, 'You 'orrible little worms, you've overslept! Get your arses into gear. No time for washing, you're late for roll-call.' Seconds later the lights were on. The red-faced sergeant glared at Susie and Katharine struggling out of bed.

'Oh hell,' whispered Susie. 'It's a woman.'

The coarse voice lost no momentum, 'Very clever, young lady. Your arse is mine for the duration. Now get up, you pathetic excuse for soldiers.'

Spike was preferable to this. Stale breath or not, he had to be easier to handle than this hard-nosed woman who swore like a common trooper.

The parade ground was barely lit. Even nature hadn't woken. Susie and Katharine filed into line with thirty others. That first day would prove to be difficult. It started with a quick breakfast, followed by a five-mile jog without full kit, just to get them used to the idea. Tomorrow it would be repeated but with kit on their backs. Weapons training was next, giving an hour's respite from exercise. Route-marching and assault courses filled the afternoon schedule. By late afternoon Katharine's muscles ached. She would never keep this up. She had two more weeks of this. She gritted her teeth, determined not to show any weakness. Susie seemed to be taking it all in her stride, coping very well with the intense physical strain.

Later that afternoon, Katharine left the camp for a solitary walk along the river. It was now the last Wednesday in January and the first break in ten days from the intense training. Winter had temporarily hidden its face. The snowdrops at the foot of the tree hung their heads; the first sign that spring was coming. It was remarkably mild for the time of year, but she knew that within days it could easily turn cold again. For now she would enjoy the respite. By the sloping bank, she reflected on the recent turn of events. Her quiet country life had been turned upside down in such a short space of time. She was desperately tired and her limbs ached. She placed a small blanket over the damp grass. Above she watched the wispy clouds across the pale blue sky. So much space in the heavens, she wondered at its mysteries. An hour later, she headed back to the hut to collect her notebook. That afternoon the lesson was on recognition of German uniform and rank. Crossing the parade ground, Spike's distant voice growled orders at some poor soul. The door to her hut was slightly ajar. She gently pushed it, containing her reaction just in time. On the bed the foul-mouthed sergeant was lying entwined with another female figure in khaki uniform. The mousey brown hair of Susie occasionally moved beneath her.

Katharine contained a gasp. Fortunately they hadn't noticed her. She turned and ran across the parade ground towards the white-washed NAAFI building.

She had seen too much.

❧

Back in Vienna, Captain Henderson was waiting for Jonathan having summoned him to the British Embassy. He stood sideways by the office window, opened his cigarette box and tapped the cigarette end on the silver lid before lighting it. Just as he took the first puff, Jonathan appeared. Jonathan could tell immediately from Captain Henderson's posture that he was in no mood for jovial humour.

'Dr Walters, please come in.' He turned to face Jonathan, moving to his desk. 'Let me get straight to the point. I understand from Sir Charles that you are to be married.'

'Yes.' Jonathan hadn't expected this line of questioning.

'To the violinist Katharine Simmons.'

'Yes.' He surveyed Captain Henderson cautiously, not sure what was coming next.

It pained Henderson to be doing this but he had to confront him. 'She is also going to be part of my team and as such I want you to look after her Jonathan.'

'Of course. How could you think anything else?'

'Don't think I don't know why you're marrying her, Jonathan.'

'You know George, I always obey orders. Someone has to cover my tracks. And as Sir Charles said, she is ideal.'

Henderson detested his smirking complacent grin. He gritted his teeth. 'Don't you have any heart or conscience, man? You are about to take serious vows in English law. She is young – with her whole life ahead of her. If you don't love her, you should reconsider.'

'I've done far worse at yours and Sir Charles's bidding.' His eyes challenged a response but knew it would be wiser to reassure him. He added quickly, 'I will take care of her.'

Henderson wasn't convinced that he would. His fist clenched in his pocket. 'You'd better, Dr Walters. If you don't, I'll be down on you at the first opportunity. If you shackle her to a life of misery, you'll have me to contend with.' He paused. 'I have considered telling her.'

'Telling her what, George? If I didn't know you better, I'd say you had feelings for that woman. You would never have made a move on her. I know you too well, you couldn't. Remember your duty, George.'

Henderson drew on his cigarette, staring beyond Jonathan's face. Jonathan was right. He couldn't break the rank of duty to King and Country. He would hate Jonathan to his dying day. He turned, looking down on the street below. It was the last day of January 1938. What would the year hold for him? A life without the woman he loved. His thoughts shot through his pain: What is it that a man should put duty and honour before the woman he loves? He would give his life for her, yet he could not have her. If he lived it all again he couldn't have changed a thing.

Chapter 6

A gentle tap on the apartment door broke through Katharine's rev-
erie. She was jolted back to April 1938. Her husband Jonathan was
gone. There was nothing she could do but wait for news. She had
to live through each day, not knowing if he was alive or still in custody. The days passed slowly, the nights even worse. Since his arrest
she was suspicious of unexpected callers, keeping a gun to hand at
all times. She heard the knock again, more persistent. She tried to
rationalise that no Gestapo raid would be like this, but it didn't take
away the fear. The clock chimed the half hour. A glance at the mantelpiece showed that it was already eleven thirty. That morning had
unexpectedly flown by. A muffled female voice called, 'Mrs Walters?'

She crept to the door. 'Who is it?'

'I need to speak with you, Mrs Walters.'

Now she recognised the urgent voice. She slipped the pistol back
in her pocket. 'I'm coming, Mrs Guttmann.'

In the five days since Jonathan and Mr Guttmann had been taken,
she hadn't gathered the nerve to visit the family. She should have
called, but her own melancholy would have emphasised the hopeless-
ness of both their situations. On the way to the British Passport Office
she had seen for herself the burnt-out shell of the bakery, looted of
all its fittings and contents. Even the gold *mezuzah*, the religious box
containing a piece of Scripture which Jews fixed to their doorposts,
had been taken. The once thriving meeting place filled with the smell
of freshly baked bread was now empty and desolate. Life had become
impossibly hard for Mrs Guttmann with three young children to
support. Now the family relied upon help from the Jewish community. As Katharine faced Mrs Guttmann at the door, the strain on
the woman's face was evident; her cheeks and eyes were hollow, skin
taught and wrinkled with worry. She had aged terribly.

'Come in.' Katharine gently closed the door behind her, 'I am so
sorry about your husband, Mrs Guttmann.'

'Thank you. Life has not been easy for us. And I'm sorry for you
too, Mrs Walters; I heard that your husband was taken as well.'

'Yes, he was. It is bad enough for us, of course, but we don't have children like you. How are they fairing?'

Mrs Guttmann paused to regain her line of thought. 'To tell you the truth, I'm worried about their safety. They've been thrown out of the state school – as have all Jewish children. They are getting only a few hours teaching a day at the local synagogue. The rest of the time they stay at home playing Monopoly. But it's not that…' She paused again. 'We've had death threats and…' Her composed face began to crack, '…only yesterday, my ten-year-old Rudi was beaten up by Hitler Youths on his way home from synagogue. Not badly, nothing broken, but it was enough to make him scared. I wonder if … I remember you mentioned once that you have something to do with visas. Please, I beg you, can you get us out Mrs Walters?'

Katharine looked at her, the depth of her sadness and suffering touched a chord. She turned and opened the middle drawer of the cupboard in the hallway. It housed a stack of forms. 'Here,' she passed one to Mrs Guttmann. 'You'll need to complete this. How many of you are there?'

'Four, including me.'

'Four, you say.' She hesitated.

Mrs Guttmann did not miss her concern. 'What is it?'

'You'll need four separate forms, but Mrs Guttmann … do you have anyone who can act as a guarantor? Do you have any relatives living in England or America?'

'No, none,' she whispered.

Katharine took three more forms from the drawer. 'Look, it isn't going to be easy to get the four of you out, but I'll do what I can. No one knows what is going to happen next. Europe is so unstable. We have to try to get you out soon.' She smiled to restore her confidence. 'As I said, I'll do what I can. If you can get these papers back to me urgently, I can act on them.'

Mrs Guttmann held out her hand. 'Thank you so much, Mrs Walters.' Katharine didn't miss the tears of gratitude in her eyes as she left the flat.

❧

April 9th and Hitler was back in the city to secure a positive result for the referendum on a united German-Austria. Everyone knew it was a foregone conclusion. No one dared vote against, each ballot paper had a name and address printed on it. Only civil war would shift the storm troopers occupying the streets and there was as much chance of that as scientist Albert Einstein returning to live in Germany. The new slogan for the referendum appeared everywhere: on ballot papers, in the newspapers and on large posters: 'We are Germans and belong to Germany and the Führer forever.'

That afternoon Katharine had agreed to meet her army training colleague. Susie had been in Vienna working for Section for just under two weeks. The female company would be good for Katharine and she was rather fond of Susie. They had been through a lot together under the rough guidance of Spike. They were scheduled to meet at two o'clock in Café Métropole on Franz-Josephs-Quai. She hadn't seen her since Jonathan's disappearance.

As Katharine entered the café, she saw Susie already seated at the far corner frantically waving in her direction. She slipped off her headscarf, smiling at her friend. Her spirits were low, shaken by the uncertainty of Jonathan's whereabouts. In the nine days since that terrible night, she could barely concentrate on anything, and had finally taken Captain Henderson's advice to bury her grief in her work. He had convinced her that her short reserves of energy were better directed at helping others to escape the regime that was strangling Vienna. As she crossed the room, her heels echoed on the cold marble floor. Captain Henderson's recent words flashed through her mind. 'I will always be there for you. If you need me, you only have to ask. I swear that behind the scenes I am doing everything possible.' She was beginning to see him in a new light. A trust between them had grown considerably; her unseemly out-burst towards him after Jonathan's arrest forgiven. Somehow, she was not sure when, but the formality between them had dissipated. Occasionally, in private, she had even called him George. She lifted her shoulders, sighed, quickly dismissing any sentimental notions of him.

Susie stood up with outstretched arms. She hugged Katharine, pleased to be reacquainted after so long. Any tighter and Katharine felt she would be completely suffocated. Susie spoke first: 'It's so good to see you. I've been really worried about you. I heard the terrible news about Jonathan. Darling, you look terrible.'

'Thank you, Susie, that makes me feel a whole lot better.' Katharine surprised herself, even managing some wry humour amidst the trauma of recent days. 'It's lovely to see you, too.'

Susie released her grip, taking one step backwards, momentarily eyeing her up and down. 'Katharine darling, you need someone to look after you. Why don't you come and stay with me for a while. I will pamper you rotten, give you time to get yourself back together.'

Katharine smiled but her red-rimmed eyes betrayed her anguish. Her optimistic tone did little to hide it. 'I can't. I've got a concert coming up at Berchtesgaden in a week's time. Oh, don't worry about me – I'm a tough old bird.'

Susie beckoned to the waiter and ordered tea and a plate of pastries. 'That should do the trick – something decadent darling, to build up your strength.' She stretched her hand across the table, touching Katharine's elbow. 'Dare I ask? What news of Jonathan?'

'None,' she stared blankly ahead.

'How are you coping? Is there anything I can do to help?' It was the first time Katharine had ever seen her so serious.

'Thank you, no. I'll be alright.' She returned Susie's touch on the arm in an absent-minded gesture of appreciation. Katharine remained distant. 'But, unfortunately, Jonathan wasn't the only one. That terrible night over seven thousand men were arrested and carted off to heaven knows where.'

'Oh, come now, Katharine darling, lets not be too melodramatic. After all, they were mostly Jews and perverts.'

'How can you say that? They're human beings, just like us.'

Susie shrugged her shoulders. 'You take me too seriously. I'm sure Jonathan was an accident and as soon as they realise their error, he will be released.'

She ignored Susie's retreating comment, glancing around to check they were not within earshot of anyone else. The café was almost deserted. Reassured, Katharine added quietly, 'There's also been a number of gruesome endings within "the family". Mother is worried sick. Rumours have it there's an intruder in our midst.'

She waited for Susie's reaction.

'I know. Mother has increased my hours and duties to weed out the "sneaking bugger" as he calls him. He must be well entrenched. These days we all have to watch our backs, darling.' She paused, fixing her gaze on Katharine. 'It's not you is it?'

Katharine's face fell, 'What! How could you?'

Susie laughed, 'You really aren't in the mood, are you? I'm sorry darling – I was only joking.' She lowered her voice again, 'But I do think we should keep an eye on that fellow Hugo.'

'Hugo?' Katharine's hand involuntarily shook, rattling the cup in its saucer.

'Ssh,' whispered Susie. 'Yes, I've been tracking him. Sir Charles's orders. Hugo has been doing some odd things recently. Remember what I told you last time we met – rumours of a nasty incident on a train?'

Katharine remembered only too well. 'Well, I don't believe a word of it. It's idle speculation which isn't healthy for anyone. Hugo is Sir Charles's shadow.'

'Exactly! And doesn't he just live in his shadow, the poor lad.'

The conversation was getting nowhere. Katharine changed direction. 'Come on Susie, tell me – what news of you?'

Susie leant closer, her soft voice a little husky. 'Darling, to tell the truth, since I last saw you, I've been promoted. I've been working at the far end of the Embassy. It may only be filing, but it's terribly important. We've got a new radio broadcasting station at the back, transmitting propaganda and all that stuff. I have to file the news reports. It's all classified of course.'

'Then why are you telling me?'

'Because my sweet, you like me have signed the Official Secrets Act, and I know you wouldn't dream of contravening that. Sir Charles would have your guts for garters … that's unless I do first.' She leant forward, winked and grasped hold of Katharine's hands. 'Oh sweetie, don't be so serious, please. I'm only teasing you.'

Katharine felt uncomfortable. Her face tensed, not knowing where to look. Susie was far too indiscreet in public, not to mention being too tactile for her liking. She preferred more distance between them. Her mind flicked back to the scene in the Nissen hut during the training. Susie had a habit of scandalous behaviour, but nothing had prepared her for the shock of seeing her entwined with the female sergeant.

Susie's sudden high-pitched laughter broke into her thoughts. 'Remember the day we had to cook that hedgehog. Spike kept telling us we'd never have a better meal. It was as tough as old boots.' Katharine couldn't suppress a giggle.

'That's better, darling. You need to laugh more often. Another cup of tea?'

Katharine nodded. Susie nattered on, 'This is about the only place you can get proper tea in Vienna – apart from the Embassy of course, where everything is done by the book, especially tea – English correctness and all that.'

An hour later they parted. Katharine concluded that Susie had made a difference. The meeting had lifted her spirits.

❧

The following week, Katharine was collected by car for her trip to Berchtesgaden. A maid had been allocated as her escort for the journey and to attend to all her needs during the stay. The next few days would be testing. One slip there and she knew she would be behind bars in the nearest German prison. Performing in Hitler's mountain retreat was somewhat daunting. He was not going to be there but that did not lessen the feeling of intimidation. Large audiences and mixing with influential political figures had never unnerved her, but this was different. As the car wound its way up the narrow road towards the summit, it was a while before the summer house came into full view. The town of Berchtesgaden was nothing like she had expected. She had seen it once on a postcard in the 1920s when her father had written to her from Linz whilst on business.

'We are here, Frau Walters,' the driver declared, turning briefly around as he stopped the car at the vast iron gates. A high white-washed wall surrounded a somewhat bland stone-built house. Through the black bars of the gate, Katherine could see guards everywhere. A large Nazi flag fluttered on its pole above the roof.

A jackbooted guard stepped forward, indicating for her to wind down the window. He proceeded to check every detail in her papers, then pulled her luggage from the boot of the car, even frisked the lining of her violin case. What he thought she could possibly hide in there was beyond her. Ten minutes passed and finally she was through the check-point. As she stepped out of the car in front of the building, the pure mountain air made her feel momentarily dizzy. The place seemed cloaked in an eerie calm as though time stood still.

She was greeted by another uniformed officer and taken into the main hall. 'Can I offer you a drink, ma'am? A whiskey perhaps?'

'Thank you, sir. That would be very welcome.'

Standing in the lofty hallway, she took in the surroundings. The white-washed complex was simple, nothing elaborate as might be expected for a man in power but the walls breathed his very presence. This very clinical place had nevertheless been touched by a female presence. A soft lavender scent penetrated the air. To the left of the main door, a tall narrow window afforded a panoramic view of snow-capped Bavarian mountains on the horizon, their slopes thickly wooded with majestic firs, the occasional tiny village in the valleys. The impossibly cloudless blue sky made an idyllic backdrop. Her eyes moved to the foreground immediately outside the window, observing the changing of the SS guard, reminiscent of the daily ceremony at Buckingham Palace. It was just as formal and precise but not as regal. Nazi officers constantly patrolled the compound, each leading a black Dobermann dog.

'Heil Hitler. Ma'am, welcome,' the voice declared behind her.

Katharine turned. 'Good day, Hauptmann.' She deduced it must be the housemaster.

'I will take you to your room, ma'am. Follow me.' He picked up her leather suitcase and led her along the narrow corridors. She could not resist glancing into some of the rooms. Their comfortable but plain furnishings gave a surprising appearance of warmth. Fresh flowers had been arranged in every one, framed photographs adorned the circular tables and sideboards, most of them military figures standing on some point of ceremony. The housemaster paused at the final door on the left. Inside, a double bed dominated the centre of the room, its floral quilted cover trailed to the floor. The sun now streamed through the latticed window, casting patterns across the polished wooden floor. A single rug lay across the fireplace.

'Fraulein Simmons,' he said. As a professional musician she still used her maiden name most of the time. 'We hope you will be comfortable here. It has been suggested you might like this room.'

'Thank you. It's perfect.'

'Ma'am, when you're ready you can take the back stairs down to the kitchen and help yourself to a snack. Dinner is served at eight o'clock sharp. And ma'am, the west wing is out of bounds, please remember that.'

Katharine nodded.

'Heil Hitler.' He retreated.

Alone in her room, Katharine pondered his words about the west wing as she began to unpack her clothes. Sir Charles had insisted on a new elegant wardrobe, telling her that no German or Austrian man could resist the charm of a smart woman. Was that why she had been given the double bed, she wondered, before dismissing the idea. An hour later it was time to find the kitchen. Orientating herself around the building was much easier than she expected. Walking along the deserted corridor, her pulse began to quicken. This was ridiculous; all she wanted was a sandwich and coffee and there would be staff there to help her. To her relief, voices were audible in soft conversation in a nearby room. Suddenly the door opened and out stepped a beautiful blonde, her accent distinctly recognisable from Berlin. She acknowledged Katharine's presence with a nod as she passed on down the corridor. A few steps later she turned and walked back. 'I do beg your pardon. How rude of me. You must be Fraulein Simmons. I suddenly realised that I knew your face from the photograph on the concert programmes. How remiss of me not to recognise you. Please, would you like to join me for coffee?' Her tiny-boned features accentuated her charm. Her lips deep crimson to match her nails, cheeks highlighted with rouge. Only her light curly hair softened her features. She was starkly beautiful, if somewhat austerely dressed in black from head to toe. Maybe she is mourning someone, thought Katharine.

'How rude of me again – I'm Claudia Kempten. I look after the place around here.'

'How do you do. Please, call me Katharine.' As Claudia moved closer to shake her hand, Katharine smelt the same lavender scent that hung in the hallway. She was clearly the feminine touch in the place.

Katharine looked directly at her. 'I recognise the name. Haven't we met before? Didn't you spend a term at Finishing School in Bath?'

'Why yes,' she threw her head back, shaking her curls. 'What a memory you have. I remember you now! Good – we can do away with formalities and consider ourselves the best of friends. Well, of course, I know what you've been doing since Finishing School; you've got quite a name as a musician!'

Katharine nodded. 'And what about you Claudia?'

Claudia tossed her head back again, curls shaking around her face, glad for the opportunity to vainly boast about her position. 'I spend most of the time here, looking after the place and organising all the entertainment and official state evenings. It's an important job.'

'That must be such fun,' prompted Katharine. 'You must get to meet such interesting people.'

Claudia giggled, 'I get to wear the most stunning outfits. It's all part of the image, of course. It's an ever-changing household.'

'Who was the man who showed me to my room earlier?' enquired Katharine.

'Ah, that must have been Fritz, the butler. Come on, let's find some coffee. Cook usually keeps a constant supply of it in the kitchen.'

She led Katharine towards the back staircase. The air became much cooler as they descended the winding stone steps to the kitchen. Inside there were no windows, only lights to dispel the gloom.

'Fancy some coffee?' she asked, lifting the slim silver pot on the oak table.

'Yes, thank you.'

The rich pungent aroma filled the room as the black steaming liquid poured into the cup. Katharine quietly surveyed her. Cook placed a tray of cucumber and würst sandwiches on the table with a side plate of pickles.

'Help yourself Katharine. There's not much else to do around here when it is quiet, except eat! It's a wonder I still have my figure.' She laughed, breaking through her austere façade.

Katharine took a sandwich. 'Thank you, Claudia.'

Claudia leant forward. 'Did you have a good journey?'

'Yes, thank you, it was very pleasant. The scenery was stunning. It makes a change to be out of the city.'

'Hmm, I agree. I want to confide something in you, Katharine. Well, it's not only that, it's also for your own protection. I wouldn't want you to make a *faux pas*. You must have seen all the speculation in the newspapers recently about Angela Raubel – or Geli as we all called her, our Führer's niece. We still take the papers here so during your stay, you must turn a blind eye to it. Don't mention it to anyone, not to the staff or the government officials who visit here some days.'

'Yes, of course. You have my word.'

Claudia's face darkened, her eyes seemed moist. 'I need someone to talk to. I'm all alone up here. There's Kurt, the estate manager. You probably heard us earlier from the corridor, just before I bumped into you. But I can't talk to him about it. That's why I'm so glad you are here. It's different girl to girl.' She took a deep breath. 'Geli and I were best friends. She was always here in the early days. Then we were separated when I went to Finishing School in England for a term. He, Herr Hitler, paid my tuition fees. But he preferred Paris for Geli. He said it would prepare her for German high society. I'm not sure whether you ever knew – she returned to Berlin and he couldn't keep his hands off her.'

Katharine remained on her guard. She couldn't let herself slip. This could be a trap. She put down her coffee, placing her hand on Claudia's arm. 'I see. Good gracious.'

Claudia's face flinched, her mouth tightened in bitterness, 'Then she slept with him. Her own uncle, how could she?' Her voice was suddenly hoarse as she spat out the next words. 'The very thought disgusted me – and still does. But, there was worse to come. She had his bastard son too.'

Katharine remained poised, showing no emotion. 'Really?' she muttered, then let out a small gasp. Claudia's smile reassured her that she had reacted correctly. Katharine looked into her steely blue eyes without betraying any feeling. She had to keep the response bland. 'Oh dear.'

'Yes, but then no one expected Geli to take her own life. *He* was devastated, or so he claimed. He had packed Geli and her bastard child off to South America, but of course he wouldn't blame himself. He arranged for her body to be brought back and buried her in an unmarked grave in Vienna's Central Cemetery. I was his only comfort for a while. It all made me rather sad even though it happened a few years ago. It has stayed with me and lives with me even through dreams. Sometimes I hate myself, really hate myself. Maybe if I had been there for her in Paris rather than England … who knows? No one has discovered what happened to the child; no one would dare ask.'

Katharine squeezed her arm in comfort. 'You couldn't do any more than you did, Claudia. Don't punish yourself. Oh, how cold your hands are, why don't you warm them by the stove.'

Claudia smiled, forcing the shadow from her face. 'What I need is female company. And now I have it … you … at least for a couple of days. It's so lovely to have a friend here again. You can't imagine what it's like to be surrounded by all these men, all the time. Come Katharine, there's something I want to show you.'

They walked across the kitchen towards the heavy oak-polished panelled door. Slightly ajar, Claudia pushed it with her shoulder. It creaked as the metal hinges ground open. A flight of wide stone steps led down to a basement. It was as black as night.

'Wait, Katharine. I need a torch.' She slipped back into the kitchen.

Alarm bells began to ring in Katharine's mind. This is it, she thought. Was it a trap? She could not back out without arousing suspicion; she had to go along with it. As her eyes adjusted to the darkness, she could just make out shapes on the wall. Claudia returned, shining the light down the steps. The mysterious shapes were revealed to be bayonets lining both walls. Two slogans and a swastika had been chalked across the stone. The air smelt musty and damp. Katharine drew the collar of her blouse up. Claudia took her hand as they descended to a set of double doors at the bottom. Claudia looked straight at her, giggling, 'This is what I want to show you. Watch this, Katharine. No one will question you because you're with me. We're now going under the west wing.'

The west wing, thought Katharine. That was out of bounds.

Claudia simultaneously pushed both doors, revealing a world buzzing with life. As they entered, the silence was instantaneous. Each man and woman stretched out their right arm in salute. '*Heil Hitler.*'

Claudia smiled at them. 'It's OK. He's not with me. Carry on as if we weren't here.' The tension drained from their faces. The background buzz resumed with the click, clicking of dials and switches. Claudia whispered, 'Isn't this an amazing world? This is his pride and joy. Isn't it exciting? Boys and their toys! I love all the maps and charts over there.'

Katharine dared to look around more closely, taking in the huge machinery stacked against the far wall. The maps on the nearest wall were not unlike the ones in Sir Charles's office back in London, except the German borders were marked in red rather than black. She noticed that the whole of Austria was shaded in blue. Looking along the map she noted that the Sudetenland was also highlighted in the same colour. How odd. Did Hitler have designs on that too? Claudia was talking nineteen to the dozen, barely pausing for breath. Katharine tried to re-focus on her chatter.

'Katharine, he loves this place more than anything else. It's where he and the boys play – sometimes all day, especially when Herr Goebbels arrives.' She started to giggle. 'And some of the night too. He calls it his OCC – Operations Control Centre.'

'Should you be showing me this, Claudia?' whispered Katharine. 'Whatever it is, it looks top secret.'

'No, don't worry about that. Neither of us knows what the hell all this stuff is, but bringing you here gives me such a thrill. I had to do it.'

It was more than Katharine could have hoped for. In the space of a couple of hours since her arrival, she had been taken completely into Claudia's confidence.

'It reminds me of the pranks we got up to at Miss Fenton's Finishing School. Remember the time we put glue in her cigarettes? And ink in her shampoo.' Katharine laughed, somewhat relaxing in her presence now.

'I want to show you something else,' said Claudia, pointing to a small glass window, only the bold Bakelite light fittings were visible through it from where they were standing. 'Come, look in here. I watch them for hours sometimes.'

Katharine peered through the glass, looking down onto a sealed room below. A large square table dominated the centre; large metal boxes full with dials and switches lined the walls. Each area had three operators wearing a set of heavy earphones. No one noticed them, far too intent on their tasks.

Claudia whispered, 'This is the special communication centre. From here Herr Hitler can keep in touch with all his ministers when he's in residence.'

Katharine feigned concern. 'Claudia, we shouldn't be looking at this. You'll get us both into trouble.'

'You're a musician, darling. I thought you'd be fascinated by all those symbols and switches. I was hoping you might be able to tell me what it all is. I've been curious for months but no one will tell me anything.'

'How should I know? I'm a violinist. It needs someone with technical knowledge.'

'And me – I just admire it when *he* brings me down here. It keeps him happy. Anyway, better not mention to anyone that you've seen it. Let's go.'

Katharine took one last cursory glance through the glass. Her heart skipped a double beat. Bent over one set of dials was Susie Norton. She was slightly turned to one side but there was no mistaking. It *was* her. Her curvy figure was recognisable anywhere. She couldn't forget her half-naked body under the sergeant. How had Sir Charles managed to install her here at the centre of Hitler's radio operations? Her legs began to feel weak; her stomach churning. Susie could turn around at any moment. The surprise might blow both their covers, although Susie did know she was playing at Berchtesgaden, but she would not expect to see Katharine in the operations room. Katharine drew back, beads of sweat at the base of her neck and on her forehead. Fortunately, Claudia hadn't noticed. Her voice penetrated Katharine's turmoil, 'Come Katharine, let's go in.'

'No, Claudia,' she spluttered. 'I'm … I'm feeling unwell with the heat down here. It's all too much. I must get some air.' She clutched her head.

'Why of course, darling. You're looking very pale. Come, we've had enough of this stuff anyway.' She led her back up to the kitchen and signalled to cook who passed a glass of iced water.

'Katharine, I'm so sorry. I've over-taxed you. I forget how stuffy and claustrophobic it is down there. It took me weeks to get used to it. You've got an important performance ahead of you this evening. Better get some rest, darling. We'll take some tea on the terrace at six o'clock, if you're feeling up to it.'

❧

An hour later Katharine lent over the balcony of the whitewashed terrace. Few were privileged to see this view. She took a long look at the Bavarian mountains stretched before her. Her body flooded with adrenalin, feeling alive and invigorated. The village of Berchtesgaden below was just visible nestling in the ridges. How quiet and peaceful it was. Behind her, a voice cleared his throat, 'On a clear day, ma'am, you can see all the way across Austria and even into Switzerland.'

She turned, recognising him immediately from his unscheduled visit to Captain Henderson's office. He hadn't taken any notice of her then, but now she had to face him head on. 'Guten tag, Herr Eichmann.'

He was sharp. He hadn't missed anything, even though he had not spoken to her on that previous occasion. 'We met, didn't we, not so long ago at the office of Captain … Henderson in Vienna. Do you work there?'

'Yes sir, I do a bit of typing. I have to supplement my earnings somehow as a musician.'

'Quite.' He surveyed her for a few minutes. 'Claudia will be joining us shortly. She says she knows you from Finishing School, what a coincidence. Come and sit under the umbrella. The July heat can get to us even at this hour.' He pulled out a chair for her. 'What do you think of the place? The Führer had it extended a few years ago. It's a welcome retreat.'

Katharine hesitated. Herr Eichmann had a fearsome reputation in political circles. Strange – the man who sat beside her now could not have been gentler or more charming. How deceptive he was. He had not shed his heavy, long grey overcoat for something casual, not even here out of the public eye. She found herself wondering if he knew about Jonathan's disappearance, whether he had had anything to do with it. He must know that the musician before him, Miss Simmons, aka Mrs Walters, was married to Dr Jonathan Walters. If he did, he wasn't mentioning it. He continued, 'This place gives us space to relax with the Führer. Anyway, Miss Simmons, I am very much looking forward to your concert this evening. We enjoy a little culture, even up here in the mountains.' He cleared his throat. 'What will you play for us this evening? Some Wagner?'

Katharine smiled reassuringly. 'I was advised on Beethoven's Violin Sonata in A Major, the *Kreutzer*. You'll love the adagio. People sometimes find slow music awful but this is an exception.'

'Under the circumstances, Beethoven is an excellent choice. Herr Hitler is rather taken by all things Austrian at the moment, not that he's here anyway but word will get back to him. He keeps apace of everything that goes on.'

Claudia's voice suddenly floated across the terrace, 'as long as there's nothing by that Jew Mahler. His work disgusts us.' She adjusted her slanting sunhat as she strolled over to them.

'The view is magnificent, isn't it? Like music itself. Its peaks and valleys stir the soul.' She pulled out a chair, nodded to Herr Eichmann, then continued her chatter about the virtues of music, intonation and the human spirit.

Herr Eichmann stood up. 'I must be going ladies. Please excuse me. I will see you later, Miss Simmons.'

With him gone, Katharine relaxed back into the chair, confident in her next comment: 'I want to introduce the audience to some contemporary British music so I've chosen two short pieces, one by Elgar, the other by Vaughan Williams.'

Claudia seemed pleased. 'I saw you looking down at the village – that's Berchtesgaden, darling. It's such a quaint place. Time stands still there.'

Katharine finished the last mouthful of coffee. 'I know. We drove through it earlier when I arrived. If you will excuse me, Claudia, I must practise for a while before the concert. I always insist on perfection in my playing.'

'Of course, darling. Go ahead.'

A final glimpse back at Claudia, and Katharine could see her touching up her dark red lipstick. Katharine smiled to herself. Claudia was certainly a character, but a likeable one.

Three hours later after supper, the drawing room of the Berghof was filling up. Nine o'clock was quite late to begin a concert, but Katharine had no choice on the scheduling. She had to keep up the contacts, raise her international profile. Therein lay her success as a musician and special operative. As she waited for the guests to take their seats, she deduced that this must be the largest room in the complex. It faced south over the main courtyard. It was whispered around the room that Eichmann was feeling unwell and might not attend the concert. All this for nothing, thought Katharine. With the guests finally seated, the preliminary welcomes made, the programme introduced, the soirée began. There was not a movement in the room; all eyes on her. She wondered how they would take to her choice of modern music. But first it was Beethoven, something safe. The slow entrance of his sonata began. Halfway through, Herr Eichmann, giving no apology, strutted down the aisle of chairs to take his place in the front row next to Herr Martin Bormann. Just once she had chance to glance from the corner of her eye. They seemed to be enjoying it.

Just after ten thirty, she finished the final piece. The select audience broke into applause. Herr Eichmann was quick to move to her side to face the gathering. 'I must apologise for arriving late this evening.' He turned his head to Katharine. 'You were an angel tonight, Miss Simmons. How privileged we are. Even the very walls of this place were moved by your magnificent playing. You are the divine embodiment of the Aryan race, ma'am, perfection incarnate.'

The adulation was a little exaggerated perhaps. He had missed the introduction. Katharine took the praise with grace. More applause followed as she curtsied to the guests and the pianist who had accompanied her. Herr Eichmann and Herr Bormann made to leave. The entire audience stood up, saluting, 'Heil Hitler, Heil Hitler.'

A short time later, back in her room, the tension of performing had taken its toll. She collapsed on the bed. What had she learnt for Sir Charles? Not much, except a surprise observation of the underground communications system. Maybe that was enough. At least she had made the contacts.

Chapter 7

Blinking in the bright sunlight, Jonathan struggled across the parade ground with the cauldron of steaming watery coffee. His arms shook with the effort. It was two months almost to the day since he had arrived. He only knew it was 1 June because he had asked one of the Capos. He had no other way of keeping track of the precise date, except to observe the change of seasons and positions of the sun. Sleep was fitful at best, stomach cramps from hunger more often than not kept him awake at night. He dared not look out the hut window to confer with the constellations. The guards would suspect him of planning an escape and that meant certain death. He rarely thought of his old life with Katharine. That was a world away. All that mattered now was survival. Every minute of every day was a bonus. Every week the camp was filling up with hundreds of new inmates. Extra huts were being built to accommodate them at the far end of the camp. During his incarceration, Jonathan kept close to Mr Guttmann who was fairing worse. The fifty-seven year old suffered from constant griping stomach pains and diarrhoea. He had become nothing but flesh and bones, his wrinkled skin jaundiced. Jonathan knew that going to the camp doctor spelt brutality for Guttmann, to be avoided at all cost. He had heard the distant screams in the night coming from the direction of the first aid hut.

'Hey you there!' A young guard was marching sharply towards him.

Jonathan stopped, slopping some of the coffee as his unsteady hands put down the heavy iron pot. Turn, obey, don't look directly into his eyes, thought Jonathan. Anything could be construed as insolence, punishable with forty-two days in solitary confinement on a puny diet of bread and water. The guard lifted his hand as if to strike him, but hesitated: 'Waste not want not. You've just spilt your portion. You'll have to go without this morning. Take that to the hut and report back to me immediately. You're wanted in the commandant's office; you and that stinking fellow Guttmann.'

Jonathan nodded. He scampered back to hut 28. Inside Guttmann was shivering, leaning over the side of his bunk being sick into his mess tin. He lifted his head, about to speak. Jonathan raised his hand,

'No don't. It's okay.' After a few moments, he helped him climb down. Guttmann was desperately weak, his ragged striped shirt covered in vomit and filth. Jonathan held him, steadily seating him in a rickety wooden chair. 'When you're ready, we need to see the commandant. Rumour has it that we're going to be Capos for the new batch of inmates that arrived early this morning.' Looking into Guttmann's eyes, he knew he had to lie to him.

Guttmann tried to lift his head. His nauseous empty stomach began retching again, bringing up putrid bile. 'I'm ready,' he managed but his voice had lost its strength. Jonathan took his frail arm. Guttmann shrugged him off. 'Let go of me. If they see you helping me, you'll be done for.'

'But you can't walk on your own. You're too weak.'

'Nonsense. Just catching my breath.' Once outside Guttmann mustered all his strength, stood upright, lifting his shoulders back and smiled. 'Thank you, Jonathan.' He veered to the left as he stumbled a few steps towards the perimeter fence. Then in one last burst of energy, he lurched forward. Jonathan could do nothing to prevent it.

'No!' he shouted. 'Guttmann, no!'

It was too late. Guttmann's body hit the electric fence, sparks sizzled as his convulsing torso flung off the wire. His body in an aura of smoke thudded to the ground. Jonathan took a few steps towards his lifeless body, white smoke gently drifting out of his nostrils and open mouth. He stared down, emotionally stunned. It seemed surreal.

A single bullet hit the ground beside him.

'*Achtung!* You there, *Stramm stehen!* Stand to attention!'

Jonathan turned, stood still, his head slightly bent down. Two more guards with drawn guns approached, their black knee-high boots clipping sharply on the gravel. 'You move one step out of line again and you die.'

'Yes, sir.' Jonathan returned a Nazi salute, hoping it would save him.

'Filth! how dare you insult the Führer. You are not fit to salute.' In one swift movement, the butt of the gun swiped across his face. The guard's contorted expression betrayed his enjoyment of the situation: 'Why aren't you working in the quarry with the rest of them?'

Jonathan held his ground; his face numb with pain. He wanted to touch his cheek to relieve the blaze. He dared not. How could they have so much hate for humanity? It defied rational comprehension. Stuttering blood, he replied, 'The commandant has asked to see me immediately,' he replied, waiting, hoping that his answer had saved him. In that moment he promised himself, however long it took, he would get even with the Nazis.

The guard raised his hand in salute, 'Heil Hitler. This time you're lucky. Just remember the camp motto: *work brings freedom.*'

Jonathan shuffled across the compound now under escort. The commandant's office seemed the only sign of hope in this God-forsaken camp because it could signal imminent release. With every passing day he was hopeful that M was hatching a plan to get him out. Standing in front of the commandant he stared ahead, remembering his training – focus on the positive. Never say more than you have to. From the corner of his eye, he noticed the photograph on the window ledge of a woman with two Hitler Youths. He presumed they were the commandant's wife and sons. On the desk beneath there was a half-full cup of coffee with biscuit resting in the saucer. The signs of normality and humanity contrasted starkly with the abnormality and inhumanity of camp life which surrounded him. He failed to comprehend how the two could co-exist.

The commandant began to pace the office. 'There's plenty of work to be done and I understand from your Capo that you're a keen worker Mr Walters. But…' His voice changed. 'You have been less than co-operative with us on the intelligence front. Do you think we're stupid? We know exactly who you are. So, we have a little job for you.' He shuffled through the papers on his desk. 'Recognise this?' He thrust the photograph at him; it was of Sir Charles.

Jonathan shook his head. His unshaven face could no longer hide his weight loss, a mirror of the reality of recent months. His gaunt haunting eyes returned to stare resolutely down at the floor.

'Are you sure about that? I wouldn't want you to make a fatal mistake. A lapse of memory could cost you your life.'

'No sir, quite sure, sir.' He remained calm on the outside, inside his guts churned like cream into butter.

'I'm moving you out of the camp.' The commandant was enjoying the power he exerted over him. 'We are about to embark on the Führer's new plan. And you will help. *Ausrottung der Juden* – destruction of the Jews.' Jonathan showed no reaction, he knew better than to look at the Nazi. Total bastards, the Führer's henchmen, the lot of them, he thought. He would find a way to avenge them, no matter what. His time would come. He *would* survive if only for retribution.

The commandant began strutting the length of the room again, unfastening, then fastening his gun holster in a gesture that signalled an atypical unease. Then the curt order echoed around the room: '*Herraus!* Get out! You leave immediately.' He turned to the guard standing in the doorway. 'Take him to line 3.'

Jonathan was escorted back across the parade ground, past the prison yard and the whitewashed wall where many prisoners were shot for disobeying simple camp rules. No evidence of the firing squads remained on the wall, all blood scrubbed away immediately by inmates and then re-painted. The smell of fresh paint filled his nostrils. The guard escorting him commented, 'You ought to eat something before you go. Heaven knows when you'll next see a morsel of bread. Wait here. I'll buy you something from the Officers' Mess.' Jonathan looked at him. It was the first and only act of kindness from a Nazi since his arrival. Was there yet hope even amidst such horror? The officer returned with bread, cake and two apples, stuffing them into Jonathan's pockets.

Finally, as they came to the exit on the eastern side of the camp, Jonathan saw a hastily dug shallow pit next to the fence, piled with naked corpses. The stench was overpowering. He tried to avert his eyes but could not avoid what lay in front of him. Guttmann's body was being shovelled onto the pile.

He turned and vomited at the perimeter. His escort came alongside him and touched his shoulder in sympathy.

3 June 1938. Inside the flat on Berggasse, Katharine walked into the sitting room with a tray of tea and biscuits. 'Here Mrs Guttmann, this should help. There's nothing like a nice cup of tea to help with the effects of shock.'

Mrs Guttmann's traumatised face tried to hold back the tears. Her hand shook as she took the tea. 'We've had to move from the bakery, Mrs Walters. Two days ago, the Gestapo raided our apartment. They turned the place upside down and confiscated our passports and documents. We're now living in one room over the far side of Leopoldstadt. They, they…' She started crying. As she turned her head, Katharine caught sight of a black bruise on her neck. She had probably been raped too. 'I'm scared, Mrs Walters. The fear haunts me every night and waking hour. We can't work without torment, can't buy things from non-Jewish shops, I have no money, it's…'

Katharine touched her arm, 'We need to get you and the children out urgently.'

Mrs Guttmann reached into her pocket, thrusting the tattered postcard at her, 'And now this. My worst fears confirmed.'

Katharine scanned the tiny black print.

Dachau, 1 June 1938
To: Mrs Guttmann

Dear Mrs Guttmann

Your husband reported sick on 25 May and was subsequently admitted to the infirmary and placed under medical supervision. He received the best possible medical attention and care. In spite of all medical efforts it was not possible to cure the illness. I offer you my condolence on this loss.

Your husband expressed no last wishes. I have directed the prisoners' property officer of my camp to forward the deceased's estate to your address.

'Oh, Mrs Walters, I can't bear it – the thought that he died in that horrific place … I've heard the rumours. We all know what's going on in the camps. He was a wonderful husband. I keep seeing his kind face before me. I walk down the street and there he is – except it isn't him of course.' She buried her face in her trembling hands, the sobs uncontrollable. Katharine gently placed her arm around her shoulders. 'I know how difficult it is, Mrs Guttmann. I do understand but you need to think of the children now and their safety. You must get those emigration forms back to me tomorrow, no later, you understand. And I'll move heaven and earth to get those visas for you.'

'Thank you, Mrs Walters. I can't thank you enough.' A faint smile pierced her lips as she left the apartment. On the stairs outside she passed Captain Henderson striding two steps at a time. He didn't make eye contact, too preoccupied with his thoughts.

Back in the apartment, Katharine felt overcome with heat and exhaustion. She moved into the sitting room, opening the window to the morning cool summer breeze. It blew refreshingly through the apartment. She barely heard the second knock on the door, followed by the firm voice of Captain Henderson. 'Katharine, are you there? Would you let me in?'

Katharine hesitated. She was not expecting him. 'Yes, of course,' she called out, then opened the door for him. As he entered, the faint fragrance of her perfume pervaded his senses. His heart skipped a beat. Neither did he miss the fatigue that held her tight, the sadness in her eyes, although he could still detect the feisty spark that he loved so much. It was there despite all the anguish of recent weeks.

She gestured for him to go into the sitting room, 'May I offer you tea, Captain Henderson? I've just brewed a pot.'

'Thank you, Katharine. That would be wonderful. I was hoping you would ask.'

She moved into the kitchen, calling through to him: 'I'm sorry I didn't make it into the office this morning. I needed a rest. I've been so exhausted recently, but I'll be there before lunchtime.' He admired her strength. A few minutes later she returned with a tray of tea. 'Come and sit down Captain Henderson. What can I do for you?'

His eyes glanced in the direction of the open window. 'Would you mind closing that please Katharine? I need to talk privately.' He watched her walk over and shut it firmly. He tried not to notice her form clinging tightly to her thin cotton blouse, her breasts gently rising with each breath. He looked away. She was still a married woman. He coughed to clear his throat.

'We've picked up something unusual on the radio waves. It appears to be coming from a closer location than usual. I hesitate to guess, but at first we thought maybe it was coming from Hitler's Summer House, especially after what you told us about the operations room at Berchtesgaden. However, Gibbons thinks it may be a lot nearer than that. I wonder whether you might give an opinion, see what you make of it, perhaps this afternoon. I would have told you earlier but...' his voice became distant. 'I didn't want to over-tax you.'

'Thank you. What's so unusual this time? We've heard a lot of traffic in the past few days. Intensive bursts and then nothing for a bit.'

He leant forward in the armchair, resting his right elbow on his knee, 'It was transmitted on a different band than usual, and one which we would not have expected. We actually stumbled across it quite by accident. It's very puzzling because we have been recording all known bands, but what is really perplexing – it's been a devil of a job to decode. That's where we need your help.' He looked at her levelly, waiting for her response.

'Have you managed to log it?'

'Yes, fortunately we have. Gibbons has noted the band frequency and times. We are assuming that whatever this is, it's important.'

'Is there anything else unusual about these new transmissions?' She sat back, discreetly eyeing his every slight movement. She felt she was beginning to understand him. It had taken months.

'Yes. They usually occur late evening, around ten or eleven o'clock, but we have also noted the occasional early morning activity at eight o'clock. Nothing seems to happen in between; nothing during office hours – naturally. More importantly, we have observed that the last few transmissions have occurred before a major night time round-up of Jews.' He paused, carefully studying her face.

Their eyes met.

She looked away, stood up and walked over to the window, fiddling with the slats of the wooden shutters. Below, children chased each other, zig zagging across the inner courtyard. Their laughter gave the city an air of normality. Through the arched entrance of the quadrangle the figures of two SS officers marched passed on their routine round. Katharine noticed how the children stopped, saluted 'Heil Hitler', their innocence shackled to the regime. The relentless presence of patrols kept any socialist demonstrations at bay. Through her dazed thoughts, Captain Henderson spoke with a deep softness, comforting her raw nerves. 'We also suspect that it is happening before one of our agents goes down.'

'What are you saying, Captain Henderson?' she knew the implications, she didn't really need to ask, she had already worked it out. She turned from the window to face him.

'Katharine,' he paused, directly avoiding the question. 'I have some other news. We believe we have located Jonathan.' There was no easy way to tell her. He waited until she appeared composed before carrying on, giving time for the news to sink in. 'He is still alive. We have reason to believe that he's in Dachau concentration camp.'

'Dachau?' she gasped. Neither appeared to find the silence between them awkward. He waited a few moments before telling her the rest. 'There's more Katharine. We think it was no accident. We believe he was compromised by the same mole that took down the others. All efforts are now focused on tracking them down. This has to be our main priority, Katharine. It's not easy because whoever it is seems to be deep within the establishment with their backs well covered. Sir Charles brought you here because of your many talents, especially your knowledge of amateur radio. Now it's time to get you on to this properly. "Do whatever it takes", Sir Charles told me last week, "You have complete autonomy to bring this miscreant down." Katharine, I … we need you on this one.'

'Fine. I'll leave with you for the Embassy now.'

He smiled. 'Thank you.'

That same afternoon it was intensely hot inside the shack on the Embassy roof. The sun had been beating down on the corrugated roof all day, heating it like an oven. Walter Gibbons was already loading the reel. 'Gee, am I glad to see you two,' he said as Katharine and Captain Henderson entered. They had spent the rest of the morning going through paperwork. Lunch was late, a cup of coffee and a sandwich before de-briefing. Katharine removed her cardigan. Gibbons carried on, 'This came in last night, it's all new. I think you need to listen to it sir, ma'am … The trouble is we can't work out whether it is army command or Luftwaffe.'

Katharine listened to the fast coded commands. Deciphering the dialect at such speed was difficult for anyone without fluent knowledge of German. She turned to both of them, 'Each transmission is followed by a response. That's unusual.' She pulled a scrap of paper from her handbag. 'Can you play that again please Mr Gibbons? Just that last bit.'

Gibbons replayed the tape. She began to scribble down the letters. Captain Henderson stood quietly watching over her shoulder. He could see a pattern beginning to emerge. 'Now I see,' he said. He bent closer to her, pointing to the four middle letters. 'That's the coded word for the Sudetenland.'

'Yes, but don't you see Captain Henderson, where the message was being sent from?'

'No.' He cleared his throat, taking his cigarette case from his pocket. Slowly he lit a cigarette, taking in the first puff.

Katharine looked confident, 'It's close, really close by. I reckon that it's being transmitted from this city. The subsequent response to each transmission is coming from Italy. That means that the transmissions are going from Vienna to Italy – Musso and his army command, to be precise. Never mind the first ones, look at the middle four letters of the next line.'

'Mussolini,' stated Gibbons. 'Of course! You're a genius, ma'am. Now your Chamberlain will have to appease him too.' He frowned. 'What does Hitler want with the Italians?'

Captain Henderson drew on his cigarette. Didn't the Americans know anything of European history? He could be forgiven. The borders had changed so often in the last hundred years that only an expert historian could follow it with any accuracy. 'We'll do the history lesson later Gibbons. For now, keep getting those codes down.' Captain Henderson turned, with authority he spoke directly to Katharine, 'Is it possible to transmit over such a distance?'

She nodded, 'With current technology, just about, but only if you have the expertise. And … that knowledge only comes from Britain at the present time.'

Captain Henderson looked beyond her, taking another drag on his cigarette. Both knew the implications. It had to be someone who had the training. He suddenly took her arm, led her to one side, out of earshot of Gibbons. He lowered his voice, 'Who's had such a level of training? Would you compile a list for me?'

'Yes, of course, but it may be a very limited list.'

'That's good. We have to start somewhere. What about that new woman who's recently come to Vienna? I haven't met her yet, what's her name … Susie Norton?'

'No, she failed the training at Blenheim and was thrown out after two weeks. She was transferred elsewhere. I'm amazed she made it here. No, it has to be someone who is proficient with both Morse and long-wave transmissions.' Katharine could not assume that Captain Henderson knew about Susie being placed in operations at Berchtesgaden. Sir Charles insisted that knowledge of his web should not be widened. She had to play safe. 'Sir Charles informed me that she has been off sick for two months and is back in England.'

'Okay, I need that list, pretty damn quick,' he replied.

Katharine took herself into the adjacent room, its smallness making it no more than an extended cupboard. The air was even stuffier than in the main part of the shack. She began compiling the list: Spike, Sir Charles, Hugo. She added a question mark next to Hugo remembering Susie's comment in the coffee house. Susie – but she had failed the training, which was strange having seen her in Hitler's bunker at Berchtesgaden. Katharine tutted and added Susie's name to the list, along with twin brothers Ernie and Bill Sandalwood who had been educated at Harrow. She scrawled Gibbons' name as an after-thought. Her list comprised of just seven names of those she knew about. They were all individuals she trusted; this was not a good start. There had to be more. She passed the names back to Captain Henderson.

He scanned it without comment and stuffed it in his pocket. She hoped to God she hadn't compromised Susie's work by including her. Sir Charles would go ballistic, but the list needed to be accurate.

❧

The following night Katharine managed to snatch a few hours sleep before the alarm went off. She had set it for 3 a.m. Getting visas for Mrs Guttmann and her family had proved more complicated than expected. She had only managed to secure two permits, one for each of the eldest children. Now she would have to smuggle Mrs Guttmann and her third child through the safe route that Captain Henderson had planned for the Freud family in the eventuality that they could not get out. Freud's papers were progressing well. Only payment of the *Reichsfluchtsteuer*, the hefty 'fleeing tax' calculated at twenty-five per cent of their assets, required of all Jews leaving Austria, was waiting to clear through Nazi channels. Then the final stamps could be issued from Eichmann's office on their new passports. Only yesterday she had confirmation that Jonathan's nephew Günter Herz had crossed the border into Belgium, en route for England. The glimmer of good news was a welcome relief.

She hastily dressed in dark colours, tying a black chiffon scarf over her head, squashing up her curls. In the sitting room, she pushed the servant's bell beside the ornate fireplace. It released the hidden hinge on the fireplace, allowing it to swing quietly open. Sir Charles had thought of everything. The outline of the panel could barely be made out. Her fingers fumbled along the thin line of the crack, feeling for movement in the wall. A slight indentation, she had it. She pushed down. Inside, the shallow cupboard was lined from top to bottom with shelves. The brown boxes on the top housed the small arms. Her eyes scanned down for where Sir Charles had filed the passports. She scrutinised the labels, her eyes fixing on the smallest box on the middle shelf marked 'X papers'. She pulled out the two books with rubber bands around them lying on the top. She thumbed through to check the names matched those that were being allocated to the Guttmanns. In the dim candlelight she saw the passport holder had already travelled widely. Authenticity was vital in reproduction. As she closed the panel, her eye caught the reflection of something shiny. She ran her fingers over the polished surface of the SS officer's badge. Her mind flashed back to Jonathan. This must have been for his use. She had to admit that she hadn't really known him. Even before their wedding he had lived a double life apart from her. Yet she had trusted Jonathan, still hoped that he would come home. She dismissed any thoughts of him. The present was more important for now. She had lives to save.

She crept out of the apartment block into the mild night air. She had just a few streets to cross. Keeping in the shadows, there was not a soul to be seen. The curfew on the Jewish population had been in force ever since the annexing three months ago. As a member of Embassy staff she was permitted to move freely, even during the curfew. Even so, she couldn't afford to take any chances. She waited in the doorway opposite the Guttmann home, checking no SS patrols were in sight. She darted across the street, giving three brief rings on the doorbell as agreed beforehand. The door opened cautiously. Mrs Guttmann peered through the tiny crack. Identity confirmed, she allowed Katharine to enter. Silently, Katharine closed the door behind her. Mrs Guttmann was looking terribly anxious, beckoning the children to keep quiet. They already had their coats on, huddled in the corner of the hall.

Katharine whispered, 'Here are your papers for the eldest two and a map of the safe route through the city. You'll need to move in twos, a few yards from each other to avoid detection. We have contacts at each marked point on the map. They know you're coming and will contact you only if you stop where indicated. They might wait a moment or two to be sure you're not being followed. If no contact is needed or apparent at any point, go on to the next and so forth. Once through the border you will be given a complete set of papers and safe passage to England for the other two children. When you get to London, a Quaker family will meet you. They will look after you.'

Mrs Guttmann managed a smile, 'How can I ever thank you?'

Katharine put her hand on her arm, 'Sssh, not now. Once I've left, give it exactly fifteen minutes and then get going, your journey has been timed. Everything will be OK. I'll see you in England one day.' With that Katharine crept back out into the street. She suppressed a cough, muffling it in her scarf. With one corner she wiped the tears from her eyes. It was hard not to become emotionally involved with these people.

Nine weeks after leaving Dachau concentration camp, the line still held a thousand prisoners. The destination, unknown to them, was rumoured to be a labour camp on the Polish border. It was now the second week of August. Weak with hunger, barely able to put one blistered foot in front of the other, Jonathan cursed the SS officers around him swigging brandy, laughing and scoffing chocolate. The ill-fitting shoes pinched his feet, wrenched off a dead body as they had passed out through the gates of Dachau. There had been no time for trying them on. It was take and go. The guilt no longer ate into his soul.

Day after day the men marched; the glare of the summer's sun mercilessly beating down. Skin burnt red raw, open sores oozed, muscles atrophied, stomach constantly burning through lack of food. Dizzy and weak, Jonathan like the rest in line could hardly move. He managed to hold in there, buffered by the men around him. He tried to keep in the centre of them, blending in, becoming almost invisible to the guards. If he stumbled, he hoped they wouldn't notice. It had already saved him twice. The constant bellow of 'Schnell, schnell' echoed around the prisoners, interspersed with the crack of a rifle when someone stumbled.

Another yard, another death. Almost a quarter had died since they started out, the route behind littered with the fallen, each with a neat bullet through the back of the skull.

'*Achtung!* Halt!' the guards shouted in unison down the line, indicating a short break was intended. A dozen SS officers began passing chunks of mouldy bread between the ranks of dejected prisoners. Each grabbed the pathetic offering, his mouth salivating at the morsel. Jonathan watched as the guards relaxed on the grass, eating and drinking. They appeared not to be watching their prisoners, but there was no chance of escape. Everyone knew it. There was nowhere to hide, even if they wanted to. Their starved bodies were too weak; they would collapse in no time. In an instant, all guns would point on the assailant, firing mercilessly, killing any prisoners in the line of fire. Co-operation was the only way to stay alive.

Half an hour later, the march resumed until after an hour the quarry gates loomed in front of them. They had finally reached Stalag Luft III: five weeks, three days, and two thousand miles after leaving Dachau concentration camp. Hundreds had died en route, but now the brutality and slave labour began in earnest.

Chapter 8

Gibbons passed the telegram to Captain Henderson. 'This arrived for you five minutes ago, sir.' Gibbons waited expectantly, hoping for a hint of what it contained. He could be somewhat prying at times, something which Henderson found irritating.

'Thank you, Gibbons.' His abruptness gave Gibbons his cue to leave. Alone again, Captain Henderson turned over the telegram. His office was immaculately tidy, an attribute due not only to his upbringing but his naval training. A place for everything and everything in its place. That was his maxim. He lived by it. There was no other way to function effectively. He picked up a silver letter opener, slipping its fine blade along the envelope, leaving a single clean cut. He liked a perfect slit. He removed the small brown telegram, sent at 7.05 a.m. from London. The bold typed letters confirmed the identity: *'Am on way. Meet you noon today. Mother.'*

Sir Charles could have given him more warning. He hadn't seen him for three months, although communication had been regular. Sir Charles astounded him. How could someone so shambolic be so effective? Apart from his sometimes over-bombastic nature, Sir Charles was efficient in his own way. Much to his chagrin Captain Henderson had to admit it, although it made working with Sir Charles somewhat difficult at times. When he entered a room, his presence felt like a tornado erupting the tranquil privacy.

Why Captain Henderson looked up at that moment was anyone's guess. Maybe he was subconsciously aware of her presence – the underlying connection between them deeper than he cared to admit. He caught sight of her passing his door.

'Katharine, do you have a minute? Come in and close the door would you?' Standing in front of him, her youthful radiant face touched a chord with him. He realised how much difference she made to his solitary life, even though he might see her only briefly each day. There was still no news of Jonathan's precise whereabouts, although it was known that he had been moved.

He pulled up another chair to his desk, 'About that other business … Have you discovered where it's coming from?'

'Yes. After a silence of nearly four weeks, there was a single transmission early this morning. This time to Germany, somewhere in the region of Munich.' She paused. He appeared not to be concentrating on the last sentence. 'Captain Henderson … Munich.'

He came around, 'Yes, sorry. Munich, you say? I have a meeting with Sir Charles this morning. He mentioned Munich recently.'

'Sir Charles? Is he in Vienna then?' She hadn't expected this news.

'Yes,' he muttered, 'never be surprised by any of his movements.' He studied her. 'Actually, could you stay for the meeting, Katharine? I need to update him and it would be good to have you. By the way, please don't use the term M to address him – not here in Vienna, do you understand?'

She nodded. Then she revealed the rest of her news, 'I've also established where the messages are being transmitted from.'

She could see that he hadn't heard the last sentence. She figured he was still thinking about Sir Charles's visit. She continued, teasing him with a mischievous sparkle in her eyes, 'Well, Captain Henderson, do you want to know where the last transmission was coming from or shall I put it in a memo?'

Her light-heartedness lifted his spirits. Unintentionally he started to chuckle. She was as surprised as he was.

'Captain Henderson, I've never heard you laugh!'

'And I have never seen you as open as you are today,' he jested.

'I'm sorry. I think I have missed something.'

He risked his reputation in the next comment, 'I do like your new blouse – the colour suits you. It has a certain touch of soft, feminine simplicity yet at the same time sophisticated. However, I think you have lost a button or two.'

She eyed him cautiously. He was not his usual self today. Something had broken through his usual reserved nature. He was so much more relaxed. 'Thank you,' she replied. 'But there aren't actually any buttons missing. It's the design; it's meant to be a little provocative. I shall take that as a compliment, Captain Henderson.' She waited for his reaction, her eager expression still challenging him. For the first time she admitted to herself he was somewhat attractive; tall and commanding. A man's man. She liked his air of authority. She knew she shouldn't be encouraging his attention; she was still a married woman. But then Jonathan was gone, possibly dead. Even before his arrest he had stopped showing her any real, intimate love. She decided she was at liberty to flirt a little as long as it went no further. It would all be superficial. The emotion would go no further. Jonathan had always appeared so frank and honest with her. The man in the room with her now was different. She was curious to know more about him, fathom him out. She wanted to penetrate his depths and know what he was capable of.

He turned away and reached for the brandy from the mahogany corner cabinet: 'Better have this ready. Sir Charles will expect some. Napoleon is his favourite brand, you know.' He continued to stare aimlessly at the bottle, 'Katharine, I'm sorry for that outburst and my forward comments just now. It's most unusual for me. It must be the heat. Please accept my apology.'

'Of course.' She felt a little disappointed. She had quite enjoyed his attention.

'That said and done,' he continued, 'you certainly brighten up the place around here.' His voice now composed, he had retreated into the 'silent service' figure she was used to. She waited, mystified. He was inscrutable again, the momentary close connection gone.

Just then, Sir Charles's deep voice could be heard bellowing down the corridor, 'Hugo, get me some aspirin, lad. I have a stinking headache. Those hotel rooms are far too stuffy … now lad!'

Katharine smirked. Nothing changed. Minutes later the bombastic figure of Sir Charles bumbled into the office, wiping his brow, his white shirt straining under his grey braces. His moustache seemed even bushier than ever. He anticipated Captain Henderson's first move. 'Ah! Brandy … excellent, thank you Henderson. A large one please.' He took the tumbler, holding it between his thumb and index finger. Katharine marvelled that his chubby fingers managed to grip it so daintily. He looked around the room, as if inspecting regimental headquarters. 'Your office is very tidy, Henderson. I approve. I wish Hugo would keep mine in such orderly fashion. That lad piles the stuff everywhere.' He chuckled. Katharine took a couple of steps towards him, 'It is lovely to see you again Sir Charles.'

He grunted. 'Well girl, are you making progress for us here? Henderson thinks you're a fine woman. He says he couldn't do without you. You might call me old school but it needs a man for a man's job.' He lowered his vast bulk into the corner chair. Captain Henderson stood there reserved but in full control of his situation. He didn't move, but uttered with authority: 'I've asked Katharine to join us for this morning's meeting Sir Charles. She has some important information for us which may relate to the mole.' Captain Henderson beckoned for her to sit in the other empty chair. 'Tell Sir Charles exactly what you've picked up, Katharine.'

She glanced briefly from one to the other, 'Sir Charles, I can confirm that the transmissions are coming from within this city. To be more precise we have located them to the east side of Vienna. We haven't yet been able to locate the exact street because each transmission is sent from a different address – they might be only a few hundred yards away from each other. It's a constantly moving target. It makes predicting the address of the next transmission very difficult. The other crucial point is that these messages could only be transmitted from an experienced operator. We believe someone who has been trained in England.'

Sir Charles began rubbing his forehead. 'Anything else?'

'Yes, the messages are currently being sent to Munich. However, we have intercepted a couple on their way to Italy, but those don't appear to have any direct relevance to the mole and operations.'

Sir Charles grunted again.

Captain Henderson interjected. 'It's what Winston Churchill has long suspected these past five years. The line is from Vienna to Munich; Munich because of the industrial plants there. We have our proof. It's all in the transliteration of the transmissions. German re-armament is taking place in a suburb of Munich.'

Sir Charles turned to Katharine, 'Well done, girl. For once you've impressed me. Not bad, not bad at all for a young girl. But then I always choose the best for my team.' He beamed, 'Now let's get down to tracing the bugger who's taking out my people.' He stood up, 'If you will, please excuse us Katharine, Captain Henderson and I have some other business to attend to.' He took her forearm and gently led her to the door, closing it firmly behind her. Waiting until he heard her footsteps down the corridor, he then turned to Captain Henderson to start the other business.

Later that afternoon, Captain Henderson watched as Katharine filed the latest emigration requests. His eyes wandered down to her dainty ankles. She hadn't noticed him standing in the doorway, her back to him. He stepped forward and coughed gently, so as not to frighten her. 'Katharine.'

She turned. 'Captain Henderson, I thought you were going to be out of the office for a few hours.'

'I was, but the Chief Rabbi cancelled our meeting. He's had to go off to do an emergency funeral; if you can call it a funeral. A mass grave has been discovered some three miles from the outskirts of Vienna, not far from the spa town Baden bei Wien. A hastily dug grave from all accounts. I have it on good authority there are nearly a hundred bodies in it. All Jewish and male, of course.'

She stared ahead. 'The ones we didn't save.'

In recent weeks he had noticed her tendency towards sombre reflection. Her usual cheerful countenance hid a depth of emotion. Occasionally she seemed quite introverted. Who could blame her? Still only twenty-five, she was so young to shoulder such responsibility. He would shelter her as much as he could, but his hands were tied. He understood her anxiety. Hadn't it also played on his conscience? He tried to reassure her. 'Katharine, they're the ones who didn't come to us for help. It is hard, but we can't save everyone. We are doing all we can.' He turned, walking towards the window. He had to find a way to tell her about Jonathan. How long could he keep it from her? He wanted to tell her that Jonathan was no more than a fraud and a cad, that he – Henderson – was the one who loved her. He always had, ever since he saw her in Bath during that school tea dance all those years ago. But such liberties were denied him, his duty uppermost. Being involved with a fellow female operative could cause all kinds of difficulties for a man in his position. Nothing could be allowed to compromise his function.

Katharine looked at him quizzically. 'Captain Henderson, a penny for your thoughts?'

'Nothing. It's nothing.' Now was not the moment.

She continued. 'This heartless country has proved worse than Germany. How can such an intellectual, cultured city have its population turn into monsters overnight? The inhumanity is intolerable. Austria has lost its soul. I can't imagine music ever being restored here again. Can't you feel the void?'

'Yes, I can, but we are British subjects and we have a duty to serve our country. We are its eyes and ears here. We can't afford the luxury of sentimentality, never mind pity. Katharine, it is important that you focus on the positive – on helping those we can. They're the ones who need us most. That's not to say you can't be concerned, but don't let it over-burden you.'

She couldn't dispel the serious mood.

'Now to other matters,' he said, passing her a cup of tea, 'One or two sugars?' She didn't miss his wry humour. 'That's better. You almost smiled. Talking of culture and music, I've had another instruction from Sir Charles. It's why I've come to see you this morning. Chancellor von Seyss-Inquart is holding an exclusive soirée, a small ball at the end of the week. You have been invited to play.'

She raised her eyes, the life in them still dulled. 'How can I? Amidst all this?'

He continued unabated: 'It is rumoured that Mussolini is attending.'

'Mussolini?'

'Yes, it's all hushed up, of course. No one is supposed to know.'

She looked at him. 'And me? What's my role besides playing the violin?'

'I'm glad you recognise that your playing is not the real reason you're there.'

'I am no longer the naive girl who started six months ago. Much has happened since then.' Her relatively sheltered life in Devon had been eclipsed by her chance meeting with Sir Charles, not that she knew then that it had been carefully orchestrated just as a composer might a concerto. Everything had panned out as Sir Charles had planned, but then that was his skill – he could pretty much predict human reactions to a given scenario. He always did his research, tried to get inside the mentality of the person he was wooing to be an agent. So far it had worked every time, except with the mole. That was his one failing. Katharine knew he took it personally and would stop at nothing to get him. No one messed with his 'family' without paying the consequences. There was too much at stake.

Captain Henderson chose not to comment on her reflection. He focused instead on the next assignment. 'First, we need you to confirm that Musso is at the ball and second, you are to get as close to him as you can. If possible, find out why he's been invited. Knowing your reputation in the music field you're bound to be introduced to him. That's why we have placed you there. We could have asked Myra Hess or Harriet Cohen. Both pianists have a substantial international reputation, but their Jewishness would place their safety in jeopardy. And … we need a sniff about looted art or gold. I might be there. It's not finally decided yet, but if I am, you're not to acknowledge me unless I instigate it, understood?'

'Yes.' Then she managed a smile, 'I'm flattered that you rank me so highly, even above Miss Hess and Cohen.'

He moved closer to her as if to whisper in her ear. He gently took her hand in an unexpected gesture of closeness. She was surprised by it.

'Katharine, about Jonathan – we have reason to believe he's been moved from Dachau. Unfortunately we have no idea yet where they've taken him. Sir Charles is onto it. I know this is difficult for you, but…'

She preferred to block Jonathan out, not talk about it. She interrupted him; her reply casual.

'You know, I am resigned to the fact that I might never see him again. I know what goes on there. I've spent all my energy these past months crying for him. To what avail? Life moves on. I know deep down he may never return to me and even if he does, he will be a different man. I have effectively lost him.'

'It may not be so. As long as he is alive, there is always hope.' He couldn't believe he was saying this to her. What else could he say? 'Katharine, you don't have to be so hard on yourself. May I suggest you need some relaxation. Why don't you take some time off? Go to the theatre before the ball at the end of the week? It will do you good.'

She stared at him for a moment or two. 'Yes, thank you. I might just do that.' His compassion and thoughtfulness touched her. He detected a warmth in her look of approval. Maybe he was making progress with her after all.

❧

Three days later on Saturday evening, Katharine caught her breath as she entered the State apartments of the Hofburg Palace. It surpassed even the splendour of the Hotel Imperial. Just months ago Herr Hitler himself had stood on its balcony as glorious victor, the nation's new hero. Two swastika banners draped from the Hofburg, a permanent reminder of the regime's presence as if the uniformed patrols were not enough. Inside, the palace was swarming with SS officers, some of them she had to admit were quite dashing, all impeccably dressed for the glittering occasion. They had turned out to do their duty, to impress one person only: Mussolini. Katharine took it all in. The Austrian chancellor walked passed, his red-white-red sash and medals worn with pride. The Italian ambassador flanked him on one side, the German ambassador on the other, their formal attire reminiscent of the pomp of the Austro-Hungarian empire. Complete with silver pickelhaube and white plumes, they represented something from a bygone age; the court formality and rectitude of Austrian life that she had once admired, abandoned to a regime that was terrorizing the country's Jews. It all made her sick. She watched as they danced, masking temporarily the culture that had disintegrated into brutality. Out of the corner of her eye, she noticed Captain Henderson in full Royal Naval mess dress with medals gleaming, conversing with three well-jewelled ladies. She recalled his words. She wouldn't acknowledge him unless he spoke to her.

The master of ceremonies for that evening asked the guests to be seated. Katharine took her place with the quartet. The music room had an intimate feel; green velvet curtains swathed in thick folds from impossibly tall windows; large onyx lamps with cream shades gave off a subtle light. Gilded chairs for the musicians had been arranged in a semi-circle on an Aubusson rug. A Bechstein concert grand piano, its lid highly polished, was positioned behind them. Tonight the programme comprised classical and modern music, both Austrian and Italian, including a work by contemporary composer Turina.

A fanfare from the back of the room caused a moment's delay. Katharine tried not to stare. Signor Benito Mussolini was escorted to the front row with the Austrian chancellor. Periodically they exchanged whispered words. Then complete silence as the audience waited. Katharine, as first violin virtuoso, lifted her bow to signal the start, all eyes on her. The music began to fill the room, the audience engrossed in pleasure for over an hour. At the end, the applause was deafening. The chancellor and Mussolini moved into the adjoining state rooms, their guests filing behind them.

Katharine began circulating, taking in the passing comments and accolades on her performance. A gentle tap on her shoulder, she turned. The Italian ambassador was already speaking, 'Signorina, Miss Simmons, the General has asked to meet you.' She looked in the direction of Mussolini. He was already gazing at her, bowing his head slightly in acknowledgement. The ambassador offered his arm. She took it, as he led her towards the guest of honour. In the far corner, Captain Henderson discreetly watched her glide across the floor. She was exceptionally elegant that evening. Her pale blue chiffon dress almost reached the ground, adorned with a single white orchid, accentuating her feminine figure. Head held high, hair swept up in a chignon at the back, her slender white neck offered a view of grace and sophistication. He contemplated how she equalled any of the women present.

Mussolini stepped forward to greet her, 'What a delightful repertoire this evening, ma'am. You do your country much honour.'

'Thank you sir, it is my pleasure.' She lowered her eyes, fluttering them slightly. Her brief curtsey exposed her cleavage giving an extra flirtatious effect. It worked. He offered her the invitation she was hoping for: 'I would like you to join us for cocktails, Miss Simmons. We have quite a table in the next room.' He nodded towards the adjoining library. Katharine followed him and his entourage. She was not the only artiste being honoured. A chic woman came alongside her, dressed in a modern style of her own. She extended her hand. Her soft voice gave only a hint of an American accent, 'Dorothy Thompson, playwright and novelist, pleased to meet you.'

'This is such an honour. I've heard a lot about you,' replied Katharine returning the handshake. She whispered, 'Aren't you the journalist and feminist thinker? The one who has the ear of the president?'

'Discretion is everything, dear girl,' she whispered, adding in a louder voice, 'No, you must be thinking of someone else.' Her smile radiated her thin dainty face. Gosh, thought Katharine, now the Americans have their eyes and ears in the room. Dorothy Thompson proceeded to sidle up to the nearest Nazi officer, a fleeting backward glance at Katharine, as she silently mouthed, 'I do so love men in uniform.'

Katharine moved on with the other guests. She could no longer see Captain Henderson amongst the throng. Amidst the buzz of conversation, she became acutely aware of one voice above the others behind her. It was the French ambassador, Monsieur Anton Fournier, offering his opinion to the circle gathered around him, all with champagne flutes in hand.

'…and from what has been rumoured in Paris, art is being plundered regularly from homes and galleries.'

Signor Carlo Renée, the Italian ambassador, leant slightly forward to be noticed, giving his cue that a comment was imminent: 'Gentlemen … Oh and pardon me, ma'am.' He nodded, acknowledging Katharine's presence as she had just come into his view. 'It's all idle gossip. I've had assurance from Herr Eichmann himself that Jews are freely taking their possessions out of the country when they leave. It's just another conspiracy plot designed to get sympathy for the Jews.'

'An amazing coincidence, isn't it,' stated Fournier with sarcasm. 'Only the other day the Sorbonne was offered two pieces by Picasso. The provenance was somewhat suspect.'

In the meantime, a clergyman had discreetly placed himself at Katharine's side. He now spoke in an English accent, 'It is mere gossip, Your Excellency. The German-Austrian government wouldn't risk plundering its own treasures.'

'Quite so, Reverend Grimes,' answered Ambassador Renée.

The Revd Grimes turned directly to Katharine. He was well known at the British Embassy. 'I see you haven't had anything to eat. Here, have this child.' He held out his left palm. A white napkin, printed with a swastika in one corner, held two delicate canapés.

'Thank you, Reverend Grimes.' She smiled back at him, noticing a tiny piece of paper just protruding from under one of the canapés. She gently lifted the other one, biting into it. The pastry seemed to crumble into a thousand pieces of ecstasy, the mushroom filling delighting her taste buds. The other remained untouched; the smoothness of the smoked salmon and cream cheese would have to wait for a quiet moment unobserved. 'The canapés are very good, sir.'

He waited before leaning towards her. 'I suggest you try the other one.'

'I will shortly, thank you.' She turned to the other guests, 'Please excuse me gentlemen, I need to move somewhere a little cooler.' Several heads nodded their approval. She left their company to make her way to double doors at the far end. Before she knew it, she was gliding down the ornamental staircase, briefly stopping to enjoy the feel of the thick red carpet under the thin soles of her shoes. She glanced back for one last look at the socialite scene. Captain Henderson was leaning on the intricate wrought iron banister; his face pensive. He appeared to be watching her. She turned, quickening her step down the stairs. At the bottom, she collected her violin and coat from the porter and dashed out of the building.

Outside, the warm summer night's air was a relief. Katharine turned to walk around the side of the palace. She made her way towards the side streets and into a quiet alley. With no one in sight, she stopped, peeled the tiny paper from the bottom of the canapé, unfolding its neat creases. She decided she might as well eat the pastry and enjoy the souvenir of the evening. As the cream cheese melted in her mouth, her eyes began to adjust to the dim light cast along the path by the full moon which momentarily peered through the clouds. There were no streetlights in the side alley and the reek of rotting rubbish along the gutters was revolting. She glanced down. The moonlight revealed a disappointing result – the paper was blank. She should have realised. The awesome occasion had played on her imagination, sending it on wild theories of conspiracies and secret agents. She stuffed it into her purse and hurried back to her apartment having decided to walk rather than take a cab.

Exhausted, but strangely elated, she finally reached Berggasse. In an ideal world, she would have moved out by now. Sigmund Freud and his family had left a few weeks ago. Now there was no real need for her to remain in that district of the city. They had been the reason why Sir Charles had allocated her and Jonathan the apartment. Glancing up at no. 19, where Freud had lived for forty-seven years, she saw the Nazi flag still stretched across the lintel. It had been mysteriously removed immediately after his departure, but someone had replaced it. And then she thought of Jonathan. The apartment still held memories of him. Maybe she should move. She resolved to approach Captain Henderson on the matter as soon as she could.

Once back in the apartment, she kicked off her shoes and stretched her toes, pinched in impossibly narrow points for far too long. She sank back into the armchair in relief, savouring the peace and quiet. The clock on the mantelpiece broke through the stillness, signalling midnight. A new day, she thought, finding herself automatically counting each strike in her head. Thoughts of the evening raced through her head. There had been something about the initial eye contact with Reverend Grimes. She had recognised him, of course, from six months earlier when he had conducted the St George's Day Commemoration for expatriate Brits at the Embassy. The more she thought about it, the more she was convinced. She reached for the tiny paper she had thrown carelessly onto the table beside her. Yes, it *was* blank but the faint fragrance of lemon still lingered. Torch in hand, she fumbled for a candle and matches in the hall cupboard. Lemon juice could be used as invisible ink, then read using heat from a candle to reveal the words. Her eyes scrutinized the faint letters:

Night train 2.30, Vienna – Brenner Pass.

Two days later, in the board room at the far end of the British Embassy, Captain Henderson addressed the half-dozen top civil servants in an emergency meeting. All were part of foreign operations in Vienna. He relied on their judgement when not at liberty to make decisions single-handedly.

'We have a problem, gentlemen. I need your advice on procedure. It concerns Sir Charles. To get to the point, he has become a liability. There are rumours circulating.'

'He's *the one*?' Henry de Brigizarre couldn't believe it. 'Sir Charles working for the Huns? But he's one of us. I was at school with him.'

'Not exactly,' replied Captain Henderson.

General Laytoncock, who was seated to his left, leant forward. 'These days you can't be surprised by anything. You don't know who is for us or against us. We all have to be vigilant.'

Captain Henderson straightened his back, 'I can assure you he has been thoroughly checked out and we can discount him working for the Nazis. Sir Charles is a loyal subject of the Crown. No gentlemen, it is something possibly more serious.'

'I consider grassing on your country grave enough,' answered de Brigizarre. 'In fact, it's damn well high treason punishable by death. You can't get any more serious than that.'

'Let's hear what Captain Henderson has to say,' replied Laytoncock.

The others nodded. De Brigizarre watched as a secretary placed a tray of tea on the table before leaving them to business. He muttered after her, 'Where are the bourbons, Sally? We always have biscuits with our tea.'

She turned. 'We have run out, sir.'

Captain Henderson smiled as she closed the door behind her. 'Back to business gentlemen. Sir Charles is proving rather unsuitable as head of Section. He's bombastic and somewhat reckless.' He guessed the bombshell might come as a complete shock; he had to prepare them slowly, give their minds time to think of possible scenarios. 'Sir Charles has proven to be, not to put too fine a point on it, somewhat indiscreet. There are rumours of – well – rape, gentlemen.'

He expected the stunned silence. He could almost hear their heartbeats pounding in their chests. Such an accusation would not have entered their heads.

'Male rape to be precise,' he added.

All were well trained. Their faces revealed nothing, but he could feel their alarm and panic. He continued, 'However, the situation is complex. We need him for a little longer. It seems to me that we can't dispense with him just yet. Operations in the east are at a critical juncture. In fact, he's never shown any other signs of being a liability. So, with regards to foreign operations he can still be trusted.'

Laytoncock broke the silence. 'Male rape? There is no such offence in English law. As I understand it, a man can rape a woman but not another male. Buggery is an imprisonable offence of course, but not male rape. It is deemed consensual, as a man in English law is expected to be able to fight off such personal intrusions. There's no case to answer, and anyway, if the petitioner tried to go public, he would also be imprisoned. It's nothing more than a bit of boarding school tomfoolery. Why not hush it up and let him get on with his job.'

Captain Henderson looked at each of them in turn, 'What do the rest of you say?' They nodded in agreement with Laytoncock.

'In that case gentlemen, can I have a show of hands – who supports me in keeping him on for the time being?'

The vote was unanimous. Sir Charles was secure for a little longer.

Captain Henderson returned to his office, pleased with the result of the board meeting. His room was stiflingly hot and airless even with the window wide open. Katharine was already waiting for him. She removed her cotton cardigan, folding it over the back of the nearest chair. He noticed her discomfort. 'Vienna in the August heat can be unbearable at times. It's on days like this that I miss England and the rain.'

Katharine agreed. She waited for his de-briefing.

'So there was nothing of any consequence to report from Saturday's ball?' he asked.

'Not exactly. I mingled with a few military men and diplomats, but no hint of the situation. I was impressed by Mussolini, even if a little intimidated by him.'

He smiled, 'You wouldn't be normal if you weren't! What would you expect from a man in his position?'

'There was nothing about gold, only reference to art.'

'Art?' He raised his eyes. 'Well, that's something. Tell me more.'

She noticed how his skin looked rugged and olive with the sunlight's rays streaming across him from the window. She had to admit it made him somewhat appealing, maybe not handsome, but definitely an attractive man. She wondered whether he had Italian blood. She carried on: 'The French ambassador made a comment about the looting of Viennese art and what was the government doing about it. His Italian counterpart denied it, of course. And…' She held out the tiny folded paper. 'This was passed to me by Reverend Grimes.'

In the silence she studied him closer, watched his every move.

'That was a bit risky, wasn't it?' he stated.

'He was very discreet. It was hidden under a canapé. And to think I could have swallowed it, it's so small.' This time he failed to notice her wry humour, too deep in thought. 'Lemon juice. It was a trick we learnt at Blenheim along with all that Morse. Anyway, it confirms your suspicions about the art. I am sure it refers to a consignment that is due out of Vienna on the 2.30 night train. Trouble is, we don't know when – it could be today, tomorrow, next week.'

'Well, we knew that Hitler was pillaging Austria's heritage. Now we may well have the proof. If we can only turn this against him, maybe leak this to the press, but it could be risky.' He turned to the map behind him, explaining to her the recent developments.

'Last week two paintings by Klimt and Schiele went missing from the Kunsthaus Wien Art Gallery. Their art expressed the erotic side of sexuality supposedly latent under every society, but their subversive interpretations are deemed by the Nazis to corrupt the Aryan mind. It's all part of creating the Nazi vision of *ein Ur-Reines Reich*, a clean cultivated German society.' He beckoned for her to come closer. 'I'd like to show you the rail route. This is the line out of Vienna – here, through the mountainous border.'

She was too close. The heat of her body took on a physical existence within his mind. Each breath of her perfume intoxicated him, further wrapping his soul into hers. He could almost feel the movement of her breasts with each of her shallow breaths. He watched as tiny beads of perspiration glinted on her forehead. He followed the line of her slender neck. There was something erotic about the way the creases at the base met her shoulders. He tried to concentrate. He wanted to take her in his arms with all the passion that was in him, but didn't – couldn't. Years of naval training had taught him impeccable discipline and self-control. That and duty. He continued his line of conversation, reluctantly stepping a little away from her.

He pointed back at the map with the end of his pencil. 'I suspect the train will take an indirect route from Vienna through the Brenner Pass then into Italy; night time as we know of course, thus avoiding suspicion.' He had regained his inner control. He smiled at her, 'And all we have to do is – confirm the correct date, and make sure that it doesn't.'

꙳

Back in England, Günter Herz surveyed the motley gathering of continentals in the waiting room of Bloomsbury House in central London. It had been the headquarters of the Jewish Refugee Committee for a number of years. Their job was to find work, and in some cases homes, for those fleeing Nazi oppression and entering Britain on visas. Looking around the bare room, he guessed the youths were all under twenty, newly arrived, barely able to speak a word of English. He clutched his agricultural permit, hoping the head of the Jewish Refugee Committee would offer him interesting work. Rumours had already spread that some refugees were working in intolerable conditions in nurseries, bent almost double in low-level greenhouses, planting daffodil bulbs in twelve-hour back-breaking shifts. He took in their profiles, reckoning they were all naive Jewish youngsters, still recovering from the trauma of being ripped away from their families and homes in Germany and Austria. He focused intently on the youth sitting next to him who was contemplating his next move on a miniature chess set balanced precariously between him and his opponent. Günter surveyed the smug opponent, weighing him up too. He was obviously from an educated background, probably privately tutored. He wouldn't cope too well with land work, especially in the suit he was wearing. Günter tapped his arm. The lad grunted at him, dismissing his interruption.

'You might be done for, unless you move that rook,' said Günter, not giving up. The lad ignored his comment.

'Where are you from?' Günter persisted in German. Various eyes around the room fixed on him, expressing an interest in the answer.

'Berlin,' replied the lad, not glancing up from the chess pieces.

Günter tried to draw him out, 'I'm from Vienna. How long have you been in England then?'

'What's it to you?' he suddenly lounged back on the bench against the cold stone wall. Günter disliked his smug self-confidence.

'Just trying to be friendly,' he replied.

The lad stared at him. 'Germans and Austrians don't get on. We are of a different mind-set.'

Günter's opening gambit was not working as well as he had hoped. 'It makes no difference now, we're all in this together.'

The lad smirked again dismissively.

Günter persevered: 'We're all refugees and we need to stick together. I bet both our fathers fought in the German or Austrian armies during the Great War and were proud of it. Now the Nazis fear and deride us Jews as well as the Communists. We had a common enemy then, just as we have now. "Stand Together And Resist" – that should be the motto for all us refugees.'

The lad sitting directly opposite piped up: 'Hey, that's good. It spells STAR as in Star of David. That's really clever. Carry on like that and you'd make a good politician, if they don't shoot you first.'

Günter smiled back, 'They don't do that here.'

'Next please,' the quiet feminine voice of an English secretary called from a half-open doorway. Günter stood up. He glanced back at the lad still focused on the chess pieces. 'Good luck! Remember, we need to stick together.' The lad acknowledged his departure with a brief tilt of the head, continuing his next move on the chessboard.

Günter entered the large boardroom. It was more intimidating than his first interview at university. Two dark-suited men sat behind a long table, waiting for him to be seated opposite. The secretary was busy taking shorthand notes on a pad. She turned a page, poised to begin, presumably with Günter's details.

'Günter Herz?' asked the grey-haired, suited gentleman. Günter surmised that he must be in charge of the proceedings.

'Yes, sir,' his English only sufficient for short replies.

'Your papers state that you are a refugee from Nazi oppression. Is that correct?'

'Yes, sir.'

'With family left behind in Vienna?'

'Yes, sir.'

'I see.' He paused, thumbing through the typed papers in front of him. 'Rumour has it that you were involved in anti-Nazi activities in Vienna. Is that true?'

'Yes, sir.'

Günter hoped the grunts from the man didn't signal disapproval. Even the secretary looked up.

The line of questioning done, the head of the committee added: 'Well, we have looked through your documents and approved your posting to a farm near Bude on the north coast of Cornwall. Here's your train ticket.' He passed it across the table. 'The farmer will meet you at the other end. You travel in two days. Keep your head down and work hard. And no trouble, is that clear?'

'Yes, sir.'

'Any questions, Mr Herz?' He was already leafing through the next set of papers, not expecting any reply.

'No, sir.'

'Then you are free to go, Mr Herz. If you have any issues as a refugee here in this country, please contact us and we will do our best to help you.'

It was the shortest interview of his life. As he left the room, his soul soared. The elated sensation of freedom finally dawned on him. He was free to leave the bustle of London and start a new life in the country.

Chapter 9

Hugo edged along the curved, raised embankment along the railway line. It was one of the few unguarded spots along the route, nine kilometres south of Vienna. Lying flat on his stomach, he would feel the first vibrations of the train even while it was still some way off. It would give him ample warning. The train was expected to leave Vienna at 2.46 a.m., passing him around 3.05. He moved towards a single row of bushes. His hand rummaged over the dry earth, thankful for the leather gloves to protect him from the prickly leaves. He touched the soft cloth of the rucksack, partially buried. He gently pulled it out, reaching into his jacket pocket for a tiny torch. He shone it into the rucksack. Two single packs of explosives with detonators and wire had been neatly packaged inside as promised.

The tick of the watch on his wrist indicated fourteen minutes twenty-five seconds until the crucial passing time of the train on the bend. Slowly he edged back along the bank, placing his head on the track. A faint vibration indicated that his target was en route. He placed the first plastic charges on what he judged to be the epicentre of the curve of the track, securing the wire over the bolt on the sleeper. Speed and accuracy was of the essence. He bellied towards the parallel track, vibrating louder now with the imminent arrival of the train. He repeated the exercise. Job done, he crawled back behind the bush, detonator in hand. There were minutes to spare.

The rhythmic chug of the train throbbed as it closed the distance. Hugo pressed the trigger. The result was instant. The track split in several places, blowing mud and debris into the air, scattering a layer of dust over him. Damn, he thought, I must remember to get further away next time. He lay on the ground, heart pumping, grit in his mouth, his eyes smarting. The train was still hurtling at top speed; the driver had no time to brake. The mighty carcass of the train rammed over the gap, its brakes squealing where they remained on the track. Its vast bulk slowly cranked off the rails, beginning to tilt. Having exceeded the point of no return, it thudded onto its side. Hugo peered through the bush, watching as the colossal fire-breathing dragon, shrouded in its own smoke and fire, lay slain on the bank.

He waited a moment, shaking the dust and debris from his body. He edged towards the side of the bush. In the darkness it was hard to tell if there were any signs of life. The acrid smell of the burning train filled his nostrils, the carriages now resting on the embankment. He crawled closer. In the grass the body of the guard, thrown on impact, lay motionless. He was dead. Hugo looked around, tuning his ear for any new sound. Nothing broke the silence. Satisfied, he flashed his torch twice to the east. Two other men were waiting in the hedge-row. They ran towards him, their black silhouettes just discernable in the dead of night.

Hugo lowered himself into the driver's compartment; it was a lot harder than he thought. The others shone their torches in his path for vital clues. Hugo felt under the driver's seat and located the slippery surface of paper. 'Rob,' he hissed. 'Shine under here.'

Silently, Robert did as he was ordered and flicked the torch on for one brief flash. Papers were strewn across the lifeless driver and his stoker, with more stacked under the seat. The stamp on the right-hand corner of each page confirmed Hugo's suspicions. The black double-headed eagle clearly corroborated his theory that these were official Nazi documents. Gathering up what he could, he stuffed the papers into his empty rucksack.

Robert glanced at his watch. They had but five minutes before the train was due to cross the next check-point; not long before suspicions would be aroused. Hugo heaved himself out of the compartment, leaving his companions to gather up the remaining papers. He scurried along the edge of the train to the rear, dragged open the heavy door of the cattle truck and clambered in. His torch illuminated the three walls, all lined with large oblong objects wrapped in brown paper and sacking. He pulled a penknife from his pocket, carefully slitting along the edge of the nearest bundle.

Art.

The carriage was full of looted paintings. Robert climbed in beside Hugo, leaving the other companion as lookout. He started taking photographs. The flash momentarily blinded Hugo, leaving flashing circles in his vision.

'That's enough,' Hugo motioned. This had been successful. Their mission confirmed what Captain Henderson had suspected. Hugo jumped out, moving to the next carriage. It was the same story. It was also packed with works of art.

A single shrill whistle pierced the night. The barking of dogs became persistent, sounding closer with every passing second. Human presence was closing in. The saboteurs turned, edging along the undergrowth before running across the next field westwards, away from the isolated village where the SS guards had been alerted.

❧

Two days after Hugo's mission, Sir Charles paced the confines of Captain Henderson's office. 'Where's Henderson?' he muttered under his breath. 'Damn it, where's the staff this morning?' He helped himself to a measure of brandy, taking one thankful gulp from the glass. He began stroking his moustache, going over in his mind the business he needed to discuss with Captain Henderson. He turned, casting his eye over the map behind him. Taking a coloured pen from the desk, his chubby hand added a red mark on the Austro-Italian border. He glanced at the clock ticking under the painting of the Battle of Waterloo. 'Where the devil are you, Henderson?'

Hugo peered around the door, 'S…sir Charles, good morning. The captain apologises. He will be with you shortly. He is on his way.'

Sir Charles stared at his young recruit standing in the doorway, 'Doesn't the man have a timepiece?' His rhetorical question required no answer.

Captain Henderson was already behind Hugo. 'Excuse me please, Hugo.'

Hugo stepped aside and made off down the corridor.

Captain Henderson placed his umbrella in the stand next to the corner cabinet. 'Morning, Sir Charles.'

'At last, Henderson. We've got business to attend to.' He cast a bundle of papers across the desk. 'These are for you. I would be grateful if you could read over them today and let me have your assessment. They're important. Now, what's new?' He proceeded to seat himself awkwardly in the chair opposite.

Captain Henderson waited for the dust to settle. He had to be open with him, give his honest assessment. It wasn't going to be easy. Clearing his throat, he said, 'Well, there is no gold.'

Sir Charles shifted in his seat, 'No gold, you say?'

'No. None. There's only art.' He cleared his throat again. 'Hugo did a fine job on that train. It won't be going anywhere for a bit.' He didn't wait for any acknowledgement before continuing, 'There aren't any surprises there. Isn't that what we expected? We knew as much from Katharine's recent intelligence. Secondly, the route is quite simple, though not obvious. The consignments are being taken through the Brenner Pass to Milan, and from there being shipped all over the world. No doubt in exchange for armaments – we have no reason to assume otherwise.'

'Damn it, Henderson. Art is only part of the story. I just know the gold is going out. I have a nose for such things and I am never wrong. It's going out from somewhere and we need to locate it pretty damn quick.' He paused. Captain Henderson wished he had better news. 'Henderson, I don't need to tell you just how important it is that we intercept the gold trains. We *have* to locate them and stop them. Art, gold – it all equals re-armament and you know Prime Minister Chamberlain has this high on his agenda, appeasement or no appeasement.'

Captain Henderson nodded, 'I understand and I've got Katharine on it. She has two urgent priorities for us at the moment – the gold and the matter of the mole. I can assure you, we are doing all we can here at the Embassy. She's the best we've got.'

Sir Charles shuffled in the chair, his heavy breathing increasing under the strain of the heat in the airless office. Captain Henderson noticed his discomfort, 'I would open the window, but that's risky Sir Charles.'

'No matter, Henderson, leave it. We can't take risks. I hadn't expected Vienna to be so hot.' He reached for the jug beside him, filling the empty brandy glass with water. 'As I was saying,' he continued between gulps, 'we have got to stop those bloody trains; increase operations, blow them all up if necessary. Get Hugo out there every night if that's what it takes. Just get me results.'

'With due respect, Sir Charles, it's not that simple. There's been a further development.' Captain Henderson waited, forming the bombshell carefully in his head, hoping to minimise a negative reaction. 'The morning after Hugo's last activities, the Gestapo unleashed a pogrom against the Jewish community. Jewish men were dragged from their homes and carted off to Buchenwald and Dachau concentration camps – around three hundred we believe. Another fifty were executed in cold blood in woods outside Vienna, not far from the site of the previous massacre. That's why I'm late this morning – I've just come from the Chief Rabbi's office.'

'The massacre is unfortunate, I agree, but we can't let it detract from doing something about the art and gold. We can't let the Germans get away with it. Speaking of Dachau, is there any more news of Jonathan?'

'No, nothing. I thought you were onto it?'

Sir Charles began rhythmically tapping his foot against the desk. It irritated Captain Henderson, though he tried to keep his cool.

Sir Charles seemed too relaxed in his response. It was unlike him. 'We were, but we lost contact with the main operative. However, we do have unconfirmed reports that Jonathan is in a labour camp somewhere near the Polish border. You'll see it in those reports I gave you just now.'

Captain Henderson glanced at the newpapers on his desk. Sir Charles stared him in the eye, 'Depending on your judgement about reliability, we may break him out.'

'Jonathan?'

'Yes.' Then Sir Charles returned to the subject of Nazi gold: 'Going back to the matter of the trains, they must be intercepted, no matter what the cost – and that's an order.'

Captain Henderson's restraint could take no more. For the first time in his life he broke the ranks of operational code; after all, the conversation was only between the two of them. His steely glare cut the atmosphere. 'Remember your place, Sir Charles. You're on my patch here. I decide what direction we take for operations. With the latest massacre I won't risk sacrificing any more Jewish lives for gold or art.'

Sir Charles weighed up the situation. He tried to lean forward, his stomach preventing him from managing more than an inch, a protruded vein began throbbing in his neck, his face flushed. 'You're a fool Henderson. How dare you cross me!'

Captain Henderson made no remark, waiting.

Sir Charles was not yet done. He lowered his tone, still seething through his teeth. 'Those trains are top priority – these are orders from the PM himself. That gold is financing the Nazi military machine and it has to be stopped. It will lead to war and the loss of hundreds of thousands of lives. What would you have us do Henderson? We must sacrifice a few lives now for the greater good of Britain and its empire.'

Captain Henderson looked at him levelly, 'Gold or no gold, war is inevitable. Everyone knows that. It's no longer a matter of if, but when. I will not sacrifice any more civilian lives for a few pieces of gold, or for that matter art. If the PM wants to formalise war with Germany, so be it, but until then I can't make my position any clearer.'

Sir Charles stood up, catching his foot on the edge of the desk, his blood-shot eyes ablaze, 'You will regret this, Henderson. We are not here to consider moral dilemmas. You forget your duty.'

Captain Henderson had the final say. 'Don't talk to me about duty.'

He watched Sir Charles bumble out of the room, his footsteps getting gradually fainter down the corridor. Winston Churchill was right. Sir Charles would have to go.

Captain Henderson hadn't left Vienna for months. It was now nearing the end of August 1938 and the Nazis' grip over the city was total. Jews had no freedom, even basic requirements of fresh food and water denied them. They were forced to pay a heavy price for daily bread, and even then they were only permitted to buy the previous day's stale loaves. Human degradation was subtle but relentless. Along the west wall of the British Embassy, the queues hadn't subsided in months. Desperate émigrés clutched papers with high expectations that they would eventually leave Austria. As long as the doors of the Embassy opened each morning, there was always hope of freedom.

In his office, Captain Henderson passed the bundle of crumpled papers across the desk.

'What do you make of these, Katharine?'

She flicked through them, glancing at the top of the pages. 'Where did you get these?'

'Let's just say a little operation. You know I can't say any more than that.' He studied her hands as she worked her way through the pile. They remained completely steady until she came to the photograph at the back. Her brief intake of breath was hardly noticeable, but he didn't miss it. There was no other hint of a reaction. Was even she becoming immune to the horror? She put the papers down, still clutching the photograph. She looked up into his eyes. 'This is Guttmann the baker from across the street. He was such a kind man. He always gave us extra croissants on Sundays.'

'I know. I am *so* sorry Katharine. It was risky but I had one of our men surreptitiously drag his body out of the burial pit in the camp. We've had our suspicions for some time now. We needed the evidence. With this, and the papers from the train the other night, we might get some of the politicians back home to sit up and take note.'

She looked down at the photograph again. 'See his forearm?'

'Yes, the tattooed symbols are on both arms. They have some kind of mystical religious symbolism. I have been told they denote ritual sacrifice.' He paused. She was already leafing through the papers again.

'What are you looking for?' he asked.

'I'm sure I recognise the symbols.' Her voice seemed awkward, even distant, 'but I can't recall where. I've seen them somewhere recently.'

Captain Henderson continued to watch her intently; her saddened face haloed by the last of the day's sunshine streaming from the window; her gaze briefly contemplative. She just managed to get the words out before her voice cracked with emotion, 'Have you managed to get word to his wife?'

'Er, not exactly.'

Captain Henderson wasn't sure how Katharine would take the news he was about to tell her. 'We have traced two of the children to London last week. They are staying with a Quaker family. Evidently, Mrs Guttmann and one child didn't make it. Their bodies were recovered by woodcutters in the forest north of Danzig.' He waited, allowing her time to digest the news. 'They had gunshot wounds to the head. How the other two children survived, heaven only knows.' The compassion in his voice tried to ease her pain. 'It's only down to your efforts that they did.'

Katharine's eyes welled with moisture, but no tears came. It was as if the pain could not be released. Silently she slipped the photo to the back of the pile. She stared out of the window, fixing her gaze on the thin telephone wires strung across the street outside. 'Will there ever be an end to this misery?'

What could he say that would ease her pain? He continued flicking through the papers on the desk. The muscles in his face twitched then relaxed.

Finally she lifted her shoulders, took a deep breath, and said more to herself than anyone: 'Enough self pity, Katharine. You can't help the dead, see to the living. Now I have to get down to work, Captain Henderson.' Her tone and attitude completely changed, it was almost matter-of-fact. 'I have more news for you on those transmissions.'

This was the woman he had come to admire so much. She was back to her usual self.

'Last night I intercepted two messages at midnight; both from the same location in the Bavarian Alps. To be more precise, I believe it was coming from Berchtesgaden – almost certainly the underground operations bunker.'

'Abwehr? You think it was from the Abwehr?'

'Yes, I'm as sure as I can be. It looks as if some of Hitler's innermost circle has relocated. The unit appears to be operating almost full time from there at the moment.'

'Excellent work, Katharine.' He walked over to the four aerial photographs pinned on a board behind him. One stood out for him. He took just a moment to examine it before sticking a coloured pin in the Berchtesgaden region.

Katharine continued, 'The nature of the message suggests that one of Hitler's top generals is particularly active. From what I've gleaned so far, the messages do refer to the movement of gold. All along we've been missing the vital clue. We know the art is going to Italy through the Brenner Pass, but the question that has eluded us is what about the gold?'

'Tell me more.'

'Switzerland,' she replied with confidence. 'The gold is being taken by train to Switzerland. From the transmissions it's apparent that around three to four hours after the midnight radio command goes out, the train leaves. That makes departure about 4 a.m.'

She had worked it all out.

He smiled. 'Of course, Swiss bank accounts. They are virtually untraceable. I should have guessed. Well done, Katharine, you're really brilliant.' Her close proximity affected him. He stepped back. Still he couldn't have her.

'Katharine, I have to tell you, we can't action this new informa-tion until we can find some way of interception without triggering further reprisals against the Jews. We will have to sit tight on this information, even from Sir Charles, until I give the all clear. For the time being, the gold will have to continue its course to Switzerland.' He stepped forward as if to touch her in appreciation. Her look of surprise stopped him in his tracks. She thought she detected a hint of frustration. Trying to cover his *faux pas*, he mumbled, 'Brilliant work Katharine', turned and left the room.

❧

3 November 1938. Hugo had been briefly sent back to London to search the files at MI6 headquarters. He had the necessary authorisation for two days work in the basement under the streets on Broadway, off Victoria Street. Captain Henderson couldn't do without him for more than four days, neither could he trust anyone else with such a sensitive task. There were no longer direct flights from Vienna to London, so he had had to travel via Prague. Captain Henderson had a hunch that the double agent had transposed secret Swiss bank accounts of the government for Nazi gold accounts. Such forgery was relatively quick to accomplish and would go undetected until it was too late. His work complete, Hugo was due to fly back later that afternoon. Walking up Horse Guards Road, he had no idea why he had been summoned by General Laytoncock to the Athenaeum Club. All he had gathered was that Laytoncock no longer operated in Vienna.

Above him, the statue of Athena gazed down, her serene protective face surveyed, even judged, the portals of power and opulence below – and him, a mere mortal amongst all this. He dismissed her presence as he nervously climbed the steps of the Club. He straightened his tie as he entered the building. An elderly porter in suit, silk waistcoat and bow tie, whisked him upstairs. At the top of the stairs, Hugo strained to see beyond him into the smoke-filled view as they entered the library. General Laytoncock spied him immediately, motioning for him to come over. 'Come and sit here, lad.' He sank back into the confines of the high-back leather chair, signalling for Hugo to do the same in the other. Taking several deep puffs on a thick cigar, his face reddened with thin thread veins. The general seemed entirely at home against the hue of the stately room.

'Thank you, s…sir,' replied Hugo, beginning to shift from foot to foot before he finally sat down. General Laytoncock surveyed him for a few moments, choosing his words carefully.

'I want to ask you something Hugo and I want an honest reply.' Hugo waited, making every effort to avoid eye contact.

'Look at me, lad.' He spoke softly but with an authority in his deep baritone voice. 'Now listen here, I need to ask you something rather delicate. How shall I put it … of course it requires your complete discretion.' He leant forward, his elbow resting on the arm of the chair. He coughed, before carrying on: 'Look, there is no easy way to say this, so I will get straight to the point. It has come to my attention that Sir Charles has been somewhat indiscreet in his behaviour.'

'I don't understand, sir.' Hugo found it easy to feign naivety.

'I'll be perfectly plain, Hugo. It has come to my attention that he has been enjoying the company of young males. To be more precise, he has violated their personage.'

Hugo stared beyond the general.

Laytoncock gently prompted him: 'Look, I understand that he's a shirt lifter. I can't put it plainer than that.'

Hugo wasn't giving anything away. He wasn't even sure Captain Henderson knew about this. He didn't want to jeopardise his position in the office. He enjoyed his job with Captain Henderson. 'I just work in the office, s…sir. My duties occupy all of my time.'

General Laytoncock persisted. 'Look Hugo, I know this must be difficult for you and I do understand. We are not questioning your integrity or loyalty to King and Country, but this is important. The incident on the Orient Express last year was serious and I have knowledge of that and more. I know what's been going on.' He sat back. Hugo's feet shuffled along the base of his chair.

The general took a large swig of whiskey, puffed twice on his cigar before resuming the conversation with Hugo. 'Why the loyalty lad? You owe nothing to Sir Charles. You could save others from the same terrible ordeal, couldn't you? I have one witness already, but I need a second to press with action. I'm aware that you have been scarred by this. Your nervous disposition makes it plain to anyone of my experience that you are in Sir Charles's grasp. I repeat – you owe him *nothing*, least of all loyalty.'

Hugo's head thumped as if it would explode. He stared ahead, mesmerised by the conversation. The cigar smoke made him feel almost heady. He wanted to run outside, ask Athena for her wise counsel. She would understand. He reassured himself he knew what to do. He could bring down Sir Charles in a single word of confirmation but that would betray his duty. He *had* been violated, but it wasn't his place to return a single act of violence, however horrific, with revenge. Blinking, he replied with confidence, 'Sir, I know nothing about what you ask. I've had the stammer since childhood. Sir Charles has always been very good to me.'

'Very well lad, if that is your answer. But remember, if you change your mind, you know where I am and you will be protected. We always look after our own.' General Laytoncock signalled for him to leave and added, almost as an afterthought, 'Er, Mr Churchill wants to see you in his office straight away. He's come up from Chartwell for the week – got some important speeches for the House.'

Hugo was already walking away. 'Yes, sir. I will go immediately.'

'Good lad.' He raised his newspaper.

Outside, never had Hugo been so pleased to breathe in the London smog. He had one more person to face before his flight back to Vienna. At this rate, he might have to delay his return.

～✤

On the first floor in Whitehall, Winston Churchill was dictating his latest speech to his secretary. Sir Charles waited patiently inside the doorway. He knew better than to interrupt the man. Churchill was one of the few men he could tolerate. Churchill nodded in his direction, acknowledging his presence briefly, gesturing for him to remain silent. He had to finish the last sentence whilst he had it in his head.

'Slow up, Mr Churchill,' Dorothy interrupted. 'I'll never get it all down.'

He paced in circles around the desk, taking several sharp puffs on his cigar, 'I do not want to lose the flow, Dorothy. This is an excellent speech.'

'Yes, but I can't keep up. Slower Mr Churchill.'

He grunted, 'Repeat back that last bit, would you Dorothy?'

'This is only the first sip, the first foretaste of a bitter cup which…'

'No, no, it's not quite right, not yet. I just can't get it.' She was used to his interruptions. He continued as she scribbled furiously, '…which will be worse year on year.' He paused, re-forming the ideas in his head. 'No Dorothy, it's just not right. Ah! I've got it … which will be proffered to us year by year. That's it!'

Sir Charles waited patiently. Churchill tapped his cigar on the edge of the desk, predicting correctly that the ash would fall neatly into the waste paper bin below. 'Repeat the whole of that final paragraph would you Dorothy?'

Dorothy lifted her scribbled transcript. 'And do not suppose that this is the end. This is only the beginning of the reckoning. This is only the first *sip, the first foretaste of a bitter cup which will be proffered to us year by year unless, by an extreme recovery of moral health and martial vigour, we arise again and take our stand for freedom as in the olden time.'*

'Brilliant. We have it Dorothy. The speech is done.'

'Yes, Mr Churchill.'

'That should ruffle a few feathers amongst the old buggers. Thank you, Dorothy. That will be all until later.' He waited for her to leave.

Closing the door, he turned to Sir Charles. 'Another speech to fall on deaf ears in the Commons.'

'It's a good one, Winston.'

'Maybe Sir Charles, but the Germans are tightening their grip on Europe and what are we doing? Chamberlain comes back from Germany with the Munich Agreement offering his suicidal ideas of peace in our time. I'll give him peace. He doesn't realise just how close Europe is to catastrophe. But you know my motto: KBO – keep buggering on. If I do not say my bit, Europe will go to the dogs without a whisper of resistance. We must be steadfast in this matter of sincere pertinence to our heritage, our freedom, our way of life.'

'Yes, I quite agree.'

Churchill passed him a half-filled glass of brandy. 'You and I have some business to attend to, Sir Charles. I will not beat about the bush. It is rather a serious matter. In short, you have become a liability. Your personal habits – I will not go into details – well, orders from above you understand. You need to retire.'

'Retire? Are they mad? … Good lord, without me operations go nowhere.'

'Remember your place, Sir Charles. We all take orders from someone.'

'What snivelling pen-pushing civil servant suggested this? They can't retire me. Operations are at a critical stage …. and …. I am M. What the devil is going on?'

Churchill picked up the smouldering cigar from the ashtray, re-lighting it. The thick pungent smell permeated every nook and cranny in the room. 'I understand this may be a shock, Sir Charles, but orders are orders. You know that. You will be well remunerated. The PM is thinking of a country estate in Suffolk. In fact, it has all been sorted for you. I understand it is a splendid place.'

Sir Charles stared in disbelief. 'What…?'

Churchill paused to survey the man in front of him. He couldn't tell him the real reason for his retirement, reveal his knowledge of the indiscretions with young lads that had percolated through the establishment. The rumours had to be suppressed. He tried a gentler approach to defuse the shock and boost his ego: 'You have served this country well. Your loyalty is unquestionable. It is simply time to have a change of scene. It will do you good. My sentiments are with you. The nature of operations is fast changing – leave it to younger blood, Sir Charles. Enjoy your retirement. You've earned it. The youngsters going into the east won't come out alive. Do you want that on your conscience? If I were you, I would graciously accept what's on offer. Enjoy the country life. When war comes, which it will, who knows what will happen. You may even be brought out of retirement.'

'Indeed, indeed,' fumbled Sir Charles in reluctant agreement. It was inevitable. He knew how things worked. He gulped the last measure of brandy, placing the glass on the desk. 'That's done then. I'll be off. See you anon, Winston.' It was a subdued Sir Charles that walked out of the office.

Churchill lifted the handset of the telephone, 'Dorothy, please send in Hugo. I take it he has arrived?'

'Yes, Mr Churchill.'

As he waited for Hugo, Churchill picked up his draft speech. He sauntered into the adjoining toilet. Standing in front of the mirror, he began to recite his masterpiece, straightening his back to fill his lung capacity. It always worked, giving him an authoritative voice. He had timed it. Seventeen minutes exactly, just long enough to ensure the backbenchers didn't fall asleep. He pondered the impact of his last masterly sentence. He became aware of Hugo in the office and peered around the bathroom door. 'I'll be with you in one minute, Hugo.' He smiled at himself in the mirror and finally emerged, walking towards Hugo, speech in hand, feeling in good spirits. 'That should do it.' He looked directly at Hugo as he cast the paper on the desk. 'Keep them on their bloody toes this afternoon.'

Hugo waited.

'Now Hugo,' Churchill lowered himself into his chair, taking two further puffs from his cigar. 'Your loyal service to King and Country has not gone unnoticed. You have learnt the job well, in fact better than anyone. His Majesty's government is impressed. Your utmost discretion and loyalty is now being recognised. In short, Hugo, you have passed the key stage. We are promoting you.'

Hugo raised his eyes, not expecting this turn of events. The shifting from foot to foot started. Churchill continued, 'You are to be the face of operations. We are trusting you to protect the boss – with immediate effect. When you arrive back in Vienna you begin your new duties. Things are deteriorating in Europe at an alarming pace. Much lies ahead of you. Good luck.'

'Thank you, sir. I will do my best.'

It was the briefest meeting of Hugo's life but the most important. As he descended the long steps outside, he reflected. It had been quite a week. Nothing had turned out quite as he expected, but then his expectations were never this high.

❧

It was 8 November before Hugo made it back to the British Embassy in Vienna. Katharine could not contain her delight at his return. 'Hugo, how lovely to see you again. It's been quite a while. How are things going?'

'Fine.' Her enthusiasm touched him.

'Something has changed. Hugo, you're looking much more confident than when I last saw you. How's Sir Charles, the old devil, is he still cursing my name?' She laughed.

'He's retired.'

She showed no reaction, just smiled back. 'It's about time, at least he won't be under my skin, blighting my existence.'

'It l…looks like I'll be working with you now, Mrs Walters. I've been promoted as the public face of operations. B…basically, I'm taking over from Sir Charles.' He had gained so much confidence; it was as if he had grown up overnight.

'That's marvellous, Hugo. Congratulations. Then you must call me Katharine.'

Hugo had liked her from the beginning. She always seemed so genuine. The woman who stood in front of him that day was a little more sophisticated than he remembered; maybe it was the new cropped haircut. It suited her.

'It has been suggested that I should use the designate title M. I never l…liked the Mother thing that Sir Charles always insisted on. It's not really me.'

'Yes, of course. Well, that's quite a turn up for the books. I approve. It's about time your loyalty was recognised.'

'Thanks, Katharine.' It now fell upon his shoulders to give her the first update as M: 'We are moving the bulk of our operational headquarters to Vienna for the f…foreseeable future. All efforts are being focused in this region of Europe now. C…can you bring me up to date with the office work?'

'Well, as you've seen, the queues outside are getting worse each day. Captain Henderson needs all the admin staff he can get just to process the paperwork. We have all been seconded for extra duties.'

As if on cue, Captain Henderson walked into the room. 'Good, I'm glad you are both here.' He flung the day's newspaper on the desk. 'Look what's happened in Paris.' The bold-typed headline stood out of the page:

NAZI DIPLOMAT SHOT IN PARIS

'Heavens, this is a serious development,' said Katharine. Hugo leant over her shoulder. He continued reading aloud, 'Ernst vom Rath was shot in Paris by a Jewish fanatic of Polish origin called Herschel Grynszpan. The German government has already made it clear that there will be consequences if vom Rath does not survive.'

Katharine looked aghast.

'We can only guess at the next move,' replied Captain Henderson levelly. 'The Nazis will use any excuse to persecute the Jewish community here and in Germany. Many of the displaced Polish Jews living in Berlin are moving into Czechoslovakia. Herr Goebbels has already described the country as "a dagger pointed at the heart of Germany".'

Hugo ventured his opinion, 'Th…this latest shooting might be used as a veiled threat to Czechoslovakia or possibly even Poland.'

'An astute observation, Hugo,' Katharine replied.

Captain Henderson glanced at Hugo, a cue for him to take a back seat. Captain Henderson carried on: 'Katharine, there's something I've been meaning to show you for a long time, but was forbidden from doing so.' He passed her a file. 'This may well be the political lever Chamberlain needs. Have a look. Just before Jonathan was taken last April, he discovered something that could rock the Nazi regime. It may even explain his arrest.'

She scanned the first page. He watched for any sign of emotion. It was the first time he had mentioned Jonathan to her in months. He wasn't certain what she would make of it. He wanted to make sure he was present when she got the news, to be there for her if she needed him.

'Prostitutes?' her voice remained level although he could still detect an element of surprise. 'Hitler slept with whores in Vienna when he was a student. It's a time bomb. If that got out it would wreck his image and bring him down. This is much worse for him than the Geli affair.'

'Precisely. It's what his top officials have been trying to suppress for years.' Captain Henderson moved closer to her. 'Skip to the third page. It's a copy of a confidential medical report that Jonathan managed to extract via the hospital here in Vienna from his counterpart at the Berlin general hospital.' He moved his finger down the page to the final paragraph. 'Here, it says that Adolf Hitler was diagnosed with the deadly sexual disease syphilis a couple of years ago. If you know anything about medicine, you will know that it leads to madness and excessive delusions of grandeur and power.'

After scanning the next two pages, she glanced up. 'What are you going to do with the information?'

'Copy it and smuggle the duplicate by special courier across the city to the American Embassy. Our allies ought to have a copy pretty damn quick. It can't go via the diplomatic bag – it's too risky. It needs to be hand-delivered.' He gave her more time to take in the information, to work through the consequences in her head before he continued. 'We believe this report must have been compromised by someone within the "family", leading to Jonathan's arrest back in April. On the night that he was taken, an unusual transmission was picked up from an area a few hundred square yards of here. It hasn't been possible to pinpoint the precise address. Ever since then, Sir Charles had set his auxiliary team on it; the one you set up in the safe house. They worked flat out to try to decode the message but they had little success until a week ago. Finally they were able to link that transmission with the regular pattern of messages recently transmitted from what we suspect to be the mole.' Throughout this, she hadn't moved an inch. He continued, 'In short, someone, probably at the hospital, discovered that Jonathan had uncovered the report. Effectively he knew too much. But locating who is proving difficult.'

Her silence gave way to anger. 'I had the knowledge to do something. Why wasn't I told?' Her eyes fired up. It was as if there was just the two of them in the room, reminiscent of the outburst after Jonathan's arrest. 'Why wasn't I trusted? This is my field of expertise and I could have helped. This might have been prevented.'

'I understand your anger, Katharine.' His voice was tender. Only she noticed it. 'But at the time Sir Charles thought it best. He was concerned for your own health and protection.'

'What do you take me for Captain Henderson? I'm not a child.'

Hugo broke his silence, 'Katharine, I believe you may misunderstand the captain. Everything that p…passed through this office had to be censored and approved by Sir Charles. I saw that with my own eyes when I worked for Sir Charles. He used his judgement with the best of intentions to protect our p…people, but ultimately the authority on that one was with Sir Charles. It has nothing to do with trust. S…sir Charles was trying to protect you. You must believe that Katharine.'

Her steely glare unnerved him, not that Hugo showed it, not now, not ever again. He had become M. Without a further word, she turned and walked out.

Chapter 10

9 November 1938. At quarter to seven that evening, Katharine hurried out of the Embassy building. Captain Henderson had advised her to go home early, aware of what was happening outside. News travelled fast. Thousands of Jewish men had been dragged from their homes, most badly beaten, then carted off to Dachau or Buchenwald concentration camps. German diplomat vom Rath had died in a Paris hospital, exactly two days after being shot at the German Embassy by a seventeen-year-old Polish Jew. Herschel Grynszpan had assassinated vom Rath in retaliation for the deportation of his family and other Polish Jews to Zbuczyn, a border town in no-man's-land between Germany and Poland. Thousands of Jews were trapped there, suffering starvation and stripped of their homes and possessions. The repercussions of the shooting had already begun for the Jews of Germany and Austria. Hitler secretly ordered mobs to attack the Jewish communities. Along the west wall of the British Embassy, the queue for visas had dispersed. It was the first time Katharine had seen it deserted since before Hitler's forces marched into the country eight months earlier. An eerie gloom hung heavy, suffocating the city. She felt the chill November night expectant with fear, and tried to quell a rising dread in her chest. The streetlights cast dark grey shadows across the pavements and doorways. Just a few steps down Braunerstrasse, she was sure someone was following her. She took a small mirror from her handbag, pretending to touch up her hair.

Nothing behind her.

The faint footsteps must have been in her mind. Still not satisfied she paused by a shop window, using its reflection to view across the street. Still nothing. She was nearly at the corner where the next street would show more signs of life. She feigned a wobble, bending down as if something was wrong with her shoe strap, looking once again discreetly behind her. Her unease subsided with each reassuring glance. Quickening her pace into Schottengasse, she turned the corner to see Hitler Youths already gathered along the shop fronts, batons in hand. Smaller groups spilled into side-alleys; shop windows freshly daubed with anti-Jewish slogans; dripping black Stars of David, not yet dry, scrawled beneath them, hanging heavy with spite.

In the distance the bells of St Stephendom struck seven. Seven usually brought luck! Not tonight. The city's tension was about to explode. In time with the bells, the youths struck at the shop windows, hammering and smashing. Glass shattered to the ground, cascading shards of raw anger onto the pavement. Above their caustic laughter, their boots crunched roughly across the walkway. Shops were now unguarded and open to the night sky. Looters moved in to steal. Katharine, stunned into morbid observation, watched them unnoticed. They would spill Jewish blood if they could. She drew her coat closely around her. More people joined the baying mob, their rhythmic chant non-stop:

> Down with the Jews!
> Down with the Jews!

The sound of breaking glass in the next side street competed with their mantras, smashing to smithereens the last remnants of a rational society. Who would dare hide Jews now? Katharine ran on.

Several streets later, she finally turned into Berggasse, gasping for breath. She glanced at the street sign, now re-painted to conform to monotype Aryan gothic lettering required by Nazi law. She unlocked the front door of her apartment block, slamming it behind her. Rushing two steps at a time up to her flat, she was thankful to shut out the night's events. In the sitting room, she shifted the table lamp to the floor and slumped down beside it, her knees to her chest, out of view. She thought of Jonathan. She missed him. It was now that she needed his reassuring hug. A slight panic welled up in her chest, adrenalin pumped through her body. Violence and destruction were being unleashed outside on an unprecedented scale. How could she possibly sleep? She got up, walked to the window and peered through the shutters. An unusual red glow across the city's skyline competed with the warm yellow of the table lamp. Above the buildings, the pall of smoke signalled the city was burning. The thickest of it trailed from the direction of Leopoldstadt, the Jewish quarter. The heart of Vienna was aflame with hatred. She could not shut out the revulsion. One by one, the names of her Jewish friends and acquaintances rolled in an orderly list before her eyes. She feared for them. She thought of Sigmund Freud and his family. They were amongst the lucky ones, safer in England's fortress, built by nature against the hand of war. The sea her natural defence. The Nazis had shown little mercy to Freud before the family left. Not a single copy of his books was left in any library or household in Austria or Germany. They had been burnt along with the books of other Jewish intellectuals. As she stared out of the window, her mind turned from Shakespeare to the words of poet Heinrich Heine:

Those who burn books will in the end burn people.

She shuddered. Was Heine right? How long before the Nazis would fulfil his prophesy? It seemed unimaginable. Then the tears came. She stood there, making no attempt to hold back the emotion that she had been suppressing. It was better out than in, or at least that's what her mother had always told her. At moments like this, she felt more like a vulnerable woman than a confident concert musician, never mind a spy. Emotion spent, she pulled herself together, mustering inner strength. Suddenly she drew back. The mole! Why hadn't she thought of it before? The mole would be transmitting tonight, of that she was certain. She had let her judgement be clouded by the terror outside, too caught up in the shock of the destruction to be clear-thinking.

She closed the shutters in each room and walked into the bathroom. A cursory glance in the mirror, she freshened her face with a splash of water and powdered her nose. Normality had to prevail on this night of aberration. Satisfied, she carefully removed the hidden clips to the left side of the mirror. Gently swinging it off the wall, the secret cupboard revealed its contents. The new radio equipment was there – Professor Q's pride and joy. He had developed the smallest set she had ever seen. She removed it and took it back into the sitting room. Hands steady, her mind resolute, she set up the apparatus. It crackled as she tuned in to the radio band. She had a map, ruler and pen at hand to draw the positioning line. The clock on the mantelpiece ticked away the hour. There was nothing but static. Disappointed, she slumped to the floor, listening to the monotonous crackle from the equipment.

Then it happened.

A distant voice was giving coded commands. She adjusted the radio. It was still no clearer. Finding the precise location of the transmission was now her highest priority. A few vital minutes were lost. But then there, she had it. It was close. Damn close.

The crackly German accent was now distinguishable, the voice familiar. She gasped. She snatched another map from under the chair, turned it over, scribbled down the coded letters. Braunerstrasse! She should have realised – it must be coming from the Embassy. It all began to make sense.

Her moment had come. This was the reason Sir Charles had sent her to Vienna. She stuffed the map into her handbag and grabbed her hat and coat.

In the next room the phone was ringing.

'Damn!' She paused. She ought to answer it. She rushed to pick up the receiver – the line was almost as bad as the radio. The voice was urgent, 'Your life is in danger. Leave now! Code Blackcock.'

The click of the receiver cut off any possible response. Her thoughts raced. She grabbed her gun from under the heavy lead umbrella stand in the hallway, placing the slim revolver in the pocket hidden flat under the left armpit of her coat. She stowed the radio equipment away safely. It took but a minute. Urgent voices on the street below were closing in. She turned off the lights and shut the door to her apartment. Hurried footsteps were already echoing through the stairwell. The rhythmic clip of their boots confirmed their rapid ascent.

Now they had come for *her*.

In the communal corridor she slipped off her shoes. Without hesitation, she crept down the back stairs. Three flights of spiralling steps. Her head felt giddy, her palms sweaty. Then out of the rear exit, she ran into the smoky night air. She pulled her shoes back on. Her nostrils filled with the pungent smoke that swept across the skyline. Deep crimson intruded upon the blackness of night, the sky ablaze. Katharine glanced up and down the deserted alley. She had to make it to the post box on the corner. She kept within the shadows and reached into her handbag. The manila double-sealed envelope was the only warning that her life had been compromised. She dropped it into the post box; her last lifeline plunged into an unknown abyss. There was no time to think about M. She prayed he would get it in time.

Across the alleyway, she spotted a lone bicycle, the object of her salvation. The owner wouldn't miss that for a few hours. She cycled hell for leather through the back streets towards the Embassy. Within the space of five minutes, she passed the burnt-out shells of three synagogues and at least a dozen Jewish shops that hadn't already been put out of business by the Nazis. Furnishings and items ransacked from synagogues and Jewish businesses lay piled high in the middle of the street, encircled by jeering youths with flame-torches, ready to set it all alight. Katharine turned into Pazmaniten-gasse, the street housing the Pazmaniten Temple, a cathedral-sized synagogue built decades earlier with the generosity of Jewish businessman Schamrek. Its former glory was gone, destroyed in one reckless night of arson; a testimony to a world that was fast disappearing under Nazi brutality and persecution.

This was a night like no other. Hitler had crossed the Rubicon. This was the point of no return for Austria's Jews.

She paused outside the gutted Pazmaniten. No one would think of looking for her here. The swarm of SS soldiers wouldn't recognise her amongst the throng of men and women gathering, excitedly waiting for the destruction of all that stood in the way of Nazi salvation. The chatter of the crowd, the smell of fire, freezing temperatures and darkness reminded her of childhood times on Guy Fawkes Night. She shuffled to the front, dragging the bicycle and stood by the railings. Through the synagogue's large, scorched oak doors hanging off their hinges, she could see a blaze of rolled parchments near the wooden Ark which had once held the sacred scriptures and their adornments. Scrolls of the Torah, the first five holy books of Moses, were burning in a funeral pyre. Their spiritual life-force extinguished by the flames of hate. She watched a piece of parchment curl, a charred text fall to the floor. She recalled a verse she had learnt at school:

How odd of God to choose the Jews,
Not so odd as those who choose a Jewish God
And reject the Jews.

The Nazis had no care for God or his Jews. She turned. She had one last task to perform. It wasn't the killing that bothered her, but the seduction.

❧

A few streets away, Hugo walked into the bathroom in the new makeshift headquarters at 2 Lambrechtgasse. Standing in the bath he removed the clips from the two-foot-long mirror above the taps. He swung it open, heaving himself up onto the mezzanine floor.

He crawled along, feeling for the light switch. He blinked in the bright light, stood up and brushed down his trousers. He closed the original door behind him, replacing the internal clips thus locking the bathroom mirror back into position. He made for the door at the end of the narrow passage. He pushed it open. Captain Henderson was already inside bent over a desk. The only light came from two small frosted lamps. Hugo passed him the manila envelope. 'Here, this arrived by our courier just now, sir. We're checking the boxes every hour now. This can only be a couple of hours old at most.'

Captain Henderson stared at the envelope. He didn't need to open it to confirm the sender. Instinctively he knew it was from her. He grabbed the paper knife. In one deft movement he slit across the top and pulled the brown paper out of its protective sheath. He knew the words of the poem by heart for he had composed it for her:

The Core of My Existence
When we both met 'most every day
my eyes and lips dared not betray
the thoughts I felt about you.
Yet now that you are far away,
My heart cries out across the distance.
You are the one for all my life, the core of my existence
I cannot live without you.

His throat tightened. He should have prevented this. 'It's Katharine. She's been compromised. Hugo, can you get me the addresses of all the safe houses please? I believe Sir Charles extended the list.'

'Yes, Captain Henderson.' Hugo began to shift from foot to foot. Conscious of it, he stopped himself. He walked into the adjoining room and began fingering through the files in a metal cabinet. It took a matter of seconds to pull out the thin folder near the back. Across the top it read: 'Do Not Remove. Waste disposal schedule.' He passed it to Captain Henderson.

Captain Henderson apologised, 'Sorry, Hugo, I quite forgot myself. You are M. I should not have imposed on you.'

Hugo felt renewed confidence as he explained the latest intelligence developments. 'The brothels have all been located as per the previous list, circumnavigating the outskirts of Vienna. However, Mrs Walters has not been informed of the new addresses yet. She only knows them as radio operational centres. We had to give her the telephone numbers so that she had direct lines to the operators to assist her radio directional finding.' He looked Captain Henderson straight in the face, 'She will be going to your address.'

'Why there, Hugo?' A hint of anger in his voice.

'It's on the edge of the city close to the train station. It makes complete sense. It was one of the last things Sir Charles got right before he retired. He believed it to be an ideal location for getting our people in and out of the city efficiently. At present, yours is the only fully functioning safe house. The other five will be up and running within a few days. We didn't need to run it past you sir, if you remember.'

Captain Henderson didn't argue. There was precious little time left. He pulled out the list of addresses, memorised them and handed the file back to Hugo. He walked over to a locked filing cupboard, almost as tall as himself, and pushed in the handle. Hearing it click he turned it once anti-clockwise, releasing the secret mechanism. It swung away from the wall. Beyond, operational engineers had constructed a labyrinth of hidden cupboards and rooms. Inside, Captain Henderson moved to the nearest desk and lifted out two passbooks. He flicked through the pages. All in order, he slipped them into his inside jacket pocket. Hugo stood in the doorway, watching, ensuring nothing was forgotten. He passed Captain Henderson a wooden chair. Climbing up, Captain Henderson felt along the top of the internal door, removing the tape across the hollowed space. He pulled out a gun and wooden box full of spare cartridges and stuffed a handful of bullets in his trouser pocket. The gun he placed in a pocket secreted in the armpit lining of his jacket. Carefully, he replaced the tape across the top of the door frame. In his mind, he went over the plan. For a moment, he could see nothing except Katharine's face. She was in danger and he had been a fool. He could have signed her off the case, sent her back to England. Now the fate of the woman he loved most in the world was hanging in the balance. He clenched his fists, his lips set. If by some stroke of fate she survived this night, he would tell her. The thoughts somersaulted through his mind. He had to re-focus. Standing down, Hugo passed him his heavy black overcoat, scarf and gloves.

Hugo looked concerned. 'Captain Henderson … sir?'

Captain Henderson came to his senses. 'If anyone asks for me, Hugo, tell them I'm visiting a neighbour in the general hospital.' He turned, marched down the corridor and out of the building. The acrid smoke bellowing from the city's forty-nine burning synagogues stung his eyes. He quickened his step towards the safe house.

❧

Outside the side entrance to the British Embassy, Katharine fumbled in her bag for the key. The church bells struck the half-hour. It was now 9.30 p.m. She opened the door, preferring to go up the back staircase. She made her way through the deserted wing; no one would know she was here. The skeleton staff worked at the other end of the building. Heading straight for Captain Henderson's office on the first floor, she figured the mole would be operating from one of three possible rooms. Only two had sophisticated enough equipment to send messages over a long distance. His office was the only place where sensitive information was collated before filing or distribution. Outside his room, she placed an ear against the door. Not a sound came from inside. She nudged it open, waiting for her eyes to adjust to the darkness. She took out a pocket torch, shining it at an angle. Its thin ray fell across the desktop. A single file was open, its papers scattered across the desk. Captain Henderson would never go home and leave his office in this state. He was far too meticulous and careful to leave anything out of place. She didn't really have time to stop. But she *had* to look.

She moved to the desk, picking up the nearest page. The right-hand corner was stamped 'Top Secret. Do not Remove'. Her eyes scanned the remaining documents, catching sight of Jonathan's signature on one page protruding from the bottom of a sheath of papers. Crouching on the floor, she shone the torch across the text. Her heart began to race; her mind replayed the events of the night Jonathan was taken. His contorted face and last words haunted her: 'I'll be back, my love.' There was still no confirmation of his whereabouts. Captain Henderson and Hugo believed he was still alive. She tried to carry on reading. A list of dates and names of German women filled the first half of the page: Eva Becker, Katarina Deutsch, and so on. She turned it over for the start of Jonathan's full report. His scrawling handwriting brought her loss flooding back. Reading on, the words intensified her torment.

18 March, Linz: reported to SS Gauleiter Deutsch at 1800 hours. Accompanied him to ceremonial opening…

Katherine scanned further down the page.

Distracted Deutsch's wife – a pretty young thing, if not rather silly. At
22.30 hours met her alone at summerhouse in grounds of German
Embassy. Task performed, seduced as requested. Extracted information
of safe passage. Mission accomplished.

The report had been countersigned by Sir Charles. Realisation slowly
dawned about Jonathan's activities; Sir Charles had even sanctioned
them. Nothing should shock her as an operative but that didn't make
it any easier. She tried to hold herself together, a numbness temporarily paralysing her.

Jonathan had betrayed her.

Behind a façade of care, he had deceived her. Jonathan, the man she
thought loved her and she him, had given himself to Nazi women.
It didn't matter whether it was in the service of duty. To her, he had
broken his vow of faithfulness. She tried to quell a rising rage, her
self-pity broken by the sound of an SS patrol marching outside in the
street. She paused, holding her breath. Had they come for her? They
passed on, the clip of their boots becoming ever faint. She sighed in
relief. Tonight she had but one task to perform.

Screwing up the page and stuffing it into her coat pocket, she
rushed back along the corridor and up the second flight of steps to
the Embassy roof. Her eyes scanned the terrace. Nothing seemed out
of place except the blazing skyline. It took a few moments to regain
her breath and composure. She crept towards the shack, hearing defi-
nite movement inside, then pushed the door open.

'Katharine! You startled me. What on earth are you doing here at
this time of night?'

Katharine's lip quivered as she moved towards the betrayer. 'That
bastard cheated on me.'

Susie came towards her, arms outstretched, 'Who, Katharine? Who
cheated on you?'

'Jonny,' she stuttered. 'I found this.' She thrust the crumpled paper
at Susie. Susie straightened out the handwritten page. Through
feigned tears Katharine continued, 'He lied to me, Susie. Our marriage was a sham.' She sobbed, 'He was having relations with other
women, Susie. As if that wasn't bad enough – with Nazi women!'

'There, there.' Susie patted her on the shoulder, moving a step
closer to comfort her. Her cool hand touched Katharine's, her human

kindness embracing. 'All men are bastards, darling. I keep telling you that.' Susie's face softened. 'I've missed you, girl.'

'Me too, Susie.' Katharine began drying her eyes with a handkerchief. 'I'm so lonely at times. I need female company, another woman to talk to.' She looked directly into Susie's steely cold eyes. 'I can't go back to my place, not tonight. There are too many memories of *him*. I don't want to … won't be alone. It's scary out there with the mobs and city burning. Can I possibly stay with you?'

For a moment she feared Susie was going to refuse. Susie's face lit up, 'Of course.' It was the cue Susie had been waiting for to hug her properly. She embraced her tightly. As she did, her hands slipped under Katharine's coat, stroking her back. Her touch felt warm over Katharine's silk blouse. Katharine deftly slipped her coat to the ground, aware that Susie could be frisking her for weapons. Susie continued; Katharine's shoulders relaxing under the soothing massage.

'You're quite tense, darling,' whispered Susie. 'I guess it's all the stress of recent weeks. It's been a hell of a time for you. In fact, for all of us.'

Katharine hesitated. Susie sensed her withdrawal. She took Katharine's hand. 'Come on, girl. Let's go back to my place for a steaming hot chocolate and you can tell me all about it. It's not far.'

Katharine's backward glance at the radio equipment confirmed it all. The faint glow had not yet fully died away from the valves. Everything tied in.

❧

Two streets on, inside the flat, Susie grabbed a bottle of vodka from the sideboard. 'Forget the hot chocolate, this is just what you need darling.' She filled two tumblers and walked into the bedroom. She motioned for Katharine to follow. Katharine tried to contain her nerves.

'Here, you can have my room tonight,' she called out. 'You need a good rest. You've been through hell.'

Katharine began walking towards the bedroom, taking in Susie's form, bent provocatively whilst straightening the covers on the bed. 'Now, come over here darling, and tell me all about it,' said Susie, patting the bed. She laughed dismissively. 'Don't be shy,' she said, coming towards her. 'How are those shoulders of yours? Still tense?'

She began to move her hands over Katharine's back, slipping them under her blouse.

Katharine held her composure. 'Susie, I … don't know.'

'Ssshhh,' ordered Susie, gently holding her finger to Katharine's lip.

Katharine had to go along with it. All she had to do was work out how to make it quick and feign pleasure. 'You don't know how good that feels, Susie.'

Susie interpreted her response as permission to explore further, softly kissing Katharine's long slender neck. In a swift movement, quicker than Katharine could take in, Susie slipped her own dress to her ankles. Then Katharine felt the buttons of her blouse undoing, Susie pressing her body against hers, pushing her onto the bed.

Through impassioned face and gritted teeth, Katharine began to caress Susie.

'That's wonderful,' groaned Susie.

'Sssh, Susie.' Inside Katharine was shaking, her thoughts racing. Tentatively she responded to Susie's hands wandering across her chest, not having been touched since Jonathan's disappearance. She closed her eyes, pretending it was Jonny. It was the only way to get through it.

Susie's voice was hoarse with sexual tension. 'Do you know how long I've wanted you? Ever since I saw you at that army camp. You walked into that hut all indignant but feminine and vulnerable. I wanted you there and then. I've lusted for you ever since. That's why I saved you, darling.' She wriggled, turned over, raising her bare arms above her head.

Katharine saw the vital confirmation she needed to quell any remnant of doubt. Under Susie's right armpit, her blood group had been tattooed. Katharine knew it was a practice carried out by all high-ranking SS officers and Nazi secret operatives. She needed no further proof. The bitch – it was *her* all along. She had to stay calm. She rolled on top of Susie and whispered, 'dearest, I need to use the loo.'

'Be quick, darling.' Susie groaned, eyes closed, still savouring the warmth of Katharine's soft body.

On the way back from the bathroom, Katharine scooped up her clothes as if to tidy them onto the chair. Keeping her back to Susie, she slipped a stiletto blade from the seam along the buttons of her cardigan. Q had cleverly designed the blade to resemble a hatpin. She clenched the thin metal in her hot palm. The point pressed upwards, concealed flat against the flesh of her forearm.

In her mind's eye she saw the disfigured face of Guttmann the baker, his wife and children with bloodstained gunshots to the forehead, then her own brother-in-law lying out in the mortuary, his feet neatly sliced off in a gruesome surgical experiment. Finally, the image of Jonny's face haunted her. A lying bastard he may have been, but still her husband. She saw them all and more. She slipped the bladed hatpin under the pillow, moved as if to embrace Susie, running her fingers down Susie's shoulders towards her breasts.

Susie was still aroused from moments earlier, in ecstasy, arching her back. 'Don't stop, keep going Katharine. Oh.'

It was now or never.

Katharine whispered softly as she slid her hand under the pillow. Gripping the cold hatpin, in one swift movement, she thrust it deep into Susie's eardrum. Susie's body buckled beneath her. Katharine held her down, muffling her scream with her free hand. The stiletto blade penetrated deeper as Susie's struggles slowly died beneath her naked form. A thin trickle of blood from the ear was all that remained of the life drained out of her.

Katharine gently untangled herself. Slowly, a little unsteady and hands stone cold from tension, she checked Susie's pulse. Definitely dead. She picked up her clothes, fumbling to put on her skirt and blouse, then her jacket. The nearby church clock tolled another hour, but she couldn't leave without searching the flat. Straightening her skirt and gathering her thoughts, she started in the sitting room. Checking all internal doors was the highest priority. There were always three safes in any one operative's house. Doors were the most popular place for documents and weapons, a hollowed-out cavity in the frame. The first safe was relatively easy to find, embedded in the door leading to the inner hallway. She pulled out the knives, then the Walther 7.63 German pistol, checking if it was loaded she placed it in her handbag. Her eyes scrutinized the skirting boards for signs of cracks. Pulling the rug back from the sideboard she located the second safe. With a screwdriver, she prised up the floorboard to reveal a small metal box, crammed with folded identity papers and money. Susie's photo was in one of the passports under the pseudonym Sandra Norris.

It took just a few minutes to find the third safe, chiselled into the top of the lounge door. Her hand felt around, the prick of a splinter from the rough frame caused her to stop a moment. She pulled out a thick wad of printed notes, removed one of the shoulder pads in her jacket and folded the money flat, manipulating them into the shoulder line. The rest were laid flat in the lining of her skirt. As she moved away, her eye caught sight of the ornate bevelled gold handle of an umbrella propped against the fireplace. It was identical to one issued to her by Q. Maybe Susie *had* been kitted out by Q as well. But how?

She picked it up, swivelled it round. Around the edge was engraved a single faint word: *Jonathan*. She drew breath. How many more revelations that night? How had Susie managed to get so close to Jonathan? Had he slept with her too? She twisted the umbrella handle and peered inside. It was some relief to discover it empty. Taking the remaining documents from the second safe, she rolled them up and pushed them into the hollowed-out umbrella handle. An eerie foreboding crept up her spine. A presence felt as if it was closing in.

It was time to leave.

Always trust your instinct she had been told in training. She turned, taking in for a final time the lifeless form of Susie sprawled naked across the bed. Katharine leant towards her one last time, moist eyes glimmering with anger.

Then the tears came – not for Susie, but for the victims; for those who had been sentenced to horrific deaths at her hands. She had done it. And now she had killed Susie and avenged them all, but her knotted stomach could cope no more. She lurched towards the sink in the corner of the bedroom. Vomit spewed out, her stomach finally ejecting its traumatised contents. In an act of ritual cleansing, she washed her hands over and over until they were almost raw. She left the apartment.

In the communal hallway it was just a few steps to the lift but it seemed to take forever. She had over-taxed herself, the emotional strain beginning to kick in. Pressing the down button, her heart raced as the lift cranked its way up.

On the ground floor, she stepped out of the lift and yawned, putting her hand up to her mouth. The concierge peered over the desk. 'A late night then, Fraulein. Is everything alright?'

'Yes, fine thank you.'

He frowned, unsure of her response.

She walked steadily towards the double exit doors. In the reflected glass panels she saw him pick up the telephone.

Out in the street, she knew she had to turn the corner before the patrols came, possibly only a matter of minutes. She lifted her head in confidence and descended the steps of the building. No attempt had been made by the city's fire brigade to put out the blazes of the synagogues, still raging in the Jewish quarter. The smuts floated in waves down the street. Turning left, Katharine quickened her pace, beginning to run towards the end of the street. The bicycle was still against the railings where she had left it earlier. The sound of male voices at the far end of the street broke the silence. They were on her trail but they hadn't seen her. She saw them head into Susie's apartment block. A few more minutes of grace were still hers.

Tying a scarf over her head, she picked up the bicycle, cycling within the shadows. She made her way towards the river; the bank of the Danube thankfully devoid of SS patrols. The lights of the city reflected sharply in the water. The silhouettes of buildings along the embankment cast elusive shapes across the shimmering river. The tranquility momentarily masked the danger she was in. There was no time for complacency. She pedalled furiously towards the one address she knew would be safe.

Chapter 11

Crossing the city seemed to take an eternity. The few SS patrols Katharine passed in the side streets were oblivious to her, too intent on the night's business. Finally, the street sign confirmed her destination and safety: Feuerbachstrasse. She threw the bicycle to the ground. Raucous laughter from the tavern spilled out onto the street. Exhausted, but strangely elated, she stumbled through the doorway into a dimly lit, hot oak-panelled room. It held an unpleasant odour of sweaty bodies mixed with pungent cigars; a string quartet played loutish music and lewd paintings clung to the walls of the saloon. Women in various states of undress leant over half-drunken men clutching thick cigars. A glance around confirmed that the place was frequented by high-ranking Nazi officers. Katharine paused momentarily, a little panicked, but then rationalised – of course she would be safe here. She would not have been given the address if not. She strained through the smoke to see beyond the bar. Making out the door in the far corner, keeping her head down, she eased her way to the back parlour. Through the partially open doorway, Captain Henderson stood, stooped over the fireplace warming his hands. He hadn't seen her. Relief flooded through her body at the sight of him. He turned suddenly at the sound of her movement. His strained face lifted, his relief tangible.

'Katharine!'

She rushed towards him. Without stopping to think, she flung herself into his arms. His chest felt strong against her body.

'I did it, I did it,' she gasped, her whispered words what he had hoped for. 'It was Susie. I should have told you about Susie and Berchtesgaden, but Sir Charles…'

He brought his lips to hers if only to silence her. She was safe and that was all that mattered to him. He held her, barely believing he had just kissed her. He was still somewhat reserved, even now. Her soft voice continued with a slight tremor, determined to tell him: 'But I've been compromised. The porter will have found her body by now. He saw me and suspected something. I need to leave Vienna.'

He reluctantly released her from his embrace. Walking back to the door, he slid across the bolt. This time there was no holding back from his confession. He took her in his arms again, held her shaking body against his chest, releasing his innermost anguish. 'Oh God, Katharine, I thought I'd never see you again.'

He drew back enough to look straight into her face, still holding her. 'Katharine, I love you.'

He had to carry on; had to tell her. 'My position normally dictates a single life. My work is too precarious, too dangerous.'

She looked at him quizzically. What was he trying to say? She felt his right fist clenched on her back.

'I am married to duty – to King and Country. There has never been room for anything else … anyone else, but the events of recent days have made me realise. My feelings run very deep, Katharine. I want to share my life with you, such as it is.' Katharine was too stunned by his declaration to respond. He took her hand with tenderness. 'What I am about to show you, you must never discuss again.'

She broke her silence. 'You can trust me.'

He knew he could.

He led her through another door into a tiny, almost empty, bleak room, filled with nothing except several old rusting filing cabinets. Again he bolted the door. He guided her over to the tallest cupboard; reaching behind, he undid the seals. It moved away easily. They walked through into the adjoining room. 'Welcome to my world, Katharine.'

The small hexagonal room was packed with operators. It was kitted out with phone lines, recording and radio equipment; numerous dials illuminated the front panel. One wall was lined with more filing cupboards, another with maps of different parts of the world. Pins stuck everywhere offering different scenarios; it reminded her fleetingly of Sir Charles's office. But that was the past. She noticed one map had operational field names marked next to specific German towns. She took it all in. The adjacent walls were covered in long shelves, heaving under piles of documents, various stamps sticking out of boxes and thousands of blank identity papers awaiting official designations. In the far corner, a bunk bed had miscellaneous paraphernalia strewn across its covers. The remaining walls of the bunker had spiralling lines of wires leading downwards to a small desk, all identical, piled high with reel to reel tape-recording machines. The operators barely had room to turn, their shoulders almost touched each other. They sat listening intently with earphones, oblivious to the presence of their neighbours.

Katharine followed Captain Henderson's eyes, resting on the tight spiral staircase leading up to a mezzanine floor. 'My home from home, Katharine,' he smiled. He led her upstairs out of earshot of the team. She looked into his rugged face. The tears welled up. 'Gosh!' she cried. 'So you are M.'

It all made sense.

'Well, yes and no. M is the designation for the family's public face. That is Hugo's job now. He interacts with all appointed political minions and various heads of the military. However, he operates under my direct guidance, as did Sir Charles until he began operating under his own steam.' She raised her eyebrows, not interrupting him. He continued: 'My designation is C. I am the absolute head of all overseas covert operations; answering to no one, not even the king or prime minister. There are wheels and cogs behind the scenes of government that you can't even begin to imagine. The heads of various military sections offer suggestions for direction or ask for my help, but only through Hugo. They never meet me. They do not control operations. I, and I alone, decide who, where and when. It falls to Hugo to recruit and organise the network of operatives.'

At that moment she felt privileged to be with him, admired his firm voice, resolute with unbridled authority. She realised that she had missed that in Jonathan, but then he had been different. 'So this is how you gather information. It's brilliant, absolutely brilliant.'

'Yes,' he replied. 'No one would ever think of looking for a fugitive or operative within a brothel; especially one that serves the needs of high-ranking German and Austrian officers. The girls here love it. We give them a level of protection they would never get working the streets. We give them free medical care whilst removing the need for pimps, so they get to keep all their earnings. The British government has little use for their income and anyway, how would we file their earnings for taxation?' He looked at her directly almost challenging a comment.

'Yes, I can see.'

'We naturally pay them bonuses for any information they can wheedle out of their clients. Each of them keeps a book, a kind of diary record. All in all it is the perfect symbiotic set up. Come, let me show you my quarters.' He took her arm, leading her from the mezzanine up to the next floor, unlocking the small wooden door in front of them. The converted room under the eaves was simple. His quarters housed a single bed, oak desk with telephone, and a chair. She noticed the absence of any papers or files. A tiny bathroom barely large enough for a bath and toilet led off to the right. The adjoining sitting room was miniscule, but had a fire crackling away in the hearth. She worked out that it must be located at the back of the house.

'Sorry, it's not exactly grand,' he said. 'But it serves a purpose.' He turned to close the door behind them. She stood motionless, waiting for his move.

This time he wouldn't lose her. He took her in his arms, held her face gently bringing his lips onto hers. They felt warm and soft. How long he had waited for this moment. He kissed with passion, years of emotion released like a dam. His chest burned, his heart pounded, stomach turning partly with nerves, partly excitement. He dared not let her go. This time it wasn't a dream. He had her. She began to respond, her lips tentatively pressed against his.

Reluctantly he released her, 'Come, let's sit nearer the fire, you're shivering. I'll go down and order some tea and brandy. It's one of the perks of living in a brothel, everything is just a holler away.'

In his temporary absence she stared blankly into the fire, sitting on the rug curled up with some cushions. She listened to the crackling of the flames on the thinly chopped kindling sticks, her lips still tingling from his kiss. She had denied her feelings for him for far too long. Having admired him ever since the concert in Vienna, she had been unwilling to admit her feelings, even to herself. It had been a gradual awakening. Now she knew in the depths of her soul that this was right. She pushed aside any thought of Jonathan, savouring the moment, feeling the heat of the fire warm her body. She unbuttoned the top of her blouse provocatively.

Captain Henderson returned with a tray, throwing the large bolt across the door behind him. Bolts and locked doors seemed to be a necessary occupational habit with him. Placing the tray on the floor beside her, he passed her the brandy first. Sitting down next to her, he watched as she lifted the glass to her open lips, sipping it slowly. He took in her feminine body, her slender arms which had seen years of violin practice, and the soft, moist lips he had just kissed. He loved everything about her, but most of all her tenacious mind.

Katharine didn't miss the change in him. There was something more than just the way he looked at her, reminding her of the first time she had seen him having missed her flight to Vienna. Fleetingly she wondered if it had all been a set-up from the beginning. She dismissed the notion as quickly as it entered her head. Deep down, she knew he was honest. Inside she was still quivering from his passion moments earlier. Placing his arm gently around her shoulder, they sat together watching the flames dance around the wood, her face flickering in the light of the fire. He watched as she removed her jacket and loosened the zip on her skirt to reveal her stockings. She pulled out the hidden documents, brushing up teasingly to his body. Reaching across him for Susie's umbrella that had fallen to the floor when he had embraced her, she removed the rest of the notes and handed them to him. Their eyes locked as their hands briefly touched. Flicking through the papers he caught sight of the eagle emblem. She didn't understand why he reacted. It was unlike him. But then he had nothing to hide with her. He jumped up, 'Oh gosh, this is not one of our fake documents. This is genuine.'

She smiled, 'I wondered as much.'

He leant down, an excuse to kiss her on the forehead. 'This document lists all the transportation details of the gold, and this page gives the Swiss bank details.' At that moment, something deep within connected them beyond the present. She felt close to him. Now it was she who couldn't hold back. She swiftly pulled him down onto her. Furiously she was undoing his tie and buttons of his shirt. She slipped her hand over his toned naked chest, felt the firmness of his muscles, excitement rising within her.

He hesitated, 'I don't think I can. Work … got to…' His protests were ignored. He had aroused her. He was trying to hold back, to be his reserved self again where he felt safe, but it was useless. He wanted her as much as she him.

'Ssh,' she reassured him.

'Oh hell,' his voice cracked with emotion. 'The Nazis can wait. I've dreamt of this moment for a lifetime. And they will never find us up here. They're only interested in the women downstairs.' He brought his lips to hers, kissed her again, their passion rekindled. He fumbled as she helped him to slip off the remainder of his clothes. She flung his shirt across the floor, pushing him gently down onto the rug. His firm hands moved into her blouse, exposing her pert breasts. As she lent over him, he brought his mouth to them, kissing her erect nipples. She groaned with pleasure, a thrill surging through her body. She felt herself pulsating below, as he moved his hand downwards.

He held her tight as she lay on his naked body, the fullness of her breasts exciting him further. The softness of her form encompassed the hardness that was his; the warmth of her body penetrated his soul. The connection burned between them. She arched her back in ecstasy beneath his touch. Frantically he kissed her again and again. He rolled her over, climbed on top, taking back control, their bodies entwined in eternity. Her hand moved down to his manhood, caressing the end in pleasure. Then he was inside her, giving himself unconditionally to her. He wanted the moment to last forever.

Their passion finally spent she lay in his arms, staring at the leaping flames in the fireplace. Physically relaxed, her mind whirled a million thoughts. She tried to sleep in his arms, but the excitement of what had happened wouldn't subside. He must have been even more exhausted than her because as she looked up at his eyes, he was already asleep. He stirred momentarily as she gently untangled herself.

Standing up, Katharine now dressed quickly, watching his slumbering naked form at her feet. A pang of guilt began to gnaw within her. Why had she done it? Had she lost her senses? She was a married woman. Jonathan's whereabouts were still unknown and he might not be dead. Never mind what he had done with other women, she had committed a cardinal sin. Two wrongs do not make a right. She was not free to give herself to Captain Henderson. She had a duty to Jonathan as his wife. Moving to the desk she scribbled a note. Hand unsteady as she wrote, she could not block out what she felt for him. Being with him was like nothing she had ever experienced before. She slipped the note next to him. About to leave, she turned back, went over to a lone wardrobe and removed a SS uniform. Grabbing a pair of long black boots that looked about right for her, she tiptoed downstairs with her bundle. She passed through the mezzanine and through the operators' room. They didn't take any notice of her, probably because she had come in with Henderson. Out in the main corridor, the brothel was deserted, the early morning raucous frivolity of the inhabitants long since spent.

Outside the tavern, Katharine paused to ascertain her direction. She took in the winter dawn, glinting through the remaining frosted leaves on the trees. In the distance, an owl hooted its dominance over the area. She shuddered in the biting cold air, pulling up her collar, straightening her crumpled skirt. The bicycle was thankfully still there. She placed the bundle of the SS uniform in the wicker basket at the front. At the rear of the building, a country lane shut off by a garden gate snaked into the distance. She lifted her bicycle over the gate, struggling to drag it across the rough terrain through the orchards. The smell of brown soggy rotting apples on the ground filled her senses with penance. She made her way through to the other side to a country road and cycled into the distance.

❧

Suppressing a yawn, Captain Henderson sat up. Katharine was nowhere to be seen. He bent down, picked up the note, not fully awake from the eventful night. Katharine's scent and warm body was still fresh in his mind. All that stood between him and happiness was Jonathan. Turning over the note, his heart leapt. He anticipated, hoped for, words of tenderness. He stared helplessly at the bold words.

I am not yet free. Till I am in your arms again. Kath.

It meant only one thing. Panic was not an emotion he had ever experienced before. This was different. He dressed hurriedly, rushed out onto the mezzanine, scanning for any evidence of her, then downstairs and out of the tavern. He looked up and down the street noticing the morning SS patrol on the corner. Curfew and the damn patrols made the streets too dangerous, especially for an unaccompanied woman. Moving around to the rear of the building, he carefully examined the ground behind the garden gate. The single track, matt and obtrusive imbedded within the frosted earth, led into the orchard behind. The size of the footprints assured him they were hers. The dragged bicycle track beside them confirmed everything. Scanning the distance, there was nothing, except a young lad with a dog herding cows out of a nearby field into a distant narrow lane. In his head, he silently cried out for her 'Katharine!' His mind in turmoil, he had waited a lifetime for her. Now she was gone. He had spent his life putting duty before everything, even the woman he loved. He had stood back silently, watched as she married a man who didn't care for her. He should have intervened then. He, the head of secret operations abroad with unlimited power, had let go of the one thing that mattered to him in the world. Even with Jonathan safely locked away, still he could not have her. Bound by a code of duty and honour, his hands were tied. He clenched his fist, biting his lower lip.

He could not live without her. The few intimate moments the previous night had taught him that much. He straightened his back, face set, determined to find her.

England. She would be heading for England.

Having slept rough in the woods, Katharine waited until nightfall before entering the station. The clock struck 10 p.m. in Praterstern Wien North, Vienna's most northerly railway station. The place was deserted except for a handful of SS officers and station guards. Katharine surreptitiously glanced down, exhausted from lack of proper sleep as much as concern at the uniform she was wearing. The grey fabric itched and rubbed against her skin, especially over her chest, pulled extra tight to hide her femininity. The swastika bands tightly clasped around each arm made the uniform feel even more uncomfortable. She had done a good job using the bicycle's mirror to remove all her make-up. Cropping her hair had proved a somewhat more difficult exercise than she had bargained for. Breathing deeply, she straightened her posture and marched across the station. At the centre, a bronze statue of Johann Strauss looked down on the new world order. He was one of her heroes. His immortal music never failed to touch a chord whenever she heard or played it. Now all she could feel was his sadness. Standing beneath his omniscient gaze, two Nazi officers leant against him, smoking and chatting, occasionally glancing with a smile in her direction. She quelled her nerves and marched confidently towards them. The knee-high black polished boots began to pinch her toes. She passed them and saluted, 'Heil Hitler'.

They nodded their approval and continued their conversation. The first incognito test successfully completed, she made her way towards the waiting train. With steely confidence in her new identity, she reassured herself she could carry it off.

A guard at the platform barrier stepped forward, 'Alles gut, Herr…?'

'Schrieber,' she replied.

'Herr Schrieber,' he confirmed, his tiny pinched mouth made him somewhat severe. 'We leave now.' He signalled to the stationmaster, then turned to her again, keeping his back to the two SS officers still under the statue. He whispered close to her ear, 'I want you in the second carriage. I have some provisions there for you. We can't afford any mistakes, not tonight of all nights. Remember the SS motto,' he grinned, 'If in doubt, shoot. Ask questions later.'

Katharine nodded. The engine revved, smoke and oil filled her nostrils. She suppressed a cough, pulled herself into the carriage and squatted down next to a huge wooden box. The guard closed the door, plunging her into darkness. The train slowly pulled out of the station.

Hand in pocket holding the loaded pistol, Captain Henderson avoided the patrols of Brown Shirts as he hurried through the back streets of Vienna's Third District towards the second safe house. Weak lights streaked through partially closed shutters onto the streets breaking the night's gloom with a milky luminosity. Hugo was just leaving the building. Captain Henderson caught his eye, stopping him in his tracks. Hugo raised his hand in acknowledgement. Henderson quickened his pace. Coming up to Hugo, he grabbed his arm, leading him firmly back into the house.

'In there, Hugo,' he hissed, guiding him towards the back kitchen now deserted of staff. 'Where is she?' he whispered through gritted teeth. 'Where's Katharine?'

Hugo had never seen him so ruffled. Hugo's own pressing voice reproached him: 'Where have you been, s…sir? I've been trying to contact you. I've left messages for you all over the place, at all the s…safe houses.' He didn't wait for Captain Henderson to answer. He spilled out the news: 'I *have* found her. She is safe.'

'Where man? Where is she? Are you sure?'

'Quite.' Hugo's authoritative response did little to reassure him. He looked down at his watch, 'She should be on the train by now. It's OK, s…sir. I've sorted everything. She's heading for the border.'

'The border?' His usual constrained voice cracked slightly. He stared him in the face. 'Which border?'

'She's on the train heading for the Brenner Pass via Innsbruck. The consignment of art is taking its usual route th…through the mountains to Milan.' Hugo read his mind immediately; anticipating his concern he added: 'Don't worry, s…sir, after the SS reprisals last month, I've had our men stand down. There will be no interception tonight. She's a woman of fortitude – we both know that. She's a survivor. It will be fine.'

Captain Henderson was not so sure. His abrupt answer surprised Hugo: 'You should have cleared it with me, Hugo. She's been compromised after the kill. It's extremely dangerous for her out there right now. She has just taken out a very senior covert Nazi operative and the authorities will be hunting her down. They won't stop until they've got her and the situation is back under their control.'

Hugo was cautious, noticing Captain Henderson's restless hands clench-fisted, suppressing his internal anger. 'I'm sorry, s…sir. There was no time. I understand … We thought it safer for her to travel by night than by day. The art train will be the last place they will ever search for her. As long as she sticks to the plan and gets off just before the border, she should be safe.'

Captain Henderson's swift response cut through the strain. 'Never mind, never mind that now. Take the truck, Hugo. We leave immediately.' He turned to go. 'With a bit of luck we can reach the border before they change guards.' Hugo stopped him.

'Er… s…sir, I have your new batman here. He will be travelling with you. I'm st…still needed at this end.'

'Very well, but by gads man, can't I go alone?'

'We can't allow that, sir. Rules are rules. I'll get him to bring the lorry to the rear. You can get acquainted on the journey.'

After a moment's silence, Captain Henderson suddenly asked: 'Hugo, what identity is she using?'

'SS officer Herr Schrieber.'

Captain Henderson smiled, temporarily relieving the tension in his face. 'Well, Hugo. That will be a challenge for her.' His tone changed, 'But, it is also the most risky. Time to go, Hugo, come on, we all have our work cut out tonight.'

The train loaded with art rattled through the mountain range, the journey long and tedious, broken by the occasional stop at irregular intervals. Katharine shone her torch intermittently to check her watch and compass, ascertaining that they must finally be nearing the border town of Gries am Brenner. The train was beginning to slow down. The brakes screeched to a halt; the carriages shuddered to a standstill. Low voices penetrated the night's silence; she couldn't hear what they were saying. Carefully she slid the carriage door just wide enough to assess her immediate surroundings. All was clear in front. She squeezed through the crack. The inhabitants of the few houses near the station were asleep, shutters closed tight on their wooden-clad houses. They would have no knowledge of the extra train that night, or if they did, they would turn a blind eye.

The boots of four German officers crunched in harmony on the gravel path as they approached the far end of the train. Katharine strained to make out their muttered conversation. One lit a cigarette, gesturing to a group of men at the other end of the platform to speed up their operation. She waited for them to unload two unmarked boxes from the last carriage; a Nazi flag draped across each. For a moment she contemplated continuing on the train to Milan, but dismissed it. Such an irrational idea wasn't viable. Once in Italy, the SS would be changed for Italian guards who could be lax, but when they chose to, they could make life difficult with their official procedures. She squatted down to lessen the impact when she jumped to the ground. Finally out of the carriage, the mountain air felt lighter, much crisper and colder. It was about a hundred yards to the signal box where she could loiter in the shadows until the train left.

The guard whistled to the driver for the train to continue its journey. Watching it fade along the track into the distance, Katharine walked nonchalantly towards the signal box. She was desperate to remove the tight boots now burning her toes. No one took any notice of her, all far too engrossed in shifting the wooden boxes into the engine shed at the far end of the siding. Behind the signal box, she exchanged the uniform for civilian clothes. In a last symbolic defiant act, she took a blade from her pocket and slit the armbands in half, right through the swastikas.

Captain Henderson walked up the steps of the Town Hall in Gries. The building was relatively insignificant for such an important centre of administration. A tiny plaque gave the only clue to its function. Making his way into the foyer, Captain Henderson took a moment to look up at the full-length portrait of Adolf Hitler filling the wall facing him. Nazi flags flanked the painting as a guard of honour. His power seemed absolute, he thought. Only another war could remove him from power, but Europe was not yet ready to take that risk, still smarting from the Great War.

'Guten Abend, mein Herr.' The young female voice behind him cut through his thoughts. 'Can I help you?' He turned. The voice behind a large desk revealed an attractive blond.

'Yes, madam. I've come on urgent business. Is the mayor here?'

'Do you have an appointment, sir?'

'No. No I don't. I know it is an intrusion, but this is rather urgent.'

She glanced at the array of medal ribbons across Captain Henderson's chest, as if noticing them for the first time. She picked up the receiver and dialled.

'Gauleiter Schrek, there's a distinguished naval gentleman here to see you by the name of…' She looked up.

'Captain Henderson,' he replied levelly.

'Captain Henderson, sir. Yes … yes, very well, I'll send him through.' She replaced the receiver. 'Last door on the left.' She pointed down the corridor.

'Thank you, madam. I'm much obliged to you.' He bowed his head in acknowledgement.

Walking down the length of the passageway, all he could think of was Katharine. First, he had to find her and then extract her safely. He knocked on the imposing door; the name plaque denoted the man's importance in the region.

'Come in!' came the response.

Gauleiter Schrek stood up as Captain Henderson entered and strode across his office. Each man eyed the other.

'Captain Henderson, good day.'

'Good day, Herr Gauleiter Schrek.'

Gauleiter Schrek moved around the desk, leaning his right hand on one corner, then motioned for Captain Henderson to be seated. 'How can I help you today?'

Captain Henderson cleared his throat. 'May I thank you sir for seeing me at such short notice without an appointment. I am very grateful.'

Gauleiter Schrek responded to the formality with a nod. A self-righteous man, full of his own importance, he enjoyed his position of power.

Henderson began to explain: 'I have orders from Herr Eichmann himself. I am to collect the latest batch of exit visas. He has specifically asked us at the British Embassy to step up Jewish emigration policy as a matter of urgency.'

'Why here, Captain? Why not Vienna?'

Captain Henderson, quick thinking as ever, replied: 'Because I understand, sir, Herr Eichmann prefers discretion, keep it away from central audit and authorities in the city. The code I was given is "Beech".'

Satisfied with the response, Gauleiter Schrek leant forward. 'Unfortunately, the papers have not yet arrived here. When they do, I assure you we will do everything we can to speed up your paperwork. You must have seen the crowds at the border. Refugees, all of them – filthy Jews. Our town is plagued by them. We can't wait to get rid of them soon enough. They worship the devil and drink the blood of children at their Passover.'

Captain Henderson thought it best to leave the smear unchallenged. He was not here to re-educate the man. It would do no good against such entrenched myths. He was as indoctrinated as every other Nazi in the country. Schrek continued: 'If those papers are due here, my assistants will know the minute they arrive. Why don't you call back tomorrow afternoon? I should have news for you by then. In the meantime, stay a while and enjoy our beautiful town.' He stood up, moved around his desk, extending his hand to signal the meeting was over. 'One thing, Captain Henderson. Please don't stray too near the border guards, they can be a little tetchy, especially about security. They have a lot to deal with each day. We leave them to get on with their own business. We do not interfere with them, if you understand what I mean.'

'Perfectly, sir. I will keep that in mind. Thank you for your time today.' Captain Henderson responded to his gesture and shook his hand. 'Until tomorrow then.'

Outside, Captain Henderson climbed back into the lorry. Without hesitation his batman started the engine. 'Where now, sir?'

Henderson took a cursory glance back at the Town Hall. Gauleiter Schrek was watching from the wings, staring across at their vehicle. 'Drive on to the Alpine Guest House – it's the best they can offer us here. We need to stake out the town.'

'Just the two of us?'

'Look, if we are to get on, you need to stop asking questions and trust me implicitly. We only need to watch the road leading to the border crossing. It's the only route out of the country for miles around. The area is surrounded by impassable mountains, and there are far too many patrols on both sides of the border to risk crossing anywhere else. No, she has to play it safe and come through. With a bit of luck she will tag onto a large group of refugees. Lose herself in the crowd. If I know her, she'll try to cross late afternoon, just before they close for daily inspection. Drive on. Let's get to the guest house before lunch.'

❧

Later that day inside the café on the corner of the square, Captain Henderson kept up his vigilant watch through the window. The endless line of refugees ahead, huddled tightly together, slowly wove its way towards the crossing. Most were weary women and young children. He noticed their broken shoes worn out from miles of walking. Most would have received their visas through his office in Vienna. How many would manage to get through the border without the guards beating them up first? He looked at them with pity. The refugee crisis was worse than most European governments cared to admit. Around him, the people chatted at the coffee tables, appearing not to have a concern in the world. He leant back in the chair, taking another sip from a fresh coffee brought by the waiter. He had been there for a couple of hours with no success so far in spotting Katharine. He tried to suppress his mounting concern. What if Hugo was wrong? He dismissed it. Hugo couldn't possibly be. He was the best for the job.

Then he saw her.

The side of her face was unmistakable. It *was* her. He almost missed her hidden in a small group of refuges. Under his breath, he muttered his relief. 'Good girl, she's learnt her stuff well.'

He stood up, walking purposely out of the café towards the group. He came alongside them, pushing his way through them. Catching up with her, he reached out for her shoulders, spun her around wrapping her in his arms.

'The boy's found his father,' one of the refugees whispered. The comment was not lost on Captain Henderson. Her disguise was authentic. He smiled to himself, realising how like a boy Katharine looked with her cropped hair and no make-up.

'It's good to see you, Captain Henderson.' Her monotone voice lacked any emotion at seeing him, no hint of her feelings for him. He had to remind himself – it wasn't a dream. He had made love to her. There had been a deep connection between them. Now it seemed a lifetime away. Through his thoughts, he barely heard her quiet words:

'I've posted some data to you that I collected in the last day or so. I think you'll find it useful.'

'Shhh, not work, not now. That's the least of your worries. Listen carefully,' he said. 'I will escort you across the border. Here, this is the address of a safe house not too far on the other side. I need to return briefly to Vienna. Duty – you understand. Here, take this. It contains tickets and money for you. When you reach England, report to the London office. We need someone of your experience to set up a new radio listening division within the family. You will be head of your own section.'

Katharine nodded, 'I understand.'

As they approached the barrier she gasped, 'Look what they're doing. They are searching and robbing everyone. Oh my, they can't do that.'

The line swelled with younger refugees, now joined by elderly ones. An older bearded man took umbrage when the guard ran his hand up the thigh of his wife. In one swift movement the SS officer swung his gun from his shoulder, the butt smashing into the man's face, knocking him backwards to the ground. Laughing, he kicked his victim relentlessly, his face and body caving into a bloody pulp.

Katharine lurched forward. 'No!'

Several guards ran out of the border hut. They turned on her. 'Get back, boy!' they shouted in her face. A truncheon headed for her stomach. Captain Henderson reacted, jumping to her defence, shielding her body with his. He took the worst of the beating.

'We're British citizens. We've got diplomatic immunity,' he yelled. It fell on deaf ears. He fumbled for his passport, tried to flash it before them. Nothing defused their anger. They kicked him harder.

The commotion aroused Gauleiter Schrek from his office. He came out, striding towards the chaotic scene. He raised his hand, bellowed: '*Achtung!*'

Silence rang through the crowd. He turned directly to Captain Henderson, bent over double in pain. 'What did I tell you, Captain? I suggest you take yourself and that young lad across the border pretty damn quick, sir.'

Captain Henderson groaned, barely lifting his head. Katharine supported him as he bent over clutching his stomach with bloodied hands. They stumbled towards the border. Three more steps and they were over it. Was this freedom? At least for Katharine, he thought. The other refugees straggling in twos and threes turned to the right and meandered slowly eastwards towards the Italian town.

Katharine continued to support Captain Henderson, his full body weight made her back ache. She helped him to a tiny brook which was gurgling its way through the valley. 'We can rest here,' she said, her voice exceptionally tender. Taking off her headscarf, she dipped the corner in the flowing water. Then she began to tend his wounds, pressing the cold material against his bruised abdomen. The blood soaked into the scarf like blotting paper. For the first time he was truly vulnerable. She bent forward and kissed him on the forehead. In spite of the pain, he intuitively moved his hand up to her face and turned it towards him. It was then that he saw her tear-stained cheeks. His tender look touched her. He gently pulled her down onto himself, grimacing as he did, his bloodied hands holding her tightly. 'It's OK,' he said. 'You wouldn't be the woman I love if you were any less caring.'

Her face was within inches of his. He could feel her warm breath. She lowered her lips, kissing him softly. Then she held his head steady between her hands as she kissed him with all the pent-up passion inside her. She had missed this. A feeling of warmth and love flooded her soul. She felt him relax beneath her. She sighed, so exhausted. It had been a long night and day. He watched as she gently succumbed to sleep; the two of them wrapped tightly together in each other's arms, oblivious to the world around them. He pulled his thick coat over them both. They held each other through the night, neither wanting to let go.

The next morning, stiff from lying on the ground, Katharine untangled herself from his arms. It felt strange to be standing alone, his warmth gone. In the weak light of dawn, she washed his pain away in the cool stream. They spoke of other gentler times. With a heavy heart, he explained, 'The safe house is about three, possibly four hours walk from here in our condition. If you're up to it, that is.'

'Darling, I am if you are.'

He could not contain his joy that she had addressed him as darling. It was confirmation enough of her love for him. But he would have to let her go, even if it was a temporary goodbye.

Four hours later, the safe house came into view. Once safely ensconced inside, with a doctor in attendance, the worst of Captain Henderson's injuries were treated. When alone again, he turned to

Katharine, taking her hand: 'You are under my protection. And …
always remember, when this damn ordeal is over, I will be there
for you.'

'I don't want to leave you,' she protested. 'Can't I come with you?'

'It's for the best. You have to trust me.'

That she did with all her heart. He was the solid rock on which
she could rely.

Preparing to leave for the final phase of her journey to England,
Katharine wondered how long it would be before she would see
him again.

Chapter 12

Late August 1939. At Rascott Farm, a few miles outside Bude in Cornwall, Günter pushed the pitchfork one last time into the ground. He had been at it since dawn, his body hardened from months of outdoor life. Dusk was still two hours away. Constant rain over the summer had ruined the land. The potato crop would not be as productive as usual, much of it rotting beneath the soil. Farm work was back-breaking, but at least he could see the fruits of his labour and it took him out of the fogs of London.

His companion Frank motioned for help with hitching the trailer to the tractor. 'You can drive,' he said to Günter. 'We'll have a devil of a job getting it through the mud, but you're better at it than me.' The tall lanky lad was a year younger than Günter. He was the farmer's middle son. The family had always treated Günter like one of their own.

'Thanks, Frank. You always leave the best jobs for me.' Günter's knowledge of English had improved significantly in the eight months since he had been on the farm. He considered himself quite proficient at the language.

Frank paused, 'I'm sorry about the news today.'

Günter shrugged his shoulders. He valued Frank's understanding and compassion. 'It's to be expected. Getting people out of Austria is impossible now.' He straightened his back, leaning on the fork handle. 'Your father did his best and I am grateful. I still live in hope that somehow…' He found it hard to finish the sentence but couldn't allow the trauma and fear to get to him. 'I keep seeing my mother's face at the station. She tried to hide her tears but I saw her hiding behind the pillar with a handkerchief. I just can't block it out.' At this point, he was miles away, transported back to the station in Nazi-occupied Vienna. He gazed towards the horizon, lush green fields rolling out as far as the eye could see. 'It's not only her I worry about, it's my father – he's the one who has Jewish relatives. When war comes, there will be no chance for him.'

Frank tried to reassure him. 'War isn't inevitable, you know.'

Günter's determined reply surprised him, his lips sharply set. 'It is from where I am standing. Don't be naive, Frank. War will come, believe you me. And when it does, where is your army? You English are totally unprepared.'

'You worry too much.' Frank bent down to turn over the newly dug potatoes. He kicked a few over. 'The crop's as good as useless this year.'

Günter persisted, 'You English are so innocently trusting and that's what I love about you, but you have no idea of the might of the Nazi war machine. I have seen it with my own eyes. Britain is not prepared for this war.'

'Maybe,' replied Frank. 'And if you *are* right, as land workers we're fine – we're in a reserved occupation. The population needs food. You have no need to worry. You will be completely safe here.'

'Until the bombs fall all around us. We must not pretend, Frank. War will affect us all. Even here, German bombers will fly over on their way to destroy the docks and harbours along this coastline. Please don't misunderstand me, I'm so grateful to you and your family for all you have given me, but I will fight. I have a duty to give something back to the country that saved my life. If it wasn't for this country, and your family of course, I would almost certainly be dead by now. If I hadn't left when I did, I would be in a concentration camp. I'm sorry Frank, but when war comes, which it will, you'll be digging potatoes alone. Somehow, I'll find a way to fight those Nazi bastards.'

Frank clapped him on the back. He couldn't win the argument, he knew that. Günter was as stubborn as a mule. 'Come on, let's go in. Ma will have made supper by now.'

❧

Captain Henderson crossed the newly mown lawn, shoulders square, heading towards the house. Stafford House wasn't bad as a retirement home for an old MI6 operative. He wouldn't mind such a place himself. It was a grand estate; the elegant tree-lined drive sweeping in front of the house added to the grandeur. Sir Charles was his last hope of finding Katharine. In the last four months since he had left duties in Vienna, he had tried in vain to locate her. Her file was missing from headquarters; no one was saying a word. She was beginning to make a habit of disappearing on him. No wonder she drove Sir

Charles to distraction. The woman was an enigma, but then weren't they all.

Finally coming up to the front porch, he rang the bell. A few minutes passed. As he waited, he thought it was just the thing to keep the old bugger happy in his dotage.

Then the door swung open. ''Ello guv,' smirked Spike. 'I knew you'd be here sooner or later. Charlie said ya would.'

'It's good to see you Spike,' he lied. He loathed him; his blackened, gapped teeth disgusted him, his manners and language uncouth. 'How is Sir Charles?'

'He's been on top form most of the time, guv. But you know 'im! Come in, you can find 'im in the Orangery at the back of the 'ouse. 'E's supping tea with some posh'uns.'

Captain Henderson made his way to the Orangery. Sir Charles was seated at an iron-lattice table, sipping a glass of red wine in the company of two elderly, well-attired ladies and a young lad. He waved enthusiastically as Captain Henderson continued his direct course towards them. The white-painted iron door creaked as he opened it.

'Ah, Henderson. What a devil of a surprise. Welcome to my humble abode.' Sir Charles unsteadily heaved his bulk, standing up. 'May I introduce you to my guests? Captain George Henderson, this is Lady Penge of Doncaster, her companion Isabel, and delightful young nephew Peter, fresh out of naval college.'

'Naval college, you say?' Captain Henderson turned to the youth, 'Which one?'

'Dartmouth, sir.'

'A fine place. That's where I trained many moons ago.' Social propriety demanded a polite response, but it momentarily distracted him from his urgent mission. With a nod of the head he signalled to Sir Charles for a word alone. Sir Charles turned to the women intently focused on him, 'Now my dears, if you will excuse us, duty calls. I thought I had dispensed with all that, but there's no rest for an old sea dog, even in retirement. Please help yourselves to cake. There's plenty of it. I'll be back shortly.'

Sir Charles negotiated the mass of plants dangling from large earthenware pots scattered everywhere. Captain Henderson followed him into the adjoining sitting room. Taking in the décor and furnishings, he realised just how comfortable Sir Charles was here, installed as a country gentleman. Silently they passed through the room into a long hallway. A stag's head gazed from above the fireplace at right angles to the main doorway and completed the stereotypical picture of the country life.

Sir Charles broke the silence: 'We'll go into the library, George. We won't be disturbed there.'

As Captain Henderson expected, the library walls were lined with dark mahogany panels, crammed from floor to ceiling with leather-bound books of all sizes. He knew Sir Charles had no intention of ever lifting a single one from the dusty shelves, except perhaps as a missile at the odd servant. It completed the image of the aristocratic gentleman.

Sir Charles moved to the desk and slowly lowered himself down, gesturing for Captain Henderson to be seated.

'I prefer to stand, Sir Charles.'

'Just as you like, George. You always were a stickler for protocol and rank. You're still as bloody-minded as ever, I see.'

Captain Henderson chose not to respond to his jibe. He got straight to the point. 'I won't beat about the bush, where is she?'

'Who?' Sir Charles ran his fingers along the edge of the desk.

'Don't give me that, I'm in no mood for games. You know full well, who.' He fixed his glare on Sir Charles, determined not to be outmanoeuvred this time.

'I'm no longer in the game, George. You know that. Don't you remember? You ordered my retirement. I'm a man of leisure now and bloody well enjoying the peace and quiet. I'm well out of the picture.'

'Damn it man, this is important. Where is she? My guts tell me that you know something – and I am never wrong about that.'

Sir Charles sat still, feigning interest in an old framed map that still needed to be fixed to the wall.

It wasn't working. Captain Henderson tried a softer touch, 'Look, I have no idea whether or not she is safe. I last saw her in Vienna.' He lied; he didn't want to disclose to him about the border incident. 'That was several months ago. As one of my staff, I have a duty to keep track of her.'

Sir Charles studied him carefully, relishing the power he had over him. 'Now Captain…'

Here it comes, thought Captain Henderson. Sir Charles never addressed him by his title. He waited. It felt as if the man held his life in his hands.

'To tell the truth, Captain, I'm bored of country life.' He looked at Captain Henderson steadily, not flinching in his steely gaze. 'If I was to find myself in a semi-retired position, brought out of my slumber for a few days a month, maybe as mentor to some of the young lads coming through … I might be of some help to you now. Then, perhaps a file that appears to have found its way accidentally into my hands can be passed to you for safe keeping.'

Captain Henderson reacted. He broke the rules, but then these were no ordinary times and she was no ordinary woman. 'You're despicable, you disgust me. I won't be blackmailed. I won't have any of it, you know that.'

'Blackmail? Who said anything about blackmail, George? I would never use that phrase. No, let's say a gentle lever to the fulcrum, shall we?'

Captain Henderson stood before him, knowing he had no choice, not if he wanted to find her. He had been frantic with worry, but not only that, he couldn't live without her. His response surprised Sir Charles. 'Agreed then, you have my word as an officer and a gentleman.'

'Well, well, George. Let's shake hands on it.' He beamed, reaching into the bottom drawer of the desk. He pulled out the papers bundled tightly together with string. He thrust them at him, 'Here, I think this is what you are looking for. I've known about you and her for some while now. It's about time you settled the past permanently. She'll never be yours until you do it. Do what you have to, George.' In one last gesture of understanding, even compassion, he added: 'Good luck old chap.'

It was not what Captain Henderson had expected at all.

'Thank you, Sir Charles.' He took the papers, glanced down at the address: Church Lane, Georgeham. It would mean travelling to Devon. He turned to leave. With one last backward glance at Sir Charles, he smiled and walked out.

❧

Captain Henderson marched up the steep narrow lane in the heart of the North Devon countryside. The six-foot-high overgrown hedges and winding narrow lanes characterised the landscape of deep valleys and hills for miles around. The faded signpost indicated that he had found his destination. Church Lane was the village's longest street, if it could be called a street. The cottage was at the top, surrounded by high firs.

He heard her music before the house came into view. It caught his breath. His throat tightened. Chopin – his favourite. It was as if Katharine knew he was coming. He stopped to savour the sweet tone, carrying him to a far-off place where the ordinary transforms to perfection. The last time he heard this piece was on the first night in Vienna when he and the Freuds had attended her concert. So much had happened since then. Above him, the transmission wires in the firs swayed gently in the summer breeze. He smiled to himself; she was probably still making contact with America or tapping into the Abwehr. His long journey finally at an end, he nervously cleared his throat, not knowing what reception he might receive.

As he approached the house, he could see the front door ajar. He felt nervous, straightened his back. He could hear footsteps in the stone passageway. He knocked and pushed the door wider. Her soft but firm voice called out from a nearby room, 'Who is it, Laura?'

'I'm not sure,' came Laura's reply. She pushed the door wide open and called back, 'It's a military gentleman, a rather handsome one, I might add.'

Captain Henderson came fully within view of the young woman limping. He glanced surreptitiously down, making sure she did not see him noticing her leg irons. This must be her sister. Katharine had mentioned her from time to time, especially after the Rear Admiral's death.

'Madam.' He bowed his head slightly in respect for such a young widow. 'We haven't met before, but I worked with your late husband. I can't tell you how sorry I am about what happened.'

'Thank you,' she replied graciously.

'Laura, who is it?' Katharine's voice sounded nearer.

Then she saw him. She froze. 'Laura, it's fine. Please, you can leave us. Captain Henderson and I have some business to discuss.'

The months of separation disintegrated before them. It was as if they had never been parted. Her face was as vibrant as he remembered. 'Let's go into the garden, shall we?' she suggested. 'It's so lovely out there this time of the year.'

He followed, the faint fragrance of her perfume intoxicating him as before. He could barely keep his nerve. He tried to re-focus his mind.

She spoke first, a little nervous and stilted, 'It's good to see you again, George.' He was acutely aware she had used his Christian name. Maybe there was hope still. She motioned for him to sit beside her on the garden bench. A robin landed close by, venturing to perch on the wooden arm of the bench, tilting its head as if to listen to what Captain Henderson was about to say.

He cleared his throat. It was now or never.

She raised her eyes expectantly. Was she holding back the tears?

'Every day I have thought of you, wanted you. I have tried to give you a life, to let go of you, but it's no use. I can't. I've been frantic with worry. I have searched for you for months, not knowing whether or not you were still alive. Not a word from you, Katharine. I've been driven mad with longing, thinking about you. I want to tell you – I love you.'

'And I you George, but it can never be. I am married.' He could read her soft eyes like a book. She *did* love him.

He ventured, 'You going off was as though what we felt that day in front of the fire meant nothing to you. How could you forget me?'

She replied steadily, 'I felt it, believe you me, George. Every waking moment of every day, I have re-lived it in my mind, wanting you and yet knowing that I can't have you. As much as I want us to be together, I know it's wrong.'

He took her hand. 'We can be together,' he replied with all the tenderness in him. 'I've brought something to show you, if it is not too late. You are not actually legally bound to Jonathan. He married you under a false name. Here look. I have the papers to prove it. Sir Charles set the whole thing up to bring you into the family. The only scrap of truth about Jonathan was his medical degree; all the rest is questionable. In English law it means you are not lawfully husband and wife. Don't you see, you are free? Whether he is alive or not, you are free to love me.'

An eternity passed. Why didn't she say a word?

The robin still perched on the bench, waiting as eagerly as he for her reaction. He had to ask her. It was what he had come for. 'Katharine, will you … will you be mine? Will you marry me?' He held his breath, almost too afraid of the reply.

'Yes,' she smiled. 'Yes George, I will.' He moved closer. He could feel the warmth of her leg pressed against his. He placed his arm around her shoulders. With the other hand, he tilted her head, bringing his lips to hers. In the passion of the embrace, his soul merged with hers. At last he had the woman he had once given up for duty.

Hugo showed no reaction to the scene in front of him as he came into their view. He had every reason to intrude on their most private of moments. Walking down the path towards them, he speeded up, almost ran, as his eye caught Captain Henderson's. He shouted across, his voice carrying towards them on the autumn breeze. 'It is official, sir. War has been declared. You are wanted on the telephone immediately.'

Captain Henderson nodded to Hugo in acknowledgement, then turned back to Katharine still held tightly in his arms. 'The devil they know exactly where I am at all times.'

She laughed, 'You would be worried if they didn't.'

By now Hugo was standing in front of them. 'Chamberlain has just broadcast to the nation. We are officially at war with Germany. God save England!' Hugo then spoke directly to Katharine, 'And your nephew-in-law Günter has just enlisted in the British army.'

'Impetuous fool,' interjected Captain Henderson. 'Doesn't he know we can't have Austrians in the British forces.' He touched Hugo's forearm, 'Just give me a minute with Katharine and then I'll come and take that phone call.'

Hugo ran back towards the cottage to tell the caller that Captain Henderson was on his way. All the wheels of military government committees would be working overtime now and that included the Secret Service.

Alone with Katharine, Captain Henderson took her hand again, 'We are still members of His Majesty's special department. Whatever this war holds for us darling, remember, you will always have me. This time, I will be there for you. You are mine to love and protect forever.'

He kissed her on the cheek, reluctantly released her hand, stood up and walked back towards the cottage. What a day it had turned out to be.

Alone with her thoughts, Katharine stared across the valley at the newly ploughed fields. The church bells began to toll. This time it was not for Vienna.